SONAYA NIGHTS

BOOK ONE

STORGY®
BOOKS

STORGY® BOOKS Ltd.
London, United Kingdom, 2020

First Published in Great Britain in 2020 by STORGY® Books

Copyright TOMAS MARCANTONIO© 2020

Tomas Marcantonio has asserted his right to be identified as the author of this work in accordance with the Copyright, Designs Patents Act 1988

London

Published by STORGY® BOOKS Ltd.
London, United Kingdom, 2020

10 9 8 7 6 5 4 3 2 1

Cover Design by Rob Pearce

Edited & Typeset by Tomek Dzido

A CIP catalogue record for this title is available from the British Library

Trade Paperback ISBN 978-1-9163258-0-7
eBook ISBN 978-1-9163258-1-4

www.storgy.com

THIS RAGGED, WASTREL THING

TOMAS MARCANTONIO

For Jung-mi, who led me through the backstreets.

"Unfortunately, the clock is ticking, the hours are going by. The past increases, the future recedes. Possibilities decreasing, regrets mounting."

- Haruki Murakami, *Dance Dance Dance* -

1

The Rivers. A spiderweb of alleys for the drunk and destitute, weaved together from stones and shadow. Winding backstreets forking off like rotten veins plunging into every shady corner. The greasy smell of glass noodles and exhaust fumes from late night scooters. Neon blinking on every grimy surface and crooked alleys disappearing into a black and sorry night. Home.

Sonaya was always a little rough around the edges, but now The Rivers are deeper, dirtier, wilder. Not that that's a bad thing; the Japanese way was always too rigid for my liking, and Sonaya's got its own mad personality. But man, you walk around the Rivers at night after eleven years away and you start wondering what the hell went wrong. This is the real Sonaya right here: alleys backed up with rusted scooters, cockroaches scuttling through pancakes of vomit, shady characters leaning on uneven walls. I fit right in, and that's not a thing to make a man feel proud.

Me and this city are one and the same. The Japanese aren't all bad, but spend too long in Sonaya and the coat hanger across your back soon disappears. You stop bowing to people and forget the niceties. The Japanese are too damn stiff; walk and think in straight lines. Sonaya's got a lot of flaws, but rigidity isn't one of them. This is a city for the flexible, and I'm damn near elastic. I don't just walk these streets; I'm bonded to their blood. Riding the plasma wave straight to the heart.

Now that I'm out I've got a lot of friends to see, and not all of them are waiting inside bottles. But hell, I'm in no rush. I'm a free man for now and every night ahead is young. But first I've got a debt to pay. There's an old saying that states a man in debt is no more than a slave, and I don't like to be a slave to anyone but my own joyous whims. There's another saying that you're a long time dead, so once I've paid my debt I'm gonna drink long and hard.

The girl's name's Jitsuko—Jiko for short. I've only met her once before, but I'm good with faces. Hair dyed red like a forest fire, skin like a winter moon, and upturned eyes like a fox. It doesn't take long for old Kosuke to find her for me.

'She's one of those Bosozoku creatures,' the old man told me. 'They make an absolute racket down in the Rivers at night, that rabble.'

I smile. Bosozoku, last of the biker gangs. Their numbers increased when the city went to shit. Just kids rebelling against nothing and everything, tearing up the streets and making a nuisance of themselves. Kosuke's right; I can hear them long before I spot their bikes. It's a good job half the city's nocturnal.

I'm down near Isorimu Station at The Cross, the five-way confluence of the Rivers' busiest streams. An old drunk with fish hook eyebrows slides along one wall, spit catching on his stubble as he screams obscenities at the holes in his leather shoes. A pair of addicts woodlouse together in a doorway and watch me pass with hungry, globular eyes. The homeless skunks wander their nightly aimless wanders, waiting for the moon to fall from the sky and crack open to cover the world in a new yolk.

All these holes are new to me. It used to be that I knew every underground bar and every kitchen that kicked rats out the back door. The blinking neon signs spell different words but the doors are as sad-looking as before; crooked basement stairs, windows dim or boarded up.

I soon find what I'm looking for: two wine bars east off The Cross, basement bars that bottle and sell the cheapest kind of grape. The apartment blocks were here long before I lost my job; their grey walls etched with rust trails bleeding from each twisted railing.

I descended the stairs to Vino Isorimu and pushed through the gnarled door. It's dark and empty; only a few flickering candles flinging light over the red oak tables. No one's waiting to show me to a table. Several girls perched on stools at the bar stop talking when they see me.

'What d'ya want?' one of them calls over. This is the hospitality of the Rivers. Another two get up and stand between me and the bar. Neither of them is Jiko.

'Got anything from Argentina?' I ask. 'I'm looking for something dry, preferably from Mendoza.'

They look at each other like cartoon bodyguards and tell me to leave. The short one's hair is dyed blonde, a bob down to her shoulders that frames her mousey cheeks and coated cherry lips. The tall one's hair is purple, with a fringe straighter than the sharp end of a cleaver; she's wearing so much black eyeliner it's like she's taken two clean punches. Together they look like an anime girl group, only with more tattoos and fewer smiles.

'I'm looking for Jiko,' I say. 'Owe her some money for a favour she did me.'

'You can just leave the money with us,' Purple says, her face as friendly as a crowbar. 'We'll make sure she gets it.'

'I'd like to see that she gets it myself.'

'Jiko's on a ride tonight,' Blonde says. 'She's fast, but the sun usually beats her home. Come back tomorrow.'

'I'll be drunk tomorrow. Jiko's money's only safe until I find some Mendoza wine.'

Purple still looks pissed but Blonde's face breaks into something like a smile.

'Wow, look at that,' I say. 'I was starting to wonder if either of you had teeth.'

'Try Sakura,' Blonde says. 'Down in the pleasure quarter. You'll find Jiko there. Follow the screaming and you can't go wrong.'

I throw her a wink and turn on my heels.

'Wait,' Blonde says. She walks over to the bar and I examine her tattoos; a mugunghwa blossom along her left arm and a tiger straddling the Korcan taegukki on the small of her back. She pours something burgundy into a glass and the tiger scowls. 'This is Sonaya,' she says. 'You'll be waiting a long time for something from Argentina. You new here?'

'Been away a while.'

She smiles and hands me the glass. I throw it down my throat like plum juice.

'Best wine I've had in eleven years,' I say, and I disappear into the night.

#

My first buzz as a free man. Who needs a job when you've got the charm of the Dag. I could sweet-talk in basement bars all night and feed on bottomless free drinks. I've got a nose that's broken in two places and a gaping hole where my ear used to be, but neither makes a damn bit of difference. The government might have me down as a five on their tax records, but talk to me nose to broken nose and you'll jot those points back up as soon as I open my mouth.

That lick of wine is tingling in my throat and I've got a stirring thirst for more. A Great White Shark with blood on his tongue, swimming in a sea of wounded seals. I better get this Jiko thing out of the way before I blow all of Kosuke's cash on the destruction of my liver. Time to dive into this new Sonaya. Deep breath now.

I prowl the pulsing lanes. One step, two step, the Sonayan waltz. You don't need a sixth sense to know where the pleasure quarter begins. Red neon blazes through the caterpillar streets, like kisses from the maroon lips of Sonaya's whore goddess. The girls and boys are all in heels and the flickering lights above their heads throw slick-hipped shadows across the walls.

'Looking for some action?' one of them asks as I pass, my eyes fixed on the shifting signs above. Japanese, Korean, English; it doesn't matter, all of them have at least one character that's blown its bulb and make the rest wink like a senile aunt.

Things sure have changed since my last visit to the pleasure quarter. It used to be just a few girls with short skirts and sly glances. Now there are different buildings to suit every desire. Homework Clubs and singing rooms and dark basements I don't even want to know about. Maybe the people in this city aren't so lonely after all.

I pick the threads of the web for a while with no sign of Sakura. There are plenty of screams for sure, but not the kind you want to hear. I stop beside a lady propped against a wall to ask for directions. She's tall and has thick purple lips; she's got heels that could take an eye out, and eyes that look like they'd enjoy watching it happen.

'You're into them young, are you?' she says, her voice gruff, like it's been trawled across the ocean floor.

'I'm just looking for someone,' I reply.

'You all are,' she says, her heavy eyes sliding to the right. I follow her gaze and find what I'm looking for down the next alley. Sakura. Cherry Blossom. It's damn ugly from outside; sickly pink and peeling paint, like someone's chewed up a bunch of cherry blossom petals and spewed all over the walls. Things don't look much better inside; flowers and frills and pink everywhere; a small reception desk covered in plush toys, a torn and tattered chaise longue and wallpaper covered in faded hearts, all of which makes you feel like you've been dropped into a giant box of confetti.

The girls on the chaise longue jolt when they see me,

each of them in school uniform; white shirts, black ties half-undone, navy socks up to their knees. Fifteen, sixteen, at most. It's strictly talking only in Homework Clubs. Smiling and leering; old suits tired of nagging wives, pretending to help with homework as girls flutter eyelashes and occasionally graze a leg. The men drink hard liquor and the girls sip juice through straws. All above board, this is as innocent as it gets. But this is just the start.

'Welcome, sir,' the oldest girl says as she slips behind the front desk and flashes me a yellow smile. Her hair is pulled back in a ponytail and secured with a white bow, her Tokyo accent lingering in the air like the sickly sweet after-taste of melted candy floss.

'Would you like a private meeting, sir? Is there a girl you usually see?'

I look around. No screams. No flashes of red. No Jiko.

'I'm looking for Jitsuko. She here?'

The girl tilts her head to one side and grants me a closer look at her grimy canines. 'I'm afraid we don't have a girl by that name, sir.'

I hear a man shouting upstairs, closely followed by the sound of a door slamming.

'Never mind,' I say.

I take the stairs one at a time. I'm no slouch but I've got a reputation to maintain. When a man loses his cool he's lost it all, like a snake shedding its skin; there's no going back. At the top of the stairs I see Jiko at the end of the corridor, dressed in black leather trousers and a tank top, the fiery rays of a Rising Sun tattoo spreading across her collarbone. She's pointing a gun at a middle-aged suit with glasses and a comb-over, and he's screaming at her like he's trying to strip the flowers off the wall. Two girls are peeking out of an open door behind him.

'Throw your wallet on the floor.' Jiko orders the suit.

Her finger hovers above the trigger, eyes firmly locked on her target. If she's seen me, then she's not letting on.

The suit swears and inches his hand inside his pocket. He removes a wallet stuffed with notes and tosses it to the floor between them. The wallet spins and slides into one of Jiko's oversized boots and she takes one hand off the gun to retrieve it. With a solitary hand, she empties the wallet and slips the wad of notes into her pocket.

'That didn't hurt *that* much, did it?' She throws the empty wallet back to the floor.

'This isn't over,' the suit says as he moves towards his wallet. 'I'll have your guts, girl.'

'Yeah, they all say that,' Jiko answers.

She lowers the gun a second too soon. She didn't see what I saw; the suit planting his feet on the floor, wiping his fingertips against his trousers. Jiko looks like she knows what she's doing, but it takes years of experience to know when a crazy cat's about to pounce. In a flash he's grasped her gun and they're wrestling like a pair of kittens over a ball of yarn, only this yarn might explode and send red furballs flying across the hall.

The schoolgirls in the doorway are screaming and I shove them inside and slam the door in their faces. I keep my eyes on the barrel of the gun and make sure I'm not in range as I approach the struggle. Jiko's surprisingly strong but the man's no mouse either. He elbows her in the face and wrestles the gun away from her as she falls to the floor with fresh bruises and blood.

Normally I wouldn't get involved, but I've got a hell of a debt to repay. Gotta wipe that dust from my shoulders before I can enjoy my freedom. I reach down to my ankle and remove Old Trusty from its sheath. My beautiful Wharncliffe blade. Been with me since my days in the force. Spent the past eleven years in a box in the basement of The Heights, but it still feels like my eleventh finger; I brandish my blade as fast as another man might scratch his nose.

Time slows down in situations like these. I haven't been a cop for years but you never lose the instincts. You see action play out like photographs, and if you're good, you can smudge your prints all over them before you reach the end of the reel. The suit's standing over Jiko and pointing her own gun at her. Whether or not he's gonna shoot, I've no idea, but I don't wait to find out. I slam Trusty's handle onto the sparse scalp in front of me, and both scalp and body tumble to the floor.

'This your first hold-up or what?' I ask Jiko.

She pushes the suit's limp body off her and I help her up.

'First one today,' she says. 'You put me off. I saw you lurking by the stairs. How'd your tax assessment turn out?'

'I got a five.'

'Congratulations. Result like that must save a man a lot of money.'

'That's why I came to find you. I told you I would.'

Jiko looks at the suit on the floor and plants a boot in his stomach. 'I hate these old pervs,' she says, shouldering past me to the room with the girls inside. She opens the door and hands them a roll of notes. 'Go home,' she says, and closes the door.

'Let's get out of here.'

2

SEVEN MONTHS TO RELEASE

Whoever designed this prison was smart. The worse the crime, the higher the cell. I'm up on sixty-third with the other murderers, and from here you get one hell of a view. The harbour, the old town, the lights on Broken Hill. The skyscrapers by the waterfront, the back alleys of the Rivers. They want us to see, see what we're missing. Maybe they're teasing us, taunting us with a world that's forever out of reach. Maybe it's to make us appreciate the city more, so we never sin again.

It's been ten years. Seven months to go, and I'm a free man. I'll finally get out of this fucking cell, but who knows if it will make a difference. Every night when the lights go out I listen to the screaming. Most of those on sixty-third have lost their minds. They howl like wolves at the moon and keep me awake. The ones with any semblance of sanity smash their skulls against stone walls. Their heads sound hollow. Maybe mine is the only one that's not.

Sometimes moonlight shines through the bars, paints black stripes across my face. I stare at the moon and think of one thing only. Ten years on and my mind still bumbles around that one night like a moth against a naked bulb that I can only beat my broken wings against. But it's never enough. My brain just flickers on and off, flashes in the dark, a film chopped up and thrown at me in fragments. No matter how hard I try to piece it all together, I always fail. I just can't work out why. I can't work out why I did it.

\#

They say that when one life ends, another begins. Prisoners never escape from The Heights, but last night a body left the building. For five seconds Song Ye-jin was free with wind in her face and lights in her eyes. This morning they were still picking up her splattered flesh and shattered bone off the pavement. They're probably still trying to wash away her blood.

New life usually means screaming babies with clear consciences and bald, pug-eyed heads. This guy walking into the mess hall doesn't fit the bill. Five foot eleven, thick-rimmed glasses, a twitchy nose. Everyone knows who he is. There aren't too many foreigners in Sonaya, and even fewer who play the game. An American in The Heights? He's already a damn celebrity.

I wouldn't usually have anything to do with the dregs below, and all they have on this guy is possession with intent to supply. That's just rabbit food in this city, hardly worth the cell. But towards the end of his first week he walks over and introduces himself, like a pimp from the seventies; khaki threads two sizes too big, a perm like a wig on a giraffe, and tortoise-shell, thick-rimmed glasses that won't last the week. He sits down opposite me during lunch and doesn't look the least bit nervous.

'Dustin Fairchild,' he holds out a hand.

I take it. 'Daganae Kawasaki.'

'I've heard of you,' he says.

'Good. Then you're not as stupid as you look.'

Whatever happens next will decide the comfort of his stay. For a moment I think he's gonna get up and clear on out, but he simply smiles, an American smile; lop-sided and overconfident.

'They told me you're a good person to know,' he says.

'I'm not. I'm a damn hurricane. You like hurricanes?'

'I like people who tell me I look stupid.'

I take a clap at my food. Plain white rice, a side of spinach. Spinach is a good day.

'You look stupid,' I repeat. 'How long you been in Sonaya?'

'Two years. Came here on work, assignment for a paper. New Jersey.'

'The Garden State. You're in the wrong city, then. See this spinach?' I pinch a leaf between my chopsticks and hold it up between us. 'There's more green on this plate than in half the Rivers. What were you writing?'

Fairchild shrugs. 'About the things that cops paid me to stop writing.'

'Let me guess. The sex trade. Drugs. Political corruption.'

'I got a bit too wrapped up in the stories, if you know what I mean,' he smiles that lopsided smile again. I like this guy. My kind of idiot.

'I'm guessing the paper isn't waiting up on you,' I say.

'I lost that gig a long time ago. Police wanted to hush me up, and to be honest, I enjoyed being hushed up. It got me into a lot of parties. They saddled me with a two-year sentence, but I'm not worried. They reckon I'll be out in a couple of months. We've got some good lawyers in the States, and anyway, I won't be short of work, not after this. A few months in The Heights, that's a book right there. They should've thrown me in here to start with. Would've saved a lot of time.'

I plough through my rice. Gotta save the spinach for last.

'I hear you've got a pretty interesting story yourself,' he says.

I look up and stare at his eyes. I try to decide which liquor bottle shares their colour. I settle on soju. 'I'm on the sixty-third floor,' I say. 'If I didn't have an interesting story I wouldn't be up there.'

Fairchild's left eye twitches. Or maybe it's a wink. 'I heard you murdered your girlfriend.'

I put my chopsticks down as slowly as I can and use my tongue to search for a stubborn grain of rice wedged in my teeth.

Fairchild holds his hands out like he's just finished a magic trick. 'What? I told you I'm a journalist.'

'And *I* told *you*, I'm a hurricane.'

#

The next time I see Fairchild I'm in my cell. The man must have some powerful friends if he's already hopping floors like a damn jack rabbit. Either that or he's got a nice stash of notes stuffed under his mattress.

My cell suits me fine. Ten foot by ten foot of cold stone. A firm mattress on the floor. Clean sheets every week. A sink with only two small chips and a working toilet without a lid. I've even got three whole walls to lean against.

I'm a damn sweetheart compared to the other deadbeats above the fiftieth floor, and that gives me the only advantage I need: weekly access to the library. I'm not a fussy reader; anything with words is fair game, I'll gobble through it just the same. I even read the newspaper when I can get my hands on it. After the government decided that commoners couldn't be trusted with the internet, papers came back in a big way, but there's only one left that does the rounds. The Daily, owned by the same hyenas who run the island. The internet was full of shit, of course, but that's all done with. Now The Daily is like The Bible; facts are 'verified' by the suits, and suddenly we're a nation of believers.

When Fairchild appears at my cell, I'm leaning against

the only wall that catches any sunlight. He even knocks on the open cell door, the softie.

'Come,' I say, not looking up. I'm reading up on the elections. Still a few months off, but there's no harm in doing my homework early. If all goes well, I might even be a free man by the time elections come around. A free man with a vote to my name, too.

'You got a minute?' Fairchild asks.

What a cutie. I scan him up and down and return to my paper. 'About a million of them,' I say. 'If I could sell them I'd buy the whole damn island.'

He enters all sheepish, and I watch his eyes dart around behind his glasses, like he's already looking for an escape route; a hole in the wall. He scratches his nose with the back of his finger.

'What's your candy, Fairchild?' I ask.

He blinks at me like he forgot I was there.

'I know what a man looks like when he goes two weeks without a fix. What's yours?'

'Nothing big,' he says. 'Just the white stuff.'

I look back at my paper but I don't read it. 'You'll have to learn to live without it. Doesn't matter how deep your pockets go, you're more likely to see a hot tub in your cell than a bag of pollen.'

He nods fiercely and sits down beside me. Look at me, I've made a friend.

'You know a guy by the name of Tsubasa?' he asks.

'One arm and hair like a banshee? Yeah, I know him. Been giving you trouble?'

Up close, Fairchild's skin doesn't look too good. His nose is pockmarked and red blotches cover his cheeks.

'He's been watching me, asking questions.'

'So what?' Poor Fairchild. Foreign boy in a foreign prison. 'Don't worry, you're not his type, if that's what you're thinking. He's a plover, that's all.'

His eyebrows scrunch up and reveal his confusion.

'The bird that flies into a crocodile's mouth to help itself to a free meal. Plaque and scraps. There are snitches like him on every floor, trying to buy their way out early, that's all. Probably knows you're an addict and is waiting for you to slip up. I suggest you don't.'

'Slip up?'

'Don't go offering cash to the wrong people. Don't visit the wrong cells. And don't ask for anything you're not gonna get.'

Fairchild stares at his knees and nods. His eyes are spinning in his sockets like marbles on the floor. Addicts suffer the most in here; you can train your brain, but the body will never listen.

'I heard about the escape,' Fairchild says.

'You call that an escape?'

'They say she was the first to ever get out.'

I turn to Fairchild and give him the look that teachers give their kids when they want them to listen. 'When I was a kid, all I wanted was to get off this island. Travel, you know, find some place better. But it didn't happen. My dad cheated on my mum, then a little later he choked on his vomit, for extra points. I could've left after that, with my mum. I could've left this place behind, started anew.'

Fairchild shrugs. 'So why didn't you?'

'Because no one really wants to escape. Song Ye-jin spent months digging a hole in her cell just so she could fly. You ever heard of purgatory? People say that this island's like purgatory. Get out of The Heights and you're still not free.'

Fairchild leans his head against the wall and we sit in silence; sucking at the cold stone walls.

'So what do you want now?' Fairchild asks.

I stand up nice and slow and stare out the window.

'I've spent ten years with my head down so I can get out of this cell. To everyone else this city might be a shithole, but they don't see what I see.'

Everything in sight is grey. Scooters zoom by, heading for

the harbour or the belly of the Rivers. One or two already have their lights on. The lights glow pretty damn well, even from way up here. Night is coming.

'What do I want? I wanna get the hell out of here and make up for lost time. And ten years is a hell of a long time.'

3

Jiko's Ducati is red like her hair and if the body has ever been scratched or damaged, then the evidence is buried beneath untold layers of paint and polish. It's a classic Bosozoku ride: the handlebars are pointed down for quick getaways through small spaces, a reminder of the days when cops only had biker gangs to worry about. There are stickers all over the fuel tank: a big Japanese flag in the centre, surrounded by the symbols of old gangs that disappeared long ago. When she revs, the motor purrs like a well-fed tiger, and we're out of the pleasure quarter and into the belly of the Rivers before we hear the sirens.

'It takes them a while,' Jiko says. 'The girls at the clubs hate the suits as much as I do. They just pretend they don't see anything.'

It's night and I'm free with nothing but wind in my face and endless open road. The lights of the Rivers blur into yellow and red and green, streaks that spit across the passing walls as we puncture clouds of stench-filled smoke. The night is waking up and Sonaya breathes again.

'Nakata's place still open?' I ask Jiko. She nods and steers towards the Rivers' scrawny northern veins. The roads are crocked and we slalom around a string of potholes; I get the feeling she'd sooner lose the flesh from her bones than scratch the paintwork on her bike. We pull over in a long corridor of fluorescent signs, a myriad of fire escapes feeding into one another, infinite wires and cables stringing the streets together. Jiko takes her time dismounting; her fingers gently caress the throttle, like a jockey sharing a tender moment with their horse after a race.

I lead Jiko through the unmarked door and down the stairs. The place hasn't changed one bit. The old record player still sits behind the bar, black leather stretches across the furniture, and the air is thick with artificial smoke; like of those old speakeasies from back in the day when people knew what jazz was and cigarettes were legal. I can barely stand up straight without brushing my mane against a maze of shimmering orbs that hang from the ceiling. Two middle-aged women in modern hanbok are conspiring in one corner; in the other corner two boys are exploring each other's necks.

'You look terrible,' Nakata says. She's standing behind her marble bar, looking at me like I never left. Short black hair streaked with violet highlights and big black eyes like an owl wired on caffeine. She's wearing a leather choker and a single earring that looks more like a wind chime. Her voice has a distinct flavour to it, like the kick of rich dark chocolate. 'Where's your ear?'

I lean against the bar and run a hand through my hair, which I've grown past my shoulders and left to matt and tangle. I shaved the side where I'm missing an ear; there's no point losing your ear if no one can see it. 'Must've misplaced it,' I say. 'How you been, Nakata?'

'Better than you from the looks of it. I heard you were getting out. What are you drinking?'

'I'll take the house special.' I glance at Jiko and she nods. 'Two.'

We take the booth in the corner beneath a black-and-white photo of a man and his sax. The smoke machine is purring away and shooting misty clouds across the tables. Fats Domino is singing about a Blueberry Hill on Nakata's old record player. She loves the old stuff that no one else remembers.

Nakata brings over two long glasses of muddy ale. I watch her as she places our drinks on the table, and as hard as she tries, she can't keep those lips of hers straight, the corners sliding up before she turns away. Damn, I *have* been missed. Twenty-four hours ago I was still in The Heights, scratching a farewell into the wall of my cell, and now I'm in heaven. I raise my glass.

'To Sonaya,' I say.

'To you,' Jiko says.

Damn right. Me and Sonaya, the two most important things in my life. I'll drink to that.

'I didn't think you'd actually try and find me,' Jiko says.

'I said I would, didn't I?'

'You think I was going to trust the word of a murderer?'

I raise my glass and let the foam caress my lips. 'You shouldn't have. It was stupid of you.'

Jiko shrugs. One of the boys in the corner squeals and we both look over, their fingers tightly interlocked and their beaming smiles oblivious to us strangers.

'I've got good instincts,' Jiko says. 'I've thought about what happened a lot. Whether I did the right thing, and whether you'd pay me back. I guess I got my answers tonight. That pig could've killed me.'

'It's done now,' I say. I don't want things to get too mushy; I've got a reputation. 'What were you doing in that place, anyway?'

'We don't make a lot of money in the bar.'

'I'm not surprised. I've seen how those girls welcome customers. I went there looking for you and all I got was some bad lip and some even worse wine.'

Jiko smiles as though as I've given the bar a five-star review. 'Ume said she met you in The Heights. She's got some big things planned and she seems to think you'll help us out. That's why she sent me in there to do you a favour.'

'Where is Ume? We've got a conversation to finish.'

Jiko shakes her head. 'Busy. The Homework Clubs are just the start, full of the wrong kind of men, and the unfortunate kind of girls. We're gonna get them girls out of those clubs one day. One day soon.'

I watch as she glugs her ale even faster than me. A cloud of smoke passes across her face.

'What have you got against the Homework Clubs?' I ask. 'I can think of worse places.'

Out of nowhere several wrinkles appear on her forehead.

'You were at the wine bar. What did *you* think of those girls?'

I shrug. 'They looked angry. Same way all girls do when they wear too much eye shadow.'

'All of those girls did time in the Homework Clubs, and some of us have done time in places even worse. We're the ones who got out. The ones who are gonna change things.'

She doesn't look at me as she gulps down more of her beer. She doesn't care what I think, and she's probably right not to. Nakata ventures out from behind the bar and tells the boys to keep things clean. The women in hanbok are staring into ancient compact mirrors and touching up their makeup for men who might never show up.

'What happened to you?' I ask.

Jiko shakes her head and pushes her chin out. 'What do you care?'

'Maybe I don't, but if Ume thinks I can be of use, I'd better know who I'm working with.'

She gives me the once over, her eyes a burnt mahogany that fades into speckled walnut toward their centre, a stark contrast to the black of her pupils. When they finally stop scanning, they settle on a point three inches above my left shoulder.

'When I was a kid, I used to wake up to the sound of

my father beating my mother. Sometimes he beat me too. Then one day he got a gun and shot her dead. Blew his own brains out shortly after. If I was at home, he would've killed me too.'

She pauses to drink more of her beer, closing her eyes to savour the taste, or force her father out of her mind.

'I was recruited by Fumiko, same as the other street girls. She taught me how to take care of myself, and a hell of a lot more. Not a lot of girls' escape Fumiko's hand, but I did, along with a few others. We're gonna be the ones to break her fingers and make her pay.'

I finish my drink and signal Nakata for two more.

'I need to speak to Ume,' I say again.

Jiko nods me away like I'm her nagging mother. 'Yeah yeah, just wait, all right? I told you she's busy. You seen Fairchild since you got out?'

'Not yet.'

'You haven't forgotten about—'

'No, I haven't forgotten.'

#

I've got a place in the Rivers. A gift from Kosuke til I get back on my feet. A small attic room above a boarding house that gets a lot of male visitors in the night. Dust throughout and a smeared window that looks out over crummy streets full of second-rate singing rooms. It's a damn palace compared to my cell on the sixty-third, but I'm not sleeping there tonight. Jiko drinks well, but she also drinks fast. Once we're done, she can barely get her key in the ignition. I'm not gonna let her kill herself so soon after I saved her life.

I grip the throttle and give it a sharp twist as Jiko rests her head on my back. It's gone three a.m. and I'm no monk myself; we sucked Nakata's barrels dry. I guide the Ducati through the back streets north of The Cross, the motor humming and forming off-key harmonies with the retching of sewer drunks and sudden bursts of synthetic music. Every rotten molecule of this city whispers a million memories into my lonely ear; I suck it up like a starved cat licking milk off a bottle cap.

I get Jiko back to her flat above the wine bar. The lights are off and none of the other girls are around, so I support her up the stairs. It's not a bad little squat for one person; four solid walls to herself, which is already more than most people. She tells me to stay and I'm in no state to argue. She switches the lights off and falls asleep fully clothed on the futon.

I stand at the window and enjoy the blissful throb of ale as it washes away the cobwebs from the dormant ventricles of my brain. The leftover scraps of the downtown party score the streets; scooters burst towards home, dissonant surges of passion erupt and echo, drunken arguments crescendo and fade away. Through a crack between concrete blocks I watch the bent-backed figure of a man as he sways and stumbles along the street, turns his head dumbly and stares at something out of sight. Eventually he trundles off, searching for a way out of the maze.

I make a pillow out of my shirt and lie down a few feet away from Jiko. My eyes have adjusted to the dark; even with her vest on, I can see more of her Rising Sun tattoo than I've any right to. I throw a blanket over her and she squints at me through one eye.

'One day soon,' she mumbles.

I put my hands behind my head and look up into the darkness.

Dust, and lots of it. That's how I like my digs. Slanted roof, a window scrubbed clean with sandpaper, moth-eaten armchairs and lumpy mattresses and lacerated naked floorboards. Perfect. The attic belonged to a local artist who went mad and killed herself, and I'm the first to move in since it happened. But it doesn't bother me. If ghosts exist, I'll greet them gladly. Quiet company is my favourite kind.

Kosuke's provided the bare necessities: a kettle with rust wounds, an ancient rice cooker with a splintered lid, a fridge half-stocked with basic greens, and crates of instant noodles. There's a pile of new underwear in the cupboard and a selection of creased shirts and trousers sagging on metal hangers. Not my style, but I've got time to replenish.

I head down to the basement liquor store beneath the greasy dumpling joint on the corner and pick up a few essentials. The toothless old lizard behind the counter fills a cardboard box with my bottles and squints as he punches in the prices. whisky, brandy, gin, soju, sake, rum, I don't care, as long as there's a good supply of booze when I need it.

'Hosting a party, are you, son?' he asks, counting the notes I pass over. For a moment I think he's gonna ask me for ID.

'Yes, sir,' I say, hauling up the box. 'I just don't know who's coming yet.'

My first nights are as quiet as expected. There's a young couple below who go at it all night, first shouting of one kind and then shouting of another. I don't have much by way of entertainment, so I listen and sit with my bottles by the window, staring out at the vast grey towers of the Rivers. I'm up all night, leaving the attic only to yellow the floors of the shared bathroom. I don't get a wink of sleep, and soon enough, I stop trying.

I lie awake thinking about the difference between the walls of this attic and the walls of my cell. I add it up every way I can, and the only conclusion I arrive at is that now I'm free to go anywhere I want, drink anything I want, see anyone I want. That might sound good to a man stuck in a cell, but after several bottles of booze, you remember that your favourite company is already inside your own head, and the difference doesn't seem so big after all. All I have to cling to is a vague thread of a thought. It's the same little creature that's been knitting away at the back of my brain since day one in The Heights. My business with Jiko is settled, but there's one more woman I have to see.

#

The next morning my head feels like the anchor of an oil tanker and my mouth tastes like I've spent the night chewing on rust. I drag myself off the damp pillow and boil some water. I rinse out my tumbler from last night and make a strong coffee; no milk, but I can live without it. I slouch into the armchair and let the coffee cool, sipping it carefully as it scolds the roof of my mouth. Ten minutes later I start to feel semi-conscious, and I make myself a second cup of coffee, just for the hell of it. I walk over to the window and watch the sun rise over the Rivers, enjoying the novelty as sunlight emerges from the ceiling of grey clouds.

There's a knock at the door. My first visitor.

'Who is it?'

'I've a message from Kosuke,' comes the reply.

Message. That's what people say when they're about to kill you. But I have little to lose. I open the door to a scrawny girl with a shaved head and a pierced ear. She's got hazel eyes that probe into me without baulking and she's wearing a grey vest that exposes her puny arms, and khaki trousers two sizes too big. Maybe twelve years old; better running messages for Kosuke than working for Fumiko, I think to myself.

'What do you want?'

'Can I come in?' she asks. Without waiting for an answer, she strides past me like I don't exist.

'It smells funny in here,' she says.

I rub my head. Feels like my first hangover in eleven years is gonna be a mean one. I better build up my tolerance fast.

'It's probably the scotch,' I say.

'No, it's worse than that. It's that musty smell. A man smell.'

I shrug and search for my booze.

'So what is it?' I ask. 'You some kind of delivery girl?'

'I've got a message from Kosuke,' she says, handing me a piece of browned paper. I take it from her and carefully unroll it. I love the old school. 'Your fingernails are dirty.'

I examine my fingernails. They look okay to me, but I've been in The Heights for eleven years and my new place smells fine to me, so what do I know?

'You can go now,' I say.

'What if you need me for a reply?'

I look at her. 'Fine, sit down. Over there.'

She approaches the armchair and frowns. I rub my eyes and try to read but end up watching the girl. She dusts down the chair and arranges herself like a cat squeezing into a box that's too small. When she's finally settled she fixes on me, like I'm a one-man play and the curtains have just gone up.

I read the note, roll it back up, and drop it on the table next to the door. 'You can go,' I say.

The girl jumps to her feet. 'Do you want me to deliver a reply? You'll have to pay me, though. The old man only paid for one-way.'

'You're good to go.'

The girl narrows her beady eyes. 'You really need to clean this place.'

I look around. 'I like it like this.'

She exits duck-footed, hands buried in her pockets.

'Well at least open the window. It's like someone died in here.'

#

A man has to make a living, especially in Sonaya, otherwise you'll end up like the sewer skunks, waking up with needles in your veins and empty bottles of booze next to your piss-stained pants. I'm better than that. I used to be someone, and I'm gonna be someone again.

It might take me a while to get back. I've got a murder to my name and thanks to Fairchild I'm missing an ear, and neither of those look good in brogues. But I've got talent. In my prime I was the best brain in the force. Sure, the sergeants never looked at me too kindly, but fat cats on thrones don't like smart kittens, especially when they're getting the kind of women I was getting in those days.

Kosuke's my only link to the world of power. Richest man in the city. He bought himself a whole apartment block down by the harbour. Did something different with each floor. A gym on twelfth, a pool on sixteenth, an arcade on thirtieth, a cinema on thirty-third. Screen golf, karaoke, restaurants, bars, aquariums, clubs, botanical gardens, artificial beaches; you name it, he's got it. With all that luxury on his doorstep he never needs to leave home, all forty floors of it. Old Kosuke's a good guy to be friends with. We go back a long way. Or at least, he went back a long way with my folks.

He starts me off small, just until I'm back in the swing of things, then he'll get me something sweet, he says. Maybe as a bod in a bank or some other fat cat firm. I doubt it, but I'll take what I'm given. Kosuke has a hand in the import-export business, but that's not how he made his money. Meat's been banned in Sonaya for over twenty years, but people still eat it. Japan's just a ferry ride away, and ferries have ample space for unmarked crates. Skunks will do anything for money, and hyenas will do anything for meat; put the two together and you've got an illegal trade with a lot of prospects. My role? That's the easy part. I'm just a delivery boy. The donkey.

I'm told to get down to the harbour, so I get clear of the Rivers and take in the strip. Hotels, bars, fancy apartments, all with sparkling neon faces and names that mean money. They look damn fine in the night, tossing long streams of pink and green and blue across the tarmacked streets and camel cream sand. Sonaya's beach is long and quiet, flanked by boys in blue who ensure only the right kind of people enjoy it. The sea itself looks better at night when the darkness disguises the oily surface and trash washed up on shore. Anyway, it doesn't matter. The point of the beach is to sit on the sand and stare at the water, imagining a means of eventual escape. Japan's across there somewhere; cleaner, greener, and without all the fat.

When the harbour's lit up, you forget what a rat hole this city is. You think you're in Singapore or Hong Kong before they went bad like everywhere else. Towering billboards display government-endorsed bullshit: special deals on substitute meat, hotels and casinos lining the strip, campaign propaganda from corrupt politicians.

I turn away and look at the sea. Peace. The harbour masts sway calmly and I pick the yacht I'd commandeer in a pinch. Blue Dragon looks nice, but a little too big for my needs. Escape: now there's a perfect match. I picture myself with the helm in my hands and the waves slapping the hull. Hell, I look good. A friend tried to teach me to sail once, but it turns out it's all ropes and knots and nautical sweat; what you really want is to sit at the stern with a glass of whisky in your hand and the wind in your face.

The Arkansas is one of the fanciest yachts in the harbour. Must be fifty feet of solid steel and a brilliant blinding white. Looks like it's never seen a single wave, let alone a storm. The name's inscribed high on the hull towards the bow, royal blue and cursive, hand-painted, from the looks of it. There's a woman sitting on deck with a glass of the good stuff and a far-off look in her eyes.

'Daganae Kawasaki,' she says. 'You're late.'

I look up at the moon like it can tell me the time. It can't, of course, but I stare it for several seconds before turning my attention back to the woman.

'Come on up,' she says. 'Careful, we've just had her painted.'

I climb aboard as gracefully as I can. The woman holds out a tiny hand, so small it could be a child's, if not for the gigantic diamond on her wedding ring. The skin on her forehead is smooth and shiny; like she's had pounds of plastic pumped into her face. Her eyes are small and twinkle like cinnamon stars between the curtains of her silky black hair. I struggle to keep my gaze on her eyes and not the outline of her black bikini, visible through her sarong.

'Have we met?' I ask.

She shakes her head. 'Aimi,' she says. 'I remember when you got arrested, what was it, fifteen years ago?'

'Eleven.'

'I was little more than a kid, but I knew who you were even *before* the murder. The stories I heard about the famous Daganae Kawasaki.'

Shucks. I'm almost blushing.

'It must have been hard for you in The Heights. I heard you were an alcoholic.'

I shrug and drag my eyes across the deck like I'm searching for something, but all I see are two tanned feet and ten small toes with perfectly painted nails.

'Anyway,' Aimi says, swivelling the glass with her slender fingers, 'you don't look too hot anymore. I suppose you had another tax assessment before your release?' She nods at my missing ear. 'I can't believe they're still doing those.'

She leans back and takes a slow sip of her drink, eyes firmly fixed on a different Dag. As much as I like attention, I didn't come all this way for the conversation. 'You got the stuff?'

Aimi continues to look me up and down. At least one of us is enjoying this. 'What did Kosuke tell you?'

'Said I had a pick-up, from here. You got the stuff?'

Aimi flashes me a glimpse of her flawless teeth. 'One week out of The Heights and you're already running mutton for Kosuke? You miss it in there, do you?' When I don't answer, her smile broadens. 'Kosuke hasn't got anything for you here.'

I chew on my bottom lip. 'Then would you mind telling me what I'm doing here?'

Without answering she gets up and descends the steps that lead below deck. She reappears from the cabin with two men close behind. Foreigners, both of them. It's a few seconds before I realise one of them is Fairchild.

'Woo, here he is!' he says when he sees me on deck. 'Looking like a ten, Dag.' He pulls me in for a one-armed hug and I get a whiff of his woody cologne and the cheap whisky on his breath. He's wearing a straw trilby with a blue and white band low over his thick-rimmed glasses, and a green and red Hawaiian shirt that might make my headache worse. Twitching like a ball of nervous energy, he steps back and examines me like we haven't seen each other in years. It's only been a few weeks since I watched him walk out of The Heights, and I seem to be the only one who remembers how things ended in there. Hell, maybe it was all in my head.

'Here, meet my boy. Stones.'

The second man steps forward and offers his hand, a gold watch on his wrist so big it would drag him to the ocean floor if he braved the cold sea.

'Peter Stones,' he says. 'Heard a hell of a lot about you, Daganae.'

I nod. Course he has.

'This is Stones' yacht,' Fairchild says. 'This is what you get for churning out shitty thriller novels. Cookie cutter plots but no one seems to notice, do they, Stones?'

Stones holds out his hands and smiles. 'I can't complain.' He puts an arm around Aimi. 'This is a hell of a city we've got here. Hard to run out of ideas. Can I get you a drink, Dag?'

'Whatever you're having,' I say.

He slaps me on the back like we're old school friends and disappears below deck. The rest of us sit down by the stern.

'Stones and Aimi been married five long years,' Fairchild says. He slips a cocktail stick between his teeth. A few months in The Heights aren't enough for a smoker to lose the habits of a lifetime. 'He was handsome back then.'

Aimi scowls. 'He's brilliant,' she says. 'But for God's sake don't ever tell him that. If his head gets any bigger, he'll fall overboard.'

Stones reappears with a bottle of scotch and three tumblers half-filled with ice. He pours the drinks and hands one to me and another to Fairchild.

'So you just got out, Dag?' he asks, leaning against the mast.

'A couple of days ago.'

'Must seem like a different city from the one you left behind, eh? Harbour alone has changed a hell of a lot in the last five years.'

'On the outside, maybe,' I say.

Stones nods, his smile unmoved. 'Fairchild tells me you're well acquainted with old man Kosuke. He's a fine cat to be friends with, that one. Just last week he bailed us out when the dogs got wind of the pollen we shipped in. Fairchild here, you should've seen him sweat. It was a picture, wasn't it, Aims? Thought you were going straight back in The Heights, didn't you, boy?'

Fairchild tries to smile but fails, gaping at his shoes like a dog with its tail between its legs. Aimi watches me closely.

'It's okay,' I say. 'I'm not a cop anymore.'

'Still,' Aimi says, looking at her husband. 'It's a fool's game.'

Stones waves a hand to dismiss any concerns. 'We only have one life, and we're gonna live it. How Fairchild went all those months without a fix I'll never know.'

Fairchild looks at me sheepishly. 'This is good stuff,' I say, holding the glass up.

'How about a refill?' Stones asks.

I drain my glass. 'Better be off. I've got a lot of people to see.'

Stones and Fairchild glance at each other. It's quick, but I don't miss that kind of thing.

'What is it?'

'There's something you should know, Dag.' Fairchild rubs his fingers together. 'That girl, Ume Uchida. The one you wanted to track down.'

I nod.

'She's dead.'

All three of them stare at me. I swivel the glass of ice in my hand.

'When?'

'Last night,' Fairchild says.

'I didn't hear anything about it. What are the cops saying?'

'Nothing, of course. Kosuke found out, who knows from where. Reckons it's all being hushed up.'

I rub my temples. My only lead, dead. I remember her face the last time I saw her. The *only* time I saw her.

'Kosuke says he knows where it happened,' Fairchild says. 'I can take you there if you want. Tomorrow, before the party.'

I lift the glass to my lips, forgetting I've already drained it as the ice clatters against my teeth. I nod at Fairchild. 'You knew her?' I ask Stones and Aimi. They shake their heads.

'Heard of her,' Stones says. 'Not exactly popular. Used to be in the circuit but got on the wrong side of the wrong people.'

I think of Jiko and her raids on the Homework Clubs. It's not hard to imagine someone wanting them gone.

'She should've left the island when she got clear of those brothels and drug dens,' Stones says. 'But she decided to cause trouble instead. Never ends well.'

Aimi stands and turns sideways, her profile clearly defined before the glistening water. 'People never realise when they should get out of this place until it's too late. Ume wasn't the first one, and she won't be the last.'

#

We're down at the mouth of the Rivers, staring at a purple stain on the ground. It's a quiet slum, not ten minutes from the jetties; an alley between two apartment blocks and a gateway to the backstreets that stretch back into the heart of the city. There's no neon here, no windows flickering with life, no staircases to basement dens; only four brick walls doused in amateur gang graffiti, a black dumpster that stinks of shit, and a purple stain that stinks of death.

'Maybe it was an overdose,' Fairchild says dismissively. 'Stones said she was an addict.'

'*Used* to be,' I correct, from down on my haunches. 'And anyway, overdoses rarely involve this much blood.'

A rat limps along the base of the wall behind Fairchild, of its front feet missing. We watch it stop in front of a cracked pipe that dribbles waste into a gutter. Unsteadily, the rat rises up on its hind legs and sniffs the air before slowly disappearing into the building's bowels.

I straighten up and Fairchild leans an elbow on my shoulder. 'So they're sending a warning,' he says. 'Whatever she was involved in, they want people to know it ain't gonna fly.'

I shake my head. 'Look around.'

He does. We both do. It's quiet, the beginning of another night in Sonaya. A cat whines in the labyrinth of the Rivers. A sour gust of salty wind kisses my mane, steering wisps of hair across my lips.

'No drones, no cameras, nothing in the papers. Whatever happened, the hyenas don't want people to know.'

The dragonflies are out; a pair hover piggyback in front of Fairchild's glasses and he bats them away.

'It smells like summer,' he says, cocktail stick perched in his teeth.

'It smells like shit.'

Fairchild smiles. 'Don't worry about this Ume girl. Just forget about her, all right? She probably didn't have anything to tell you, anyway. From what I hear, she was a waste of space.'

Forget about Ume? Her words have been banging around my skull for the past six months, and just as I set out to find her, she gets knocked off.

Fairchild removes his glasses, cleans the lenses with a silk cloth from his shirt pocket, and slips them back on his hooked and freckled nose. 'You ready for the party?'

I look out over the harbour masts and see Kosuke's pad, towering above the other sleek apartments behind the marina. The party's up on the roof, and the neon lights are already pulsating. There's a pool and bar, naturally, and a club on the floor below. Kosuke sure knows how to throw a party.

'They say it's not a party in Sonaya until someone's dead,' Fairchild says, glancing back at the purple stain on the floor. We set off towards the harbour.

'Then I guess this one started early.'

5

The teardrop pool in the middle of the roof is glowing pink beneath a blanket of mist. A string of grey-cushioned sun loungers stretches its circumference, conquered by lazy guests who sip bright cocktails while comparing costly nose jobs. A long white bar runs the length of the back wall faced by a stream of round leather stools with gleaming chrome legs. Guests who aren't mingling around the pool lean against the iron railings that ring the roof, watching and judging everyone else.

Kosuke knows the best people and the best night for a party. Saturday, the start of summer, kids gliding across the harbour road on glistening bikes beneath the glow of the first summer moon. On a night like this the whole city wants in, but it's only the better half that's welcome at Kosuke's place.

All the richest guys are here, but Kosuke isn't all about the money people. He knows what he's doing. He's got actors and musicians and the whole damn wild crowd out, young up-and-coming delicates who know how to party and fuck-all else. All the best ex-pats, too; a bunch of artists, that lot. Writers, painters, poets, musicians. Something about the city inspires creativity, apparently. They haven't been here long enough to know any better.

A cluster of girls in bikinis circle the pool. I've never seen them before; Kosuke's probably hired them to encourage the ugly suits to believe there's a chance they might wake up tomorrow with dainty fingers running through their chest hair. A couple of girls balance silver trays of bubbly drinks. Champagne, naturally, and I grab two flutes from the off; I've never been blessed with patience. Kosuke has eighties ballads blaring out from the speakers, but no one cares. His party, his music. It's all good as long as the champagne keeps flowing and no one's dead.

I'm standing at the bar with Stones. Blood vessels are already bursting in his pale, steel-blue eyes. He's holding two glasses, so Aimi's probably picking up some gear for him.

'How's the book coming?' I ask. It's the only question I can think to ask a writer, and it's probably the only question they don't want to answer.

'It's not,' he says, pointing his glass towards the party, 'how's a man supposed to write with so many distractions? You ever been married, Dag?'

'No. I murdered the only woman I ever loved.'

Deadpan Dag. Free for kids' parties.

Stones just sips his drink and arches an eyebrow. 'Damn.'

'Damn indeed.' I like to keep people on their toes. Stones takes it, though, recovers well enough.

'Don't get married, Dag, it'll only hold you back.'

'I won't,' I say. 'I'm a free man now, and I'm not looking to change that any time soon.'

Stones clinks his glass against mine and the champagne sinks down my gullet like liquid glory. He finishes his drink and lines up the next. Three women dressed in white shirts and black bow ties stir and shake cocktails behind the bar. As soon as they place them on the marble counter, greedy hands fly in and swipe them away.

'Ah, Dag,' he says. 'Have you ever had the pleasure?'

I look at the woman striding towards us. Black, big lips,

short hair like a schoolboy. Her large almond eyes are like pools of bronze that have been melted over scorching flames and left to slowly simmer. She has beautiful skin and a walk that could floor a rhino. The silk dress that clings to her body doesn't do much damage, either.

'Sara Barnes,' I say. She nods and leans on the bar beside me. Her perfume is so sweet I feel a sudden need to brush my teeth.

'You two met already?' Stones asks.

Me and Sara look at each other, like a couple deciding who should tell the story. Sara breaks first. 'Dag was one of my projects,' she says. 'He was supposed to give me the scoop of the century, but he didn't live up to the hype. Did you, Dag?' She smiles sarcastically.

Stones looks between us. I just smile and raise my glass. 'I never live up to anything.'

We fall silent and watch the party. Everyone's wearing their finest: silk shirts and expensive cuff-links; sumptuous dresses so thin the slightest touch could rip them open. I'm not one for formalities; I like to keep things down to earth. Black cargo pants, brown leather boots, grey shirt unbuttoned to the base of my chest, sleeves rolled up. If anyone asks, I'm fresh out of prison. It's a conversation starter.

'How's the story coming then, Barnes?' Stones asks. 'Any progress?'

See. It's the question that needs to be asked. Sara shakes her head and broods. She holds her glass up to her lips like a microphone. 'Sonaya's not the easiest nut to crack,' she says. She's drinking whisky and holding it well.

'You need to get out more, Barnes,' Stones says with bravado. 'A basement's no place to write. You've gotta *live* if you wanna write. Heck, living is *why* you write.' He cracks me on the back like we're in some secret club; like I'm the mastermind behind his success.

'It's not a basement,' Sara says coolly. 'It's a studio.'

Stones raises his eyebrows at me like we're conspiring kids in a head teacher's office.

'Your man Fairchild's enjoying himself,' Sara says to me. I look around; Fairchild's in with a group of locals, his hand hovering beside the lower back of an elegant lady way out of his league. She spots his hand and slides away.

'To hell with him,' I say. I'm getting lit and I want something to happen. These people only talk; goldfish opening and closing their mouths, nothing but empty bubbles flying out. I search the crowd for someone I know or someone who might shake this party up. The youngsters are trying too hard with their jewellery and colourful cocktails stuffed with umbrellas; the suits are doing their duty rounds and licking each other's business cards; the druggies are stealing the show so far, but they'll crash soon and end up little use to anyone. Seems like I'm the only one here with a third dimension, and even I don't know how deep it goes.

Then I see him in the middle of a smiling circle. The man I lost out to. An average guy, with two ears and everything. A policeman, or at least he used to be. He's in a sleek grey suit that matches the aging tips of his side-swept hair. His eyes are like drops of ink in water. The woman beside him says something and he smiles weakly, but his eyes stay fixed on his glass. He knows I'm watching, I can tell. But he doesn't look up. I leave the bar.

'Where you going?' Stones asks. I hold up a hand. Later.

Kosuke's leaning on the railings and talking to a woman in a short white dress who doesn't look a day over twenty. From way up here you can just make out the row of hotels along the beach, the shimmering reflections of neon on the surface of the water.

'Kosuke,' I say, and slide up beside him. He asks the girl for another drink and watches her disappear like a dinosaur grinning at the meteor.

'Why's he here?' I demand, looking out over the harbour. Kosuke turns to me with his wonky eyes. He's in a tux that's wasted on his potato shape; his thick, greying hair smells like money. He smiles with teeth that might once have been his; the smile of a sad clown who needs help applying his make-up.

'The widower,' he replies.

'That guy messed up my life,' I say.

'*You* messed up your life, Dag.'

He's right. 'Anyway, why's he here?'

'He helped me with some important matters, and to be perfectly honest I didn't have much choice, so you'll just have to get used to the idea, Dag. This isn't the same world you left behind; you're not the bell of the ball anymore. You're not even the pumpkin.' He watches me as I quietly seethe at the sky and finally places a hand on my shoulder. 'There'll be no trouble tonight, Dag,' he warns.

I look deep into the old man's bad eye. He's done more for me than anyone else and I'm not about to forget it.

'It wouldn't be a party without trouble.' I drop my glass over the railings and walk away. I imagine the sound of the glass shattering forty stories below.

#

Fairchild's watching the girls with the lust of a lion at the watering hole. They're all wearing red bikinis and sarongs, sitting by the edge of the pool with their feet in the water. As they feign and pose, the blue light from the water makes their wide grins glow.

'Terrible party,' Fairchild says. We both know he's lying, but he wants something to happen, same as me. Two girls break away from the crowd and I don't need to be good with faces to recognise them. One has blonde hair, and the other purple. The blonde girl's carrying a tray of champagne flutes and she subtly shakes her head as they approach. The message is loud and clear: I've never seen them before.

'How about a tour?' Fairchild asks, giving me the most obvious elbow of all time.

The girl's just smile; Kosuke must be paying them well. The smile doesn't sit well under Purple's sullen eyes, but Fairchild fails to notice. They don't clean up too bad, these biker girls, and it's only Fairchild's pathetic grin that draws my attention away from their neck-lines.

We take the stairs beside the bar and head down to the bowling alley. Fairchild flicks the light switch as I shimmy behind the bar and turn the music on. The lanes are empty and it's just the four of us, the other guests still partying on the roof, for now. I open a bottle of champagne and stick another one on ice by our table. I keep my eyes on Blonde and wait for an explanation, but whatever part these girls are playing, they're not ready to remove their masks.

The girls keep hitting gutterballs but don't seem to care; they just shrug and smile and sip at their drinks. Fairchild's lapping it up like a randy Labrador as he throws strike after strike and whoops with delight. Whatever the girls are up to, he's blind to it. Purple sits on his lap and they start necking shots, and pretty soon they've lost interest in bowling altogether. Blonde takes me by the hand and leads me down another flight of stairs. I don't ask any questions.

We stop on the thirty-third floor; the cinema. I reach for the lights but Blonde shakes her head and enters the darkness.

I take a seat in the front row and sup at my champagne flute. Blonde sits down next to me and takes my glass and drains it in one. There's no movie or music and we sit in silence, projecting our own sad stories onto the screen.

'I'm guessing Kosuke thinks you're here for the money,' I say. 'I thought you girls were done with that world.'

Blonde sighs and rests her head on my shoulder like we're at a drive-in. 'If we knew how much he paid girls to walk around in bikinis we might've done this a long time ago. But you're right. That's not why we're here.'

'Ume,' I say.

'We don't know who did it. No one seems to know,

and that means the people involved are important. And if they're important, there's a good chance they're here. I recognise half of the men from when I was younger, working the Homework Clubs. Some of them from Fumiko's brothels. *They* don't remember, though. Dressed like this, I could have three eyes and a forked tongue and they still wouldn't notice my face.'

I offer a small laugh to the darkness. 'So what's your plan? You gonna go round asking everyone what they were doing two nights ago?'

The noise from above is filtering through the floors; the party's progressed to round two.

'Jiko warned you about Fairchild, didn't she?' Blonde says.

'Fairchild may be a lot of things, but he's not a murderer. Why would he do it?'

'I don't know, but we might be about to find out.'

'So what, you're meant to distract me while Purple plays Fairchild?'

She puts a hand on my chest. 'You've been locked up a long time.'

'Get off,' I say, pushing her hand away. She laughs and sounds five years younger.

'Jiko said you were more of a gentleman than you looked. You feeling old, Dag, is that what it is?'

I don't know what it is. Maybe I am feeling old. 'Where is Jiko anyway?'

'Ever heard of the Roses? They pretty much run the Rivers these days. Just a mercenary group, when it comes down to it. They get their hands dirty when the government runs out of soap. Jiko thinks if the hyenas were behind Ume's death, the Roses won't have been too far away.'

My eyes have adjusted to the dark and I turn to face her big black eyes. 'You really think the government had something to do with Ume's death?'

'I don't know what you heard about Ume—or about us,

but we're not exactly friends of the law. Ume burned down one of Fumiko's whorehouses.'

'Yeah, and she went to The Heights for it. If that's all it was, they could've kept her locked up, fabricated charges, whatever. It would've been easy.'

Blonde shrugs and turns away. Something tells me the same thought has crossed her mind. 'Well that's what we're gonna find out.'

We sit in silence for a few moments.

'Ume said something to me, back in The Heights. Did she tell you what I did?'

'You mean killing your girlfriend? Everyone knows about that.'

The music upstairs revs up a notch.

'My glass is empty,' I say, standing up. 'Let's get back to the party.'

#

We head back to the bowling alley but by the time we're there it's completely deserted, just empty champagne bottles and upturned glasses, so we continue upstairs. When we reach the club it's heaving; disco lights blinking, dance floor bursting, sofas draped with guests in varied states of inebriated decay. Blonde comes up behind me, kisses me on the cheek and walks off. I watch her leave and approach Sara, stood at the bar.

'Aren't you a little old for treats like that?' she asks. She feigns tiredness, but I know she's enjoying the party; she's still here. 'Doesn't it get boring?'

I keep my eyes on the back of Blonde's head as she disappears in the crowd and resumes her performance. 'I'm bored of everything,' I say.

We observe the dancefloor. The music is terrible, the dancing too.

'Where's Stones?' I ask.

'Him and Aimi have pulled out the coke. As if he needed it.'

'You're not joining them?'

'I don't partake.'

'You don't partake in life,' I say.

Sara stares at me with those cold, dark eyes. 'You feeling sore about something, Dag? That little treat get you all worked up, did she?'

'She's not a treat,' I say. But maybe she's got a point; something's definitely not right.

Sara places her glass on the bar and leans towards me. I freeze as her breath caresses my cheek and the scent of her perfume shoots up my nose like an explosion of rose petals. She skirts the skin where my ear used to be and whispers something into the hole, but I can't hear anything with all this racket.

'Talk to my good ear,' I tell her.

She brings her face across mine so our noses graze, then whispers into my lonely ear.

'You'll always be a fool,' she says.

I pull my face away and stare at her.

The scream pierces the air before I can respond. The music stops and the lights come on. A few people groan and grumble but most of them search for the source of the scream or an explanation. I hear Stones above the din, calling for the lights to be killed. I drain my drink while I still have a chance; Sara's mercury eyes express signs of interest.

Everyone knows something's gone wrong. A death, I'd say, judging by the pale pallor of Kosuke's face. I'm amazed how surprised everyone is. This is Sonaya, after all. Commotion erupts in the club, so Kosuke instructs everyone to return to the roof. It feels like a school assembly, except these particular students prefer to scurry and snatch drinks from the bar or huddle in heaps by the pool.

Kosuke is stood at the front like a dolled-up hamster with a gun to its head. 'A girl has died,' he informs the crowd. Several guests place their hands over their mouths, but not me. 'The doors have been locked and the police are on their way. No one is permitted to leave the building until they're done with their questioning.'

Kosuke scans the crowd and wants to say more, but how do you follow up a speech like that? Sorry? Thank you? A girl's fucking dead. In the end he just wobbles his fleshy jowls and turns back to the bar.

No one asks where the body is because everyone knows. I look over the railing but it's pitch black and impossible to see anything. Forty floors is a long way to fall.

Whispers ripple through the crowd, but it's all speculation. Kosuke's woman from earlier tells Aimi that someone saw the girl jump. A boisterous suit with a blotchy face claims she was pushed.

'Who was she?' Aimi asks, but no one knows. One of the bikini girls, someone says. That's when I go find Sara, who pushes a drink into my chest.

'People will have seen you with that blonde swan,' she says. She doesn't sound overly concerned. 'The cops will be after you if it's her.'

'You saw her leave me alive,' I say. I'm not worried. Not yet.

Someone taps me on the shoulder and I spin around to see Fairchild. He has that familiar look on his face. The Fairchild look. 'It's not your girl, Dag—it's mine. Purple. It's my girl, Dag.'

I roll my eyes and Sara takes that as her cue to leave. 'What happened?'

'Nothing,' Fairchild says, his eyes scared stiff of another stint in The Heights. 'Dag, we need to get out of here before the cops arrive.' He rubs his face like he's trying to scrub the last hour away. I wish he'd stay still, but he's got all the twitchy energy of a candy-guzzling kid.

'There's only one way out of this building,' I say, looking at the crowd gathered along the railing. 'And you don't wanna take it. Just tell me what happened.'

Fairchild flops to the floor and starts muttering to himself, swallows like he's trying to take a bowling ball down his gullet. A liability, as always. I leave him to it and search for Kosuke. I find him at the bar surrounded by hangers-on, but he tells them to disperse when he sees me approaching. He pulls me behind the bar and into the store room. It's as big as my attic and stocked with almost as much booze.

'What do you know?' he asks me.

'One of your pretty little swans,' I say. 'Went off with Fairchild and never came back. We need to get him out of here.'

Kosuke's blotched hamster cheeks drain of colour. 'Did he do it?'

To be honest, I've no idea. 'We need to get him out of here,' I say again.

'I can't let anyone out, Dag. They'll be here any second now. Do you know how much trouble I'm in already?' He looks like a fat schoolboy whose party's been crashed by bullies.

'The cops will take your money, like they always do,' I say. 'They're only interested in the killer, Kosuke, and I wanna make sure it's not Fairchild.'

Kosuke looks around. Boxes of champagne, wine, whisky, beer, but no answers.

'He can go downstairs,' he says at last. 'But I can't do any more. If Fairchild's done something wrong, he's on his own.'

'Thirty-nine floors should be plenty enough to hide in,' I say.

'Go for thirty,' he says. 'Fuses are blown.'

I place my hand on his shoulder. Good guy, old Kosuke.

I come out from behind the bar. The party's over. The roof is gloomy as fuck without the neon lights and booming music, just a bunch of rich folks sitting around, feigning concern for the girl but scared for themselves. Stones and Aimi are next to the pool. They've probably thrown their snow over the railing already; the richest have the most to lose. A couple of drones circle above the pool; I'm only surprised they weren't here all along.

I find Fairchild standing alone and holding a scotch, the glass shaking in his hands, his complexion doing a green clash job with his darting eyes.

'Let's go,' I say, grabbing his elbow and guiding him towards the stairs. We pass Kosuke, and his stern look tells me the police are in. We've got a thirty-nine floor playground to hide in and a pack of pigs on our tails. Finally, the party's started.

6

SIX MONTHS TO RELEASE

The Heights might be the only prison in the world with a bar. I'm not talking about a party bar with strobe lights and music and endless brands of whisky lined up in bottles. Sonaya's a city for the lonesome, and a honsool is a bar for lonely souls. Good behaviour gets you a one night pass every six months, but the booze is only half the appeal. Conjugal visits in The Heights are only for the lucky few with special friends or long time lovers; the honsool is for everyone.

With booze and women on offer, a lot of guys gobble their visits up right away and spend the next six months yearning for the next one. Me? Well, let's just say that I've got my cell and a good imagination. I've been tucking my passes away in my pocket, and now I've got six months to play with and twenty honsool visits to cash in. They're strictly once a week, so it's time to come out to play. Right now, I'm just about the richest man in The Heights.

#

On the ninetieth floor I'm led through the men's door and greeted by a penguin suit. His hair's slicked back so fiercely a typhoon wouldn't blow a single strand out of place. He smiles, bows, extends an invitational hand. As soon as I enter the smell of sake hits me in the face and I'm half-drunk already. Ten years suddenly seems like an eternity.

The bar is a long and narrow room with a low ceiling and a row of booths separated by oak partitions, lit by dim glass orbs fixed along the back wall. It's the same design as the honsool's in the city; they exploded on the scene when technology was still man's best friend. Now most of the tech is gone, but the loneliness remains, like a dull hangover that pounds at the back of your head for a cruel eternity.

I take a seat in the farthest booth, flip a salute to the penguin and look around. The walls surrounding me are covered in calling cards for the hopeful hookers of the city. Fuck knows why; maybe to get me in the mood. The cards look ancient; frayed at the edges and splashed with stains you pray is sake. On the table in front of me is an empty shot glass, some crushed pretzels in a tiny tray, a grubby plate of dried squid, and a tube of toothpicks.

The penguin returns with a ceramic bottle of steaming sake. He presents it to me in both hands like it's a fine wine. I nod and he pours me a shot and leaves the bottle behind. He says he'll count the toothpicks before I leave; like I'll use them to build a ladder and escape from my cell. Enjoy your stay, he says. Damn right I will.

I pick up the glass of sake with my forefinger and thumb, hold it up to my nose, and close my eyes and inhale. Ten years sober and I don't even have a badge to show for it. Going cold turkey can drive a man insane, especially a man who used to wash down his breakfast with Irish milk. I made it, though. Patience of a saint, me. I let the rim of the glass settle on the soft cushion of my lower lip. The scent of the sake shoots up my nose like a damn firework show. Cheers to me, Dag - The Teetotal Machine. Farewell old boy, can't say I'll miss you. Bottom's up.

The sake caresses my tongue with a faint sweet splash, and I relish the acidic burn as it slips down my throat. It's as beautiful as I remember, and I've got two full bottles waiting to go. This is gonna be one hell of a night, and a damn fun final six months. I slug another shot before I hear noises from the other side of the partition in front of me. I'd almost forgotten I wasn't alone.

I hear a female voice converse with the suit as he pours her shot and repeats the toothpick story. I can't see her, of course. I could open the panel in the partition but I still wouldn't be able to see her; it takes two to play this game. I hear her shot glass slam back down on the table and consider saying something but decide against it. I pour myself a third and neck it. Time to talk.

'How long you been inside?'

She doesn't answer straight away. Maybe she's playing it cool. Or maybe she's not the talkative type. Either way suits me fine. Leave me alone with this bottle for long enough and I'll forget that she ever existed.

'Six months,' comes the eventual reply. From the way she talks I can tell she's grinding on a toothpick. I wish I'd shoved a toothpick in my mouth before I'd offered my opening line. It sounds like you know what you're doing if you've got a toothpick hanging between your incisors. Too late now.

'So it's your first time, too,' I say. 'Cheers to us.'

She doesn't say anything, so I pour myself another shot and slug it down. I hear her follow my lead and slam a shot too.

'Cheers to us,' she finally says in a gravelly voice, like maybe she's old enough to remember the taste of cigarettes. I stare at the photos of hookers lining the walls and choose the one I think best suits her voice: short hair, full in the face, thirty. Not ugly, not pretty. The kind of woman you walk past on the street and never think about ever again. I look at the picture when I talk and almost feel bad about it. Almost.

I hear the woman slug another shot. She's as thirsty as I am.

'What are you in for?' I ask.

'Arson,' she says.

I let that one sit between us while I tear off a strip of squid, slow and subtle, like a god tearing the world in half while the sleeping snore along.

'No one died. I'm getting out soon.'

I chew on the squid and pour myself another drink. The squid's tough and it takes me a while to break it down, but once it's swallowed I wedge a toothpick between my teeth.

'Congratulations,' I say. 'Maybe I'll see you on the outside.'

'Maybe.'

I thought *I* was a bloodless stone when it came to conversation, but this woman's something else. I crunch on some pretzels but they dry me out so I throw another blast of sake down my throat. I've already polished off a bottle and there's only one more to come. Better slow it down. *Slow it down?* Fuck that. I signal for service and the penguin duly delivers. Another salute, and I'm back to feeling good and warm. I trickle my glass full; the sound of a shot glass being filled is about the most wonderful sound in the world.

'Don't you wanna know what *I'm* in for?' I ask the partition.

'I know what you're in for,' the partition replies.

I let the words hang over my glass, then pick it up and rest the rim on my lip again. Take your time, old boy.

'What is it then?'

She slugs a shot before answering.

'You're in here because Hana died.'

I set the glass down in front of me.

'She didn't die,' I say. 'I killed her.'

The woman calls the penguin over and orders her second

bottle. When it arrives she takes her sweet time pouring herself a shot.

'I killed her,' I say again. 'You hear me?'

'You must have done. You pleaded guilty.'

I examine the pictures again, but this time none of them match the voice. To hell with it; I knock twice on the partition. Nothing. I take a deep breath and slither another glass full. I'm down to half a bottle. Slow down, Dag, you fool.

We sit in silence and I stare at the wall. I don't like being reminded of Hana, and I definitely don't like my almost empty bottle. I'm blaming the wall for both.

'How d'you know who I am?' I ask.

Whatever's going on over the wall must be more exciting than the questions I'm throwing at it. It's another long thirty seconds before I get an answer.

'I saw your name on the list, that's all,' the woman says. 'You'd think there'd be a ton of takers for a guy who was a ten, but you'd be wrong. I guess a wife beater isn't the kind of man a woman wants to spend a night with.'

'I'm no wife beater.'

'You killed her, you said it yourself. Killing, beating, which is worse?'

This woman's boiling my blood. I knock on the wall again. Two knocks finally come back my way. I slide the partition up and wait for her side to open too, and when it does I see her face through the metal grate, the only thing now separating us.

She looks nothing like the women on the wall; dark chestnut skin, jade-black hair and a cherry blossom tattoo on her neck. Her forehead's too big and her mermaid eyes are too far apart. If we met before The Heights, then I don't remember her. When she finally drags her eyes up to meet mine she doesn't react to the sight of my face.

'So what's this?' she says, picking up another toothpick and slipping it effortlessly between her lips; definitely a former smoker. 'The part where we slink off and spend the night together? Do our bit for the dwindling population of this shithole country?'

Now it's my turn to be the silent one.

'I'm almost out anyway,' she says. 'I don't need to get pregnant to speed up the process.'

I slug another shot but keep my eyes firmly fixed on hers through the metal screen. It feels like a confessional box, but with sinners sat on either side and no forgiving priest in sight.

'The hell do you know about Hana?' I ask.

She smiles slyly, the corners of her mouth curling up.

'You know The Taegukki down in the Rivers?'

Know it? I used to sink soju in there like it was water.

'My mum used to take me there in the evenings when I was a kid. I remember the way the men looked at her, like she was the most beautiful woman in the world. She would always complain about my dad working late, and the men in Taegukki would tell her to leave him and run away with them. She laughed them off and looked at me, like I was the one holding her back.'

'Heartbreaking,' I say. Suddenly we're onto childhood stories and now she won't shut up.

'My dad would get home from the office at two or three in the morning. Mum would be passed out—drunk—but I always woke up, made him come to my room and tuck me in, say goodnight. I could never sleep until he tucked me in. Then one night we were in The Taegukki and mum drank more than usual. Her face was red and blotchy and she could hardly stand. The owner closed up the bar, sent everyone home, but my mum told me we were staying. They turned out the lights, didn't even send me away or into the back room. I just lay in the dark on one of the benches, listening to the sound of their breathing. Now whenever I'm alone in the dark, that's all I can hear.'

I chew on the last of my squid. 'Your dad ever find out?'

'He must have. He hung himself a week later.'

We both sink a drink.

'But do you know what's funny? My mum knew exactly what she was doing, despite all the drink, and I blamed her for my dad's death. But she had no idea how I found out. Can you imagine that? She didn't even remember I was there, in the same room, crying in the darkness.'

I look at her through the grate. 'Cute story, but what's it got to do with me?'

'You were pretty well known back then for being a whale. They used to say that if you were left on the beach at night and the East Sea was made of whisky, the next morning we'd be able to walk to Japan.'

Yeah, they did say that. Dag the whale, swallower of oceans.

'A lot of people drink,' I say.

'And a lot of people drink too much. I know as well as anyone how drink can make you do things you'd never normally do, and how it can wipe memories from the brain. How much will you remember tomorrow, Dag? How much do you remember of that night ten years ago?'

'If you think you know something, just come out and say it.'

She looks up to the ceiling and I follow her gaze. There's a flashing red light above my head; you're never alone in The Heights.

'You've got six months left, right?' she says. 'A lot's changed in the ten years you've been stuck in here, Dag, but your reputation hasn't. You might just find yourself a fox again, and there'll be a pack of hungry hounds on your tail.'

I look back at the flashing light. I wish I could smash it to pieces and put a stop to all of these riddles. If there's any meaning or truth to what she's saying, I'll find out once I'm out of this damn monolith. I've waited ten years for a drink, but now the prospect of waiting six months for information seems like a kind of torture.

'Now, you wanna finish this or what?' she asks.

I throw the last shot down my throat and smack my lips. Everyone knows the bedrooms are bugged, and that can only mean my night is over.

'I'm a ten,' I say. 'And I'm not that desperate, so if you're done with all your fun, so am I. By the way,' I add, standing up, 'what's your name?'

'Ume,' she says. 'Ume Uchida.'

7

Thirty-eight, thirty-seven, thirty-six. We don't stop until we reach the thirtieth floor, the old arcade. Kosuke has all the classic games, all the latest consoles, too. Slot machines, grab machines, simulators; you name it, he's got it. Fairchild and I skulk into a corner and collapse on a sofa in the darkness. We watch the elevator lights flash in ascending order. The police are on their way to the roof.

I look at Fairchild as he breathes fast and heavy, eyes shut tight. 'Tell me.'

'I didn't kill her,' he says. 'I swear it.'

'Then why the hell are we hiding here? Hardly shines the light of innocence on us, disappearing as soon as the cops show up.'

If this is all a show then Fairchild's one fine actor; I could fill a tumbler with all the sweat streaming down his face.

'I heard someone say it was the girl with purple hair, so I panicked.' He's spitting words like a machine gun. 'But I didn't do anything, Dag—hell no—I swear. She kept asking questions and got all angry when I didn't have answers. Kept going on and on about Ume. Seemed to think I had something to do with it—but I've got alibis, yes sir. I was with Kosuke and Stones the night it happened. I told her to ask them herself if she didn't believe me. I told her. But she stormed off and went back upstairs. I never saw her after that, Dag, honest.'

I rub my temples like I'm trying to rub myself out of the building. His story sounds about right, though. Purple hardly looked like a bag of fun, even without all the leather.

The elevator light flashes thirty-nine. They'll be on the roof now, Kosuke greeting them with his special practiced charm. I wonder how long it will take them to discover two ex-cons are at the party. Not that anybody need tell them.

'They said she was on the panel, Dag,' Fairchild says.

'Purple? Whose panel?'

'Yours.'

I think back to that morning in The Heights. The dark room. The girl at the mirror. 'No, she wasn't,' I say.

'It doesn't matter. If they say she was, she was.'

One in four murdered women in Sonaya are panel girls, and the first people the police suspect are the men they've rated. Bribes, blackmail, threats; those ratings cause more ripples than a cannonball in the deep end.

'I got a five rating,' I say. 'No one's ever killed because of a five. An ugly man has no motive.'

'Everyone has a motive,' Fairchild says.

The elevator numbers start flashing again. They're coming down. Hasty footsteps and shouts echo in the stairway. The swinging beams of blazing torches puncture the darkness like rabid fireflies.

'What do we do?' Fairchild asks.

A pack of dogs begin to bark; deep, guttural howls from drooling, muscular hunting machines. The kind of dogs that can smell a guilty thought and would rip through your skull to tear your brain to shreds.

'They'll scour every floor,' I say. 'We need to get back to the roof.'

'We'll never get past them.'

'The cops won't leave without a suspect, so we better give 'em one, or else it's one of us. And I'll throw you to them myself before I hold my hands up.'

Fairchild is sweating like a blue-flamed candle.

THIS RAGGED, WASTREL THING

Two shadows enter the room and I hold my breath as Fairchild's eyes roll into the back of his skull.

'Turn the lights on,' one of them says.

'Electrics are out,' the other replies. It's Kosuke. 'Some kids blew the fuse last week. The alarm still works, though. If anyone came in here, I'd know about it.'

Good old Kosuke.

'What's below?' the cop asks.

'Pool, sauna, hot tubs. Go on down. I'll make sure it's clear here.'

The cop hesitates before trudging back to the stairwell, leaving Kosuke alone in the darkness.

'Kosuke,' I whisper, craning my neck around the slot machines. He's standing in the doorway and hurries over when he sees my face.

'What happened?' Kosuke asks.

'They're saying she was on my panel. And with my rap for murder I'm suspect number one.'

'They're after *both* of you. Fairchild was with her the last time she was seen alive. Honestly, Dustin, couldn't you have kept your donkey head down for once in your life?'

'I didn't do anything,' Fairchild barks. 'Just get us the hell out of here.'

'The entire building is on lockdown,' Kosuke says, shaking his head. 'Your only way out is the same way the girl went.'

We sit in silence with the ghosts of the arcade. First Ume, now Purple; if it carries on like this, there's another girl at the party we need to find—and fast.

'Get us back to the roof,' I say.

'The cops are still there.'

'How many?'

'Two, guarding the other guests. The rest are searching the floors below.'

'Then get us up there while the coast is clear.'

Kosuke looks from me to Fairchild. 'Fine. Come on.'

The club is empty again but the lights are on and the place is a mess; streaks of coke abandoned on every available surface, upturned glasses and empty bottles smothering the sodden floor. Fairchild snatches a bottle of beer as we run for the exit and hurdle up the stairs towards the roof.

'What are you gonna do?' he asks, taking a swig from the bottle and handing it to me.

I have no idea.

'Get those cops out the way,' I say to Kosuke.

He disappears and I hear the guests moving around, Stones' voice louder than most. Party finished too damn early for him, no doubt. Heavy footsteps approach the stairs and I pull Fairchild into the women's toilet in the hall. Through the gap I watch two cops descend the stairs and enter the club; Kosuke must have told them something was going on below.

As soon as they're out of sight, we burst out onto the roof. I half the expect the other guests to call for our heads when they see us appear, but it seems that no one's too desperate to go home yet. I search the staring faces. Sara blinks, barely acknowledging me. Stones smiles and raises his glass. Then I catch a flash of blonde hair by the pool.

'Hey,' I still don't know her name. 'Blonde.' She looks up. I grab her arm and pull her over to the railing, away from curious eyes and ears. Fairchild and Kosuke follow close behind.

'What the hell happened?' I ask her.

I feel the crowd glaring at us, so I signal to my only allies. Sara grabs a tray of drinks from the poolside bar and does the rounds while Stones steps behind the decks and turns the music back on. We won't have long before the police return.

'What happened?' I ask again, squeezing the girl's arm.

She scowls. 'How the hell should I know?'

'Let the poor girl alone, Dag,' Kosuke says.

I see the grimace on Blonde's face, my fingers clamped

onto her arm. I release her, step back and stare at my hands. When I finally look up I notice the girl behind Kosuke; Purple. She's alive. For a split second I think it's over, it was all a mistake. But then I see the look on Kosuke's face.

'How did someone get thrown from here without anyone seeing?' I ask.

I look at the girls and Kosuke, and then at the silent crowd. Everyone's staring at me. I'm the only one who doesn't know whatever it is.

'Don't be a fool, Dag,' Kosuke says. 'There's nobody down there, there never was. It's you, Dag. They want you.'

I grab hold of his shoulders and shake him wildly. 'Why? He didn't give me any choice.'

I'm about to ask who *he* is when it all comes crashing together.

'Why did you let him in?'

'I had no choice, Dag. He's a sergeant now. He could finish me. He wants *you*. He's wanted to get his hands on you ever since you got out—and long before.'

'So you sold me out, you old fool.' I wanna smash his face in. Smash the whole goddamn place up. Smash them all. 'Where is he, the coward? Why doesn't he arrest me himself?'

Five cops burst through the door with their feral hounds, snarling Dobermans busting a gut to break free of their leashes. This time the guests barely drop the glasses from their lips. This is a Sonaya party, and they're bored of the drawn-out drama. The men in blue find me straight away; there's nowhere left to run.

'Dustin Fairchild, Daganae Kawasaki, you're under arrest on suspicion of the murder of Ume Uchida.'

Ume Uchida. No wonder they kept it so quiet. They were just waiting for a chance to pin it on someone.

I look at Fairchild sitting on the floor with his head in his hands; he shouldn't worry, he'll get out of this now. If that bastard sergeant's involved they'll blame it on me for sure. I search for him in the crowd; everyone's watching the arrest like it's a mildly interesting opera, their champagne flutes still glued to their hands. Blonde and Purple are alone in looking surprised; at least I wasn't the only one in the dark. Somewhere behind them I find his face. Goichi Fujii: the man whose wife I killed. The man who won her love and stole her away from my world. I see the hatred in his eyes. A sergeant now, eh? And what better way to assert his power than a good old fashioned shake-down, with a side of state corruption.

The police start to close in, so I search for a way out. Fairchild's already holding his wrists out and I look to Kosuke for one last favour. Get me out of here, old man. I did my time.

'One moment, officers,' he says. 'This man is deaf, as you can clearly see.' My one good ear is hidden by my greasy mane, but this is still a long shot by any fool's standards. 'You can't just arrest him, he has no idea what's going on.'

The leading officer hesitates. Fujii is too far away to hear what's going on, but he's clearly concerned by the delay in my arrest.

'I'm sure everything can be explained at the station,' the man says.

So boring. I'll have to make my move any second.

'His interpreter is over there,' Kosuke says to the officers. I wonder if anyone's smart enough to simulate sign language. 'I really must insist—especially before you make an arrest under my roof—or *on* my roof,' he corrects. Kosuke whispers in my good ear. 'Thirty eight, trash chute. Now.'

He pushes me away from the officers and they swiftly raise their guns and call us back. Kosuke turns to face them, hands raised in a display of innocence. Music erupts from the speakers and the strobe lighting kicks in, and suddenly there's a commotion around the arresting officers that gives me the time and space to break away. I must still have some friends at this party.

Head down, I drive into the crowd. Safety in numbers; they can't shoot me now. My hand soars to my ankle and I unsheathe my faithful knife, Old Trusty drawn and ready by my side. The man who ruined my life shouts for the music and the lights to cease, but no one listens to him. The knife pierces his flesh before he even knows I'm in front of him. It's not a party until someone's dead, and I might just have got this party started. I'm flying towards the stairs before the screaming starts, but there's still one person to pass.

Sara stands with her arms folded at the entrance to the stairwell. I don't have time for this.

'Hold them off as long as you can,' I say.

She looks disappointed. What does she want me to do? I became a butcher eleven goddamn years ago, and I'll forever be a butcher.

'Maybe now you'll have something to write about,' I say.

She stands aside and I head for thirty-eight.

The trash chute is truly where I belong. A rat chute for a rat. What a fitting exit for murdering little me. And when I reach the bottom, where then? My time in Sonaya is done for sure.

8

Sonaya's not the best place to be a wanted man. The cops here don't knock on doors, they shoot them into splinters and then search for bodies in the smoke. My room in the Rivers is nothing more than a cube of cheese sitting under a metal hammer. Guess who the hungry mouse is. Never mind. There are a lot of places to conceal yourself in this city, and I know enough people who don't mind looking the other way.

I can't be dragging them into my trouble, though. Word is that Fairchild's out on bail and that means he's a no-go. Better give him a few weeks to lose that red flag above his head. The only person I can count on right now is Kosuke. He did the dogs in blue a favour so now he's in their good books, and he's got plenty of holes for his friends to hide in.

He offers me an array of basement bars in the heart of the Rivers and I know which one I want. Nakata sets me up with a mattress in the back room behind the bar and the faux bookcase. There's almost enough room to stretch out and sleep if I angle my legs right. I'm not complaining. Anything's better than a cell in The Heights.

Nakata doesn't talk to me much and I don't blame her; I'm a walking time bomb with bad omens buried in my pockets. Nakata just wants her quiet nights in plumes of artificial smoke, pulling records out of sleeves and pretending she's somewhere in the past. She puts up with me, though. Passes on messages, lets me know the latest. Nakata's well connected; she owns one of those old-school pager things, despite the fact they're expensive and extremely dangerous; everyone knows the government monitors every goddamn message. There's a three year waiting list and the application process is a fucking nightmare. Still, at least some people are allowed to communicate.

Anyway, Kosuke's passed on word that I'm to stay under the radar, and I'm all too happy to oblige. Sergeant Goichi Fujii is nursing a nasty wound to his gut in a downtown hospital bed, but Kosuke's reckons he'll survive to scheme a new revenge. Now I've got an attempted murder rap to go with the fabricated one. If I wanna stick around Kosuke thinks I should change my appearance. I guess I can kiss goodbye to the office job. For a few sweet days, I had a clean slate. It was good while it lasted.

'It doesn't matter now if you killed Ume or not,' Nakata says. She places my beer in front of me. I sit on a stool at the end of the bar and inhale the aroma as Nakata sprinkles cinnamon over my beer. 'Stabbing a sergeant? Even for you, Dag, that's dumb. They'll double the number of drones in the sky until they get you.'

She slides a record from the shelf behind her and gazes at it adoringly like it's a newborn baby. She runs a palm over the cover and slowly removes the record from its sleeve. Otis Redding. There's two young bucks in the corner who have probably never even heard of Old Otis before. They're dolled up in slick navy suits, blanketed in smoke and braying like ugly donkeys.

'It's not good for business,' Nakata says, returning to her open newspaper. 'Drones hovering over every roof. Murders on the quiet. The Rivers are running red these days.'

I can smell the cheap paper and faded ink from across the bar. Damn, what a fine smell.

'People always need beer,' I say, kissing the cinnamon off the rim of my glass. 'You don't need to worry.'

These days politics is all about the gimmicks; some new problem to solve, a new policy to present. Drones are only one of them; billed as the saviours of the city; eyes in the sky to keep the wolves from the fence and the startled sheep on their toes. I'm still getting used to them, same as everything else that's changed. Environment's the latest item on the ironing board; pretty soon we've got a city-wide blackout, and everyone thinks it will save the last polar bears. Thankfully, the citizens of Sonaya still have some priorities. When the previous government tried to introduce prohibition, the PM was threatened with assassination. God bless our booze.

'We never should have left,' Nakata says, folding the paper and dropping it on the bar.

I don't need to ask; half the city has buyer's remorse. Independence was so attractive back then.

'Damn it, though,' I say, drink in hand. 'Do you remember those days, Nakata? The protests, the parties.' She smiles as she pours fresh ales and Otis sings about his lonely arms. 'Those were some of the best damn days of my life.'

Nakata ferries the drinks to the kids and returns with a dreamy look in her chocolate eyes.

'The parties lasted for days,' she says, shaking her head.

I raise my glass and toast; nostalgia's a damn fine drug. 'Ex-pats came pouring in. Hell, this was the place to be.' I hand my empty glass to Nakata and she returns it to the tap. 'How the hell did everything go so wrong?'

Nakata refills my glass, her smile nowhere to be seen. Cinnamon snows down onto the foam of my beer and the spicy aroma devours the whole bar. I take a healthy hit and stare into the smoke.

It's amazing how much someone can change in twenty years. Back then, Nakata was a little firecracker, electric blue hair, spiky like a porcupine's back. She had better prospects most Sonayan women, but independence didn't work out for her. As soon as her parents caught her in bed with another woman, they cut her loose. They were religious types, and when Sonaya went out on its own the church became a way for people to make sense of it all. Sonaya was supposed to be a progressive city, but some things never change. Nakata lost everything; her family, her home, her place at university, and eventually, some of that punk in her soul.

Now she's staring through the smoke, same as me.

'Damn, those parties, though.'

#

Nakata's put on The Moody Blues and the echo of the piano follows me up the stairs as I leave the bar. Out of one darkness and into another. I take to the alleys; pulsing neon eyes and swinging signs that paint distorted shadows on crumbling, crooked walls; towering claws itching to dive in and drag me into another world. Drones don't see much down here. Half of those that enter never leave. My kind of community spirit.

The brothels and basement bars are slowly waking up. A sour-boned chef lifts the lid of his rusted pot and a rush of smoke escapes from his steaming dumplings. I glare at him as I pass through the dissipating cloud;He glares back with cold eyes that suck all the heat from his filthy shoebox kitchen. Out of nowhere a faceless child scuttles past, hobbling like an imp and cackling between hunched shoulders. I watch it disappear into the smoke. Suddenly I'm aware of every shifty eye, every silhouette that lingers a second too long behind splintered and unwashed windows. So this is how it feels to be a wanted man.

Kosuke's right; I need a new look. There aren't many men like me around; shaggy hair, one good ear and a face you can't forget. I'll ask one of Fumiko's girls to fix me up. The old girl must be pushing eighty now, but the government encourages the earthworms to toil until they're too damn tired to get out of bed anymore. This was part of Tokyo's plan to combat the ageing population: stagger retirement and keep old folks in simple jobs. It might have worked, too, if Sonaya hadn't dropped to its knees once Japan cut us loose.

Fumiko runs the biggest brothels deep in the Rivers and she knows how to keep things discreet; has her crooked fingers in a lot of crooked pies. She's short of teeth and morals, with long grey hair tied back in a witch's bun, and eyes like scythes that could slice your balls off with one clean swing. She was on the panel for Kosuke's tax assessment a few years back. The rich fool bribed the entire panel to guarantee a low score. As if he needed to, the boss-eyed git.

'What do you want, Kawasaki?' she croaks from the corner of The Cross. Charming as ever. 'Finally ready to pay for it, are you?' She's sitting on a wooden chair in front of a flashing advert for the government's biggest pachinko parlour; coins are raining down behind her head, her grey bun reflecting the golden lights like a flaming matchstick.

'Tens never pay, lady. Once a ten, always a ten. I just need a new face.'

She laughs, all gums and gullet, like an intestine struggling to expel a naked mole rat. A sound that would make any man cringe. 'Fancy losing the other ear, do you?'

I'm getting impatient. I can't stand around talking in the open all night. There are too many eyes around, and a few too many glances coming my way. I push past the old lady and she gets up and follows me down the creaking stairs to one of her seedy studios. Black walls adorned with grubby mirrors line the hall and doors lead off in all directions; a dingy warren for bunnies who've lost their way. Fumiko leans on a gnarled walking stick and pushes open the first door on the right, ushers me onto a stool. The room is small, black, with a naked bulb swinging from the ceiling, just enough light to bring my hazel eyes to life. The old woman circles me like a prehistoric shark.

'Let's lose the mane,' she says, fingering my hair so it

catches on her gnarled brown nails. 'And we'll ink your face. How does that sound?'

'Like music to my ear,' I say. 'Just get it done—fast. I'm a busy man.'

'You're a *wanted* man is what you are.'

She rings a brass bell that dangles beside the door. The sound reminds me of feeding time at The Heights. A few seconds later the door creaks open and a skinny girl squeezes in.

'Deal with this one,' Fumiko says, pointing a claw at me. 'Special customer, an old friend of mine.'

The girl creeps up and lines her shoulders up with mine, examining our reflection in the mirror. 'Tax assessment?'

'Murderer,' Fumiko answers. The girl blinks but doesn't falter. 'And that means he's sweet nectar for the drones. Ink him. Pluck his feathers.' She lands on a stool against the back wall, her cane burrowed between her legs. The girl runs her long slender fingers through my locks.

Fumiko laughs like a drowning lizard. 'Hellfire, you look like your father, Kawasaki. He was the first foreigner I ever saw. You can't imagine how the girls went crazy for him. Your mother was one lucky woman.'

'They were both as unlucky as each other,' I say. 'Careful near my ear,' I add to the girl with scissors in my hair. 'I'd like to keep this one.'

The girl doesn't reply. She's got a jaw that could sharpen the dullest blade, her face covered in so many piercings she could pass for a Christmas tree if you stuck her out in the square and lit her up. She could be anywhere between fifteen and thirty, but I'd venture to guess she's not yet legal. When girls become women, they don't stay in Fumiko's basements for long; they get 'promoted' to the bigger establishments with silk curtains at the windows.

'So you killed Ume?' Fumiko asks with her eyes closed. She's like an underground spider that's evolved to live without sight. 'If that's true, you did me a favour.'

'Friend of yours, was she?'

'She didn't have many friends, I'm afraid. Burned down one of my smaller establishments in the western Rivers. She used to work there when the sun was younger. Too many bad memories, perhaps.'

I watch the girl lop off chunks of my handsome mane. She lets them drop over my shoulders and onto the floor.

'I can't say that she'll be missed,' Fumiko says. 'Didn't play by the rules, if you know what I mean. She had fire in her belly, though, I'll give her that.' She burps; short and sharp. 'Still,' she goes on, 'it wouldn't do me any harm to hand you in, would it, Dag? Never hurts to stay on the right side of the pigpen.'

I look at the reflection of her wrinkled smile.

'How does it feel to have a murderer's hair in your hands, Min-su?' Fumiko asks. The girl doesn't flinch; like she never even heard her.

'The cops know you run a cocoon?' I ask Fumiko. 'Bribes might blind them from your brothels, but how would they feel about this little side-business of yours?'

The lizard in Fumiko's throat slithers closer towards death. 'Don't fool yourself into thinking that I care about those dogs. There isn't much that scares a woman who's this close to the end. There's only one reason I'm not turning you in, Kawasaki, and it's because I can see your father in those big brown eyes of yours.'

She croaks out a laugh, and it turns into a cough. 'Don't worry, Kawasaki, I won't regale you with tales of the past. I'll leave it to your imagination.'

I move to stand, but the girl behind me pushes down on my shoulders.

'Sit down, Kawasaki,' Fumiko says, 'I'm only teasing. You're too easy.'

I stare at my reflection in the mirror. The hair is gone. That one ear looks even lonelier now.

'Min-su,' Fumiko barks. 'Get the needle. Time for your first tattoo.'

#

Look at me, a new man. Chameleon Dag. Tribal lines spiral up my neck and curl around the hole of my missing ear. The mane's gone too; military style for the win. Now I'm just another one of those tattooed freaks you see at night; the ones who perch by gutters and ask passersby for beer. Whatever, I'll take it. Once a ten, always a ten.

I bury my hands in my baggy pockets and don't bother to confine my boots to the shadows. The Cross is the hive at the centre of the Rivers and the bees are blindly hunting pollen. I stand in the centre of the buzzing swarm, bang in the bullseye of the square as rogue planets circle round their sun, their orbits chopped up by the dark. I watch them move and take a slow, deep breath. A drone passes overhead but doesn't stop to throw a spotlight on the crowd. I've sold my looks and bought myself some time. I'm a unicorn no more, but I don't care; I've still got the sharp cheekbones of my Brooklyn pops and the hazel eyes of dear old mum, Tokyo's finest beauty. You can't take those away. Not ever.

I rip the plastic film off my neck as I head back to Nakata's bar. The night's still young and that only makes me feel older. Dag, you dinosaur. Eleven years can weigh on a man more than you'd think. I sail down the basement stairs, yearning for the smoke to veil me from my audience. I've only just moved in, but Nakata's basement already feels like home.

I return to my stool and Nakata says she's got a present for me. She's got some smart remarks about my new look, too, but I quickly put an end to those.

'One of Kosuke's carrier pigeons,' she whispers, nodding to a kid at the other end of the bar. A pigeon of the streets, and just as clean. Sharp black eyes and high cheekbones; pale face, coloured tattoo on his neck. He's wearing a dirty baseball cap with the Yomiuri Giants logo stitched on the front, a Japanese ball team from twenty years ago. I take one look at him and turn back to Nakata.

'I don't want it. You keep him.'

Nakata bites her bottom lip to keep from smiling. 'What's the problem, you don't like kids?'

'I like that noise they make.'

'What noise?'

'That noise they make when they're far away.'

Nakata gives me a look and I reluctantly get to my feet. 'How old do you have to be for a tattoo nowadays?' I ask the kid, motioning for him to move. He's probably only thirteen. 'Who did that scrawny little thing anyway?' His tattoo is some kind of flower, the sort the gangs of the Rivers have. Probably wants to make himself look tough. Stupid little thing.

'Probably the same guy that did yours,' the kid throws back at me.

I smile. 'Well now we look as stupid as each other. What's your name, kid?'

'Shinji.'

'What do you have for me, Shinji?'

Nakata looks over the only other customers, a couple in the corner: a balding suit in his fifties, his fat fingers in the hair of a girl who could be his daughter. Gene Pitney's on the record player complaining about something holding onto his heart; we won't be heard.

'This is from the German,' the kid says, sliding his hand across the bar. I reach out and discreetly scoop up the card that Shinji leaves behind.

'Bernd still here, is he? I sure have a lot of friends these days.'

'Kosuke has a lot of friends,' Nakata reminds me.

I examine the black plastic card and stare at the square barcode imprinted in the centre.

'A key,' I say to the kid. He replies with a sarcastic round of applause. Nakata smiles and fills a glass with fresh beer from the tap.

'Kosuke said you were interested in a woman called Ume Uchida,' the kid says.

'I was,' I reply, sipping at the froth of my drink. 'Now she's dead and I'm the one they want to rot for it.'

'That's what the fat man said. But if it's proof you're after, all you need to know is the right people. Se the drones outside? You gain access to them, you gain access to Sonaya. You can even find out when and where your enemy last took a stinking shit.'

I look at the card in my hand; suddenly full of possibility. I half expect it to wink at me.

'You telling me this is a keycard to access Surveillance?'

'Kosuke said you already know the details of her death,' Shinji says. 'So it's all there waiting for you. From the sound of it, this could solve all your problems. Might not grow your ear back, but everything else...'

I consider whether or not to smack him. I decide on the latter; first impressions and all that.

'So what? Bernd and Kosuke expect me to waltz into City Hall and hack into their systems?'

Shinji shrugs. His smug little face is begging for a beating.

'There might be a good night for it soon,' Nakata says.

I stare at the keycard. I always did love polar bears.

9

Earth Hour, they're calling it. Pathetic. They think an hour without electricity will save them from global warming and their guilty consciences. Wrong again. The monthly hour of darkness begins tonight, eleven sharp, and as usual I'll be one step ahead of everyone else.

I know exactly how it's gonna go down. The sheep will return to their tiny studios from brain-dead jobs, cook plastic meals in humming microwaves. They'll suck up every watt they can until the lights go out and their appliances slip into unconsciousness. They'll light their candles, sit and stare. Most people won't have a clue what to do next. They can't live without televisions or computer games. Reading a book by candlelight? Not that easy, especially when books are so damn hard to find. What does the government expect people to do? Dust off their guitars and sing hymns? Get drunk and fuck? The lucky ones, maybe. But not me. There are far better opportunities out there for a man who knows the streets. A city in darkness and an hour-long pass to run wild. Happy birthday, Dag, don't waste it.

It's ten forty-five and I'm at Isorimu Station. Everyone else is getting the hell out of here, and I don't blame them. This isn't the place to be when the lights go out—or even when the lights are on, unless you enjoy stepping on syringes or being shadowed by the drunk and deranged. Not that

I'm worried about that kind of thing; when you look like me, trouble tends to stay away.

The last train is due any minute now. The station will empty and soon everything will turn to black, and that's when things will get interesting.

Shinji's down there already, sitting on the floor with his back against the red brick wall. He's spinning his mangy baseball cap on one finger; when he sees me he speedily slaps it on his head, but not before I see the cat-scratch scar that splits his close-cropped hair in two.

'You're late,' he says.

Cheeky shit. Must have been a long time on the streets.

'I've never seen a temporary tattoo last so long,' I say, looking at his neck. 'Or is it because you haven't showered?'

He's itching to reply but my eyes tell him to keep his mouth shut. I asked Kosuke for an extra pair of hands, not a big mouth.

A gust of stale wind signals the approach of the last train and the station trembles as it rattles up beside the platform and finally hisses to a stop. I wish they'd rebuild this ancient underground. The Pipe, they call it. Looks like shit. The respectables wouldn't be caught dead down here. They'd be robbed before their polished shoes crossed the caution line.

The doors stutter open and there's hardly anyone on board. An old crone with a wrinkled face like a dried prune and a shabby headscarf gets off in front of us. I pull Shinji back; he almost steps on her feet as he tries to push past. The old dear smiles at me and fires a dirty look at the boy.

'Gentleman of The Pipe,' Shinji mocks. I shove him onto the train. Too cocky, this one.

There are only two people left in the carriage. One is a skunk in brown leather, asleep across five seats with his hood up and face down, reeking of piss and booze. Further down is an old gent in a pin-striped suit, newspaper spread across his lap; he's straight-backed and super slick with a neatly trimmed silver beard. His line of vision doesn't veer from his paper as the boy and I sit directly opposite him.

'Smells like piss,' the boy says.

The Pipe always smells like piss. A revolving toilet for the scum of the city. Thankfully, we've only got three stops to travel. The hand straps are swinging wildly and a rattling orchestra is playing out of sight; nuts and bolts loosening, or maybe it's the rusted wheels fixing to fall off.

Shinji can't keep still, fidgeting in his seat and pacing up the aisle, leaning against the carriage doors with his cap down and fists in his pockets. He's a runtish little thing, but I have to give it to him; he knows how to look like a nutter. I settle in and watch Silver Beard's sharp little eyes scanning the government's black and white lies. He catches me looking and offers a chivalrous smile before licking his index finger and turning the page. He cracks the newspaper open on his lap with such force that Shinji looks our way.

An announcement breaks the silence in three languages: end of the line. Earth Hour's about to begin. Shinji's already stood by the doors, waiting for them to open; kids have no patience these days. The hobo's still asleep. Someone will be along soon enough to kick him off the train. Or if he's lucky, he might sleep through the night. But Silver Beard isn't moving.

'End of the line, old man,' I call across the carriage. The doors open and Shinji jumps out onto the platform. The beard looks up at me and smiles. Don't know how these morons end up in their cushty office jobs. 'Lights'll go out soon,' I say. He continues smiling, like a simpleton. Shinji calls for me to get off, but I can't pull myself away from the old man. Then something changes deep in his eyes.

'Then you'd better get moving, Daganae,' he replies at last.

Damn. Don't like it when a suit knows my name; it's never good news.

'Five minutes till lights out, Kawasaki,' the beard continues, folding his newspaper across his lap. 'Watch out for the tigers. They can see in the dark.'

I don't hang around for an explanation; in a flash I'm off the train and racing up the subway steps with Shinji close behind.

'Who the hell was that?' the kid asks.

How the hell should I know? Nothing's ever simple when you're me.

#

'Stick to the plan,' I say.

I'm out of breath. Damn subway stairs.

'What was that about tigers?' Shinji asks.

'Just shut it and keep up.'

Kids, always asking too many questions. We emerge at street level beside The Pulse, the shallow stream that snakes through the business district in the heart of the city. Used to be a quaint little creek a long time ago, but the government souped it up and now it burns at night with endless chains of fairy lights. Shady folk sink bottles of booze beneath the cover of crumbling bridges, hypnotized by the glowing banks and gov-run buildings that tower high above.

We follow the shimmering promenade until we reach the fountain in front of City Hall. I used to work around here once upon a time, before the handsome tax and the heartbreak and everything went wrong. Back then the fountain spurted water and wasn't just a rain collector covered in a layer of grime.

'We breaking in or what?' the kid asks.

Have to wait for the lights to go out. 'What time is it?'

'Any minute now,' he says, sitting down on the weathered stone of the fountain wall.

'Get up. People are after us.'

'No one's after me. They're after you.'

'Then piss off home and leave me alone,' I say. I can't be bothered with his lip. He probably doesn't have a home to go to, anyway.

Then the lights go out. Just like that. The moon is full, but it's trapped behind a sky of smog; you've never seen a city so damn black. Earth Hour begins, and a shiver of excitement slides down my vagabond spine.

'Look,' Shinji says, pointing at the nearest apartment block, a sleek black tower built entirely from glass; swanky homes for the office zombies. It's clear from the flickering lights within that candles are being lit.

The roar of helicopter rotors erupts nearby, and we hit the deck. The government will send its drones out, too. A little darkness won't stop them from seeing everything.

'Let's go,' the kid says.

'Hold it.'

Now it's my turn to sit tight. Total darkness. I'm not gonna be caught by tigers; I'm gonna become one myself.

'What you doing?'

'Shut up and keep your ears open. Adjust your eyes, quick. I'm gonna need more than one pair tonight.'

I get up just as he gets comfortable; gotta keep him on his toes. I head past the fountain to the entrance of the building, bold as brass, like I never lost my job all those years ago. Doors are padlocked; no one's relying on electricity tonight. We go round back to the frozen revolving doors where suits used to smoke their breaks away. Man, I still remember the taste of cigarettes. Haven't seen one in twenty years; hyenas would have you think they're weapons of war.

'How do we get in?' the kid asks.

I pick up a metal table from the patio and throw it through the glass. No alarms tonight. No security guards either. Yet.

We head on in. The lobby is empty, reception unmanned. Our footsteps bounce off the marble floor and echo in the foyer, closely followed by further footsteps and a swinging torch beam emerging from the stairway. Shinji follows me as we jump behind the reception desk and duck out of sight.

'I thought torches weren't allowed,' the kid whispers.

Damn kid. Didn't know he was so naive. This is a government building; as if the government would follow its own rules. I hold a finger to my lips to silence him. A guard appears and waves his—*her* torch. Her eyes will never adjust like that. Advantage Dag. Just don't look at the light.

'No lights allowed,' I call out. Improvisation. Following my gut.

'Who's there?' she asks. Her voice is breathless and she swings her torch wildly. She's coming our way.

I mime instructions to the boy; on my signal, run to the stairs. He nods. Seems like this kid gets me.

'Now' my eyes command.

The boy leaps to his feet and legs it. The guard's too concerned about catching him in the beam of her torch to even think about giving chase. And this little pigeon flies fast.

'Who's that?' the guard screams at the boy's back.

I'm behind her in a flash. A swift smack to the back of the head and she drops like a stone. Should keep her out for a while.

'You hit a girl,' Shinji says, all surprised.

I switch off the guard's torch and shove it in my pocket. 'What did you want me to do? Distract her with flowers? Equality, boy, equality.'

We start on the stairs and climb twenty floors. I take it slow; not as young as I used to be.

The kid leans against a wall to catch his breath. 'You gonna watch it again?' he finally asks.

'Watch what?'

'You killing your girlfriend.'

Enough's enough. I grab him by the scruff of his neck and pin him against the wall, his feet twitching above the floor. My eyes do the talking, and finally, he understands. I release my grip and he slides down to the floor and adjusts his cap. It's the first time I've seen anything like fear in his eyes.

'Is that you, Daganae?' Someone calls from below, all calm and polite, like a parent checking their kid is home from school. 'Mr. Kawasaki? We're here.'

Damn. Must be the tigers. The kid glares at me.

'Up', I command.

This time we're bounding up the stairs as fast as we can. Sounds like two on our tails, could be more. The kid falls over, and he's meant to be the sprite one.

'The torch,' he says, as I pull him up.

'No.' There's something comforting about the darkness and I don't wanna destroy it.

We finally reach the thirtieth floor. Drone surveillance. All I need to do is slip inside, lock the door, and pry. Somewhere on those computers is the proof I was framed. I search my pockets for the key, but it's gone. Damn. I must have dropped it during our race up the stairs. The footsteps below are gaining on us. I try the door but it's locked. I shoulder barge it. Nothing. We try the door on thirty-one. Locked. Everything is locked. This staircase is my entire world now.

The tigers are gaining; I can hear them.

'The roof,' the kid says, and he's off, taking two steps at a time.

I'd rather not go to the roof. Nothing good happens on rooftops, but we don't have a choice.

The kid's already there when I reach the top of the stairs. He's staring at the door like he's expecting it to burst into flame, but there's no time to hesitate. Dag the Brave. I push it open. We're up. And someone's already there.

#

Silver Beard. Of course. A helicopter behind him. Silver in his hand, too. A Nambu, semi-automatic, aimed squarely at a bagged head. The body's wrapped in tarnished leather and tied to a chair.

'You took your time, Kawasaki,' Silver Beard says.

There's nowhere to run; I hate rooftops. Two tigers burst through the door behind us. Burly soldiers garbed in black; night vision goggles and guns the size of bulldozers.

'Before we begin,' I say, 'why don't we let the kid go. He's just a skunk, doesn't know anything.'

Dag the Martyr. Shame they don't give awards to guys like me.

'Oh' Silver Beard replies, smiling with his twinkling eyes. 'I think he knows more than you give him credit for.'

Shinji approaches the old man, all cool like. He reaches into his pocket and pulls out my keycard, holds it up to the moonlight. The flower tattoo; I should've known. Fooled by a damn thirteen-year-old? I must be getting soft.

'Nothing personal, Dag,' Shinji says, accepting a wad of cash from Silver Beard. 'But it pays to be on the right side.'

Not so smart after all. There is no right side in Sonaya, kid.

'Recognise this one?' Silver Beard asks, waggling his gun beside the bagged head. 'Thought we'd invite someone special, someone who means something to you. Wasn't easy, though. You don't have many friends, do you, Dag?'

Shit. Who have I dragged into this? My first thought comes as a surprise even to me, and Silver Beard reads it.

'Oh, no no no,' he says. 'You're not thinking of that little biker girl, are you? You're getting soft, Dag. But don't worry, we let you take care of her yourself. We merely dressed her up and sent her on an evening stroll downstairs. Just like you to kill before you check the face.'

Damn, the security guard. But I didn't kill her, just knocked her out. I think.

'Oh, come on, Dag,' Silver Beard says, disappointed. 'You saw him this evening, sleeping on the train. Didn't you recognise your brother in crime?'

He removes the bag. Dustin Fairchild. Unconscious, glasses askew on a bruised and broken face. Better him than

Jiko, I try to convince myself. Fairchild has a knack of finding his way out of trouble. Should have recognised him on the train, though. Getting sloppy. Soft *and* sloppy.

I slowly reach for my ankle and the Beretta I borrowed from Nakata, but it's gone. Shit. Damn stairs. Or Shinji. All I've got is Old Trusty, and that won't stand a chance against two cocked and loaded guns.

'What do you want?' I ask, straightening up. Let's get down to business. 'If you thought I'd give myself up for this worthless punk, you thought wrong.' Brave face and all that. 'You wanna put me back in The Heights? No way. I've done my time. I had nothing to do with Ume's death.'

'Well, the law doesn't quite agree with you on that one, Dag,' Silver Beard says. 'But we're not here to do their dirty work. If the law wants you, they can catch you themselves. They were hoping to do it tonight, but I guess we got to you first.'

'Tonight?'

That sly smile again. 'If you want to catch a spider switch off the lights and wait for it to scuttle out of its hole.'

Earth Hour. Nice cover. I wondered when the hyenas started caring about the environment. So much for the polar bears.

'So what is it, then?' I ask. 'What do you want?'

Silver Beard offers me a level stare. 'The girl,' he says. 'Where is she?'

I don't need to fake the smile. 'Which one? I know a few.'

He cocks his gun. The two behind me follow suit. '*The girl*, Daganae.'

I look around at each of them. Cluelessness doesn't suit me.

'We're powerful people, Kawasaki,' Silver Beard says, tilting his head. 'Surely you can't expect to stab a sergeant and get away with it. He's a well-connected man, and he looks after his own. Only this job, well, it's personal. He'd prefer it taken care of quietly before they try and send you back inside.'

So that's what this is. A protection racket. I give them

what they want and they leave me haemorrhaging on the pavement. It's an old story, only I haven't studied the synopsis.

'I've no idea who you're talking about,' I repeat. I'm fucked either way.

'We're not playing around, Kawasaki.'

I laugh. Gotta try and keep things cool.

Silver Beard spins his gun and smashes the handle into Fairchild's face. His nose spreads over his face like jam on bread and blood streams down his chin. Silver Beard looks at me and I just shrug. One of the tigers steps past me and Silver Beard nods. He heaves the butt of his rifle into Fairchild's stomach and his body slumps forward. Then another, and another, until Fairchild tumbles to the floor. There's blood all over Shinji's crummy shoes; he throws up on the spot, and I'm not far from doing the same.

Silver Beard reaches into his inner jacket pocket and pulls out a red, stemless rose. He drops it onto Fairchild's crumpled body; it rolls off his torso and falls into the puddle of blood on the floor. So these are the Roses I've heard so much about.

'Not even this snake pit of a government will let you get away with killing an ex-pat,' I say. 'They don't like the publicity. You're done for tonight.'

Big Mouth Dag.

The beard has Shinji by the neck before I can blink, gun pointed at the little traitor's head.

'We're not done yet, Dag,' Silver Beard says. 'Maybe you're right. Maybe Fairchild's the wrong brain for this bullet. This kid, though? Who'd miss him?'

'Why should I care about that little shit?' I ask. The kid's got one of their tattoos on his neck; they wouldn't kill one of their own.

Bang. Gunfire. Blood.

The tiger who was standing over Fairchild falls to the ground, his brain blasted across the rooftop. I turn around to see who fired the gun, but catch only a flash of red hair disappearing behind the door. Silver Beard uses Shinji as a shield and points his Nambu over the kid's shoulder. The other tiger fires at the door, but Jiko's safely tucked behind it. All I've got is my knife. I might as well be naked. Suddenly everything goes silent.

'Come out with your hands up' Silver Beard barks. 'Or the boy dies. Kawasaki, too. Three.'

I check the door. Nothing. Jiko could be halfway out the building by now. Shinji's squealing like a pig, snot down to his lips.

'Two.'

No sign of movement. See you later, pigeon boy.

'One.'

I'm braced for the sound of the bullet piercing the boy's skull when a spotlight slaloms over the rooftop like a swinging chandelier.

'Everyone drop your weapons,' a distant voice orders.

I look up; it's a drone, and a big one. Lights flash twenty feet above as the searchlight paints bright circles on the roof.

Silver Beard throws Shinji to the floor like a kid spitting out gum. He scrambles aboard the helicopter with his tiger while I drag the blasted kid to the door. Fairchild will have to deal with the fallout of this himself; right now he's dead weight and he'll only slow me down. The voice from the drone barks more orders but this party's over and we're clearing out. The chopper's off the ground and slicing through the sky towards the coast. The drone hesitates, unsure of who to follow. I pull Shinji through the door and see the drone give chase to Silver Beard's chopper. Two bloody bodies remain on the roof and you can bet more drones will appear to clean up the mess. I just hope the police are busy with other spiders tonight. I lean against the door and catch my breath, Shinji a defeated mess at my feet.

'You took my gun,' I say to the quiet stairwell.

Jiko's standing in the shadows one floor down. My eyes are still adjusting, but I can make out her face.

'You tried to knock me out,' she says. 'I swiped this from your ankle during your sermon on feminism.'

This really hasn't been my finest display. 'Any more bullets in there?' I ask.

Jiko looks at the gun. She probably doesn't know.

'Stick one in this kid's skull if there are,' I say, nodding to Shinji, whimpering on his knees.

Sirens blare outside.

'You'd better run,' I say. '*You're* probably more wanted than I am right now.'

Jiko stares at me hard. Fine; misery and company and all that.

'Well, let's go then,' I say.

I grab the boy by his collar and drag him to his feet. I believe in second chances; I've had my fair share.

'Twenty minutes of darkness left,' Jiko says as we begin our descent.

A twenty minute free pass. Run wild. Live fast. Happy birthday, Dag, don't waste it.

10

FIVE MONTHS TO RELEASE

I'm sitting in a square room with mirrors surrounding me on all sides: walls, floor, ceiling. I know I should be wondering who's behind them, but all I can think about is how I still look like a ten after all this time. From the side, from the back, from the front. Don't get me wrong, I'm not arrogant. When you're a ten, you're a ten. It's a fact.

I've got a few new greys in this mane of mine. A few more of them peppered into the stubble, but I'm not worried; if anything, they give me an extra edge. A wolf with a slither of dignity in his fur. I'm still admiring the fine line of my jaw when a hidden door within the mirrors opens and the journalist walks in.

I know who she is; I like to keep abreast of the ex-pat community. Foreign journalists don't last long in Sonaya; either the hyenas in government don't like what they're doing and shut them up, or they like their work too much, like in Fairchild's case, and then there's no going back. This one's been here for a while now, if my memory serves. And it doesn't always.

'Daganae Kawasaki,' she says.

I love it when people say my name like that. Like I'm the eighth wonder of the world.

She closes the door behind her and we're back in the land of mirrors. I'm starting to like this room; you can examine a person from every conceivable angle. She approaches the table and keeps her eyes locked on mine like a cat stalking a mouse. Gobble me up, girl, I taste mighty fine.

'Sara Barnes,' I say.

I can see by the way she hovers behind the chair that I've caught her off guard.

'Please, have a seat,' I say.

Damn I'm a gentleman. All I need is a roaring fire and a bottle of the good stuff and I'd be the perfect host. Welcome to my world of mirrors, Ms. Barnes.

She pulls out the chair and sits down, removes a pocket-sized pad and a ballpoint pen from her shoulder bag. All that separates us is a single pane of glass that cuts through the middle of the room and moulds itself around the table.

'Rags in the States still using pen and paper, are they?'

Barnes looks at the thing in her hand. 'I'm old-fashioned,' she says.

'Then shouldn't you buy me a drink before we begin?'

I smile at her. She smiles back. Look at us, we're having a tea party.

'What are *you* in for, then?' I ask. It's an old joke I play with the guards.

'You seem to know who I am,' she says. 'But do you know who I work for?'

I shrug.

'I'm told you're friends with Dustin Fairchild, so you must know he lost his job.'

'So you took his place. You from New Jersey, too?'

'Manhattan. I've heard you're getting out soon. You'll have a tax assessment before you leave, is that correct?'

I nod.

'You still think you'll be a ten?'

I shrug. 'I've aged pretty well.'

There's a hint of a smile on her lips. She doesn't disagree at any rate.

'It was hard enough for you to get a job when you were just a ten. Now you're a ten and a murderer. How do you rate your prospects?'

'I'll find a way to make things work.'

She doesn't bother writing that down.

'Just because Fairchild lost his way doesn't mean the rest of us have given up on this city,' Barnes says. 'I'm working on a historical piece: Events that Shaped Sonaya.'

'I'm flattered,' I say. 'But I didn't have anything to do with the shaping of this sewer.'

She shakes her head. 'No, but you were involved in the city's most famous murder case of the last fifty years. The death of a prospective prime minister? That's big news wherever you're from.'

'So read the reports.'

'I have. Many times. But I want to hear *your* side of the story. The famous Daganae Kawasaki. The ten who murdered his girlfriend because she left him for another man. I don't know about here, but that's the kind of story that sells in America, Mr. Kawasaki. Kitchen sink stuff, you know. Better than plain old political intrigue.'

I shuffle back on my chair but can't get comfortable. Meanwhile, Barnes is sitting at ease and looking pretty pleased with herself; I glance around the room to find her smug face repeated a hundred times over.

'Can I ask you a question?' I lean in. 'How many people are on the other side of these mirrors?'

Barnes looks at the mirrored wall to her right as if she can see right through it.

'Three or four.'

'I've got a clean record,' I say. 'No fights, no resistance, not a blotch. Five months to release. They know I'm not going to do anything today to jeopardise that.'

Barnes hardly blinks. She's got a solid stare.

'Why do you think they've got so many people watching us?' I ask. I lower my voice, just for effect. 'Are they here for me, or for you?'

She spins the pen between her thumb and forefinger.

'Why don't you tell me what happened,' she says. 'In your own words.'

I lean back. 'I hope you don't have plans for this evening.'

#

'I was good,' I say. '*Real* good. I had everything. You understand me? *Everything*. I was good at my job and everyone knew it. Don't get me wrong, I wasn't a saint, but I was better than most. I didn't take bribes, and I played by the book. If I'd stayed on, I would've made detective. No doubt about that. But the ratings changed everything.'

'How old were you?'

'Twenty-three.'

I can tell she's trying to picture me without the wrinkles and sprinkles of grey. If she's doing it right, she's looking at a pretty fine portrait.

'They said it was because of the low birth rate,' I continue. 'No one was fucking anymore, that was the problem. The guys weren't picking up girls in bars; they were dating video game characters. The women were after careers; they didn't want to hook up with geeks only to quit their jobs as soon as they became pregnant. The population was falling by one percent every year—and those aren't healthy numbers.

'That's when some genius in government came up with the handsome tax. They didn't want guys like me to have such an advantage, you see. The ugly guys weren't getting any, I guess, and guys like me were getting loads. They wanted to even up the playing field.'

'And you got a ten average,' Sara says. 'How did you feel?'

'Mixed feelings, I guess you could say. But it doesn't matter how *I* felt—the fact is their stupid tax didn't work. After a couple of years it wasn't just your average guy who was getting taxed, but their employers too. So companies didn't want good-looking guys working for them anymore; it cost too much money. Why hire a ten when you can hire a five for half the price? You've no idea how hard it was for a ten to find work. Lose your job because you're too good-looking? Fucked up. A guy can get pretty desperate in a situation like that.'

'But you had a girlfriend by then, right?'

'Correct. I used to get around pretty well, but she came along and tried to make an honest of me.'

'Hana.'

'Yes, Hana. Smart, pretty, didn't stand for my shit. She was going places, all right, and I thought I was going with her.'

'So what happened?'

'I'm getting to that. Tens aren't that common, you know. There weren't many of us then and there's less of us now. In those days, if you were a ten people knew about it. People knew who you were. There was a big scene back then, the city was on the up and I was one of the faces deemed fit for the ride. Let's just say I enjoyed myself. I drank this city dry. And if you drink as much as me, you make mistakes.'

Sara looks up from her notebook. 'What mistakes did you make?'

'I threw it away, that's what I did. I had the world in the palm of my hand and I crushed it to pieces.'

I stare at Barnes but she doesn't say anything, pen poised above her pad.

'I cheated on her.'

'With who?'

'Oh, back then she was little more than a punk kid. Dyed hair and black lipstick and a bike that bellowed through the night; she was nothing like her sister.'

For the briefest of moments Sara Barnes isn't a journalist anymore; she's a girl in the playground chewing on the latest gossip. 'Her sister? You cheated on Hana with her sister?'

'I guess that's the part of the story that didn't get out. She was a fiery one, for sure. A trash-talking teen with rebellion seeping out of her pores. Young guy scared of commitment? A punk girl like her was the perfect distraction.

'All it took was one conversation with Hana to send me running. One small talk about the future, proper plans, a wedding. One meeting with her old man to send me to the bar and start doubting everything. The old square thought I was a waste of space, see. I'd just lost my job to a guy with a beer belly and a pug nose; half my skills but half the taxes. But Hana always had faith in me; she told her father we would make it work, no matter what. No one had ever put such faith in me before.'

'Faith and pressure,' Sara adds.

I nod. 'I drank long and hard, drowning in a bar run by a friend of mine, big panda named Ganzo. I chewed his ear off that night. Until Ryoko came down the stairs. She was twenty-one, drunk and jealous. Jealous of her sister. Of her sister's job, her prospects, her ten-rated boyfriend. I should've known better, but back then I was young and stupid. So I lost control. We drank too much, stumbled home. Hana caught us together, and that was it. The start of Dag's road to ruin. One moment of weakness.'

I watch Sara's pen dance across her pad.

'Did you try to get her back?'

'Within a few weeks Hana was seeing some square on the rebound. A cop.'

'You knew him?'

'I knew *of* him. About the same age as me but nowhere near as gifted. Goichi Fujii. Ambitious and ordinary, the perfect combination to professionally progress. They became steady pretty quickly, but I was convinced we weren't done. I tried to get her back for months, and it almost happened, but she couldn't forgive me. Couldn't trust me. They married soon after.

'Then one night I got a message with instructions to meet Hana down by the lighthouse, the place we used to go when we first started dating. I thought it meant something. Thought maybe she'd changed her mind about Fujii. But I wasn't exactly stable in those days. That night I was so smashed I don't even know how I got there.'

'And what happened?'

I watch Sara's pen again. I'm searching the dusty tunnels of my mind, but all I can see are the same grainy images I've been thumbing through for the past ten years, and I'm not even sure if they're real anymore.

'All I remember is firing the gun. The puddle of blood around Hana's head. And running. I remember the running, all right. I remember that much.'

I look up at Barnes. She finishes scribbling and stares at me.

'That surprise you?' I ask. 'How bad a person can be? Cheated on her, killed her, ran away. Didn't even have the guts to stay with her as she bled out on the street. That's the kind of person I was. That's the kind of person I am.'

'When I came in here,' Barnes drawls, 'I didn't expect to meet any angels plucking harps behind bars. This is The Heights.'

I nod.

'How long you been a journalist?'

'Why?'

I shrug. 'This is easier than I thought, that's all.'

'People like to talk about themselves. They like the attention. My part is easy, I just guide the pen.'

'I don't think you've been at it long,' I say. 'You don't question like a journalist. You're too soft.' Follow me, girl, let's waltz through this maze of mirrors.

Barnes' expression doesn't change. Whatever she is, she's good. But I won't let her know it.

'So you pleaded guilty even though you can't remember what it happened,' Barnes says. 'You really don't remember why she wanted to meet you or what she might have said? Was it about the baby?'

I take a deep breath, crack my knuckles, and stand. 'Feels

like we're alone, doesn't it?' I say. I walk over to the mirror on my left, cup my hands around my eyes to check if I can see what—or who—is on the other side. No good; it's too bright in here. 'Feels like we can say whatever we want and no one will hear us.'

Barnes clicks her pen and drops it on the pad. 'If you really can't face up to what happened, that's fine,' she says. 'I'll tell my boss you weren't as interesting as everyone makes out, that your story's not worth printing. No skin off mine.'

I turn back from the mirror and stare at her.

'It must be hard being an ex-pat in Sonaya. Artists, musicians, writers. They've all got something, haven't they? Passion, inspiration. But what have you got, Sara?'

'I'm not here to talk about me.'

'Indulge me. People like to talk about themselves, you said so yourself. Tell me about Sara Barnes.'

Her eyes are pinned on me and if she's rattled she doesn't show it.

'I read that you're here alone. Not many people would accept an assignment abroad, especially in a shithole like Sonaya. What happened? Boyfriend break up with you? Looking for a fresh start?'

Sara Barnes purses her lips. Her jaws tense. She picks up her pen. 'Do you remember seeing Hana fall to the ground? Do you remember the crack of her skull against the pavement?'

'Journalists don't have much of a reputation here, you know,' I say. 'Especially foreign ones. Not after the likes of Fairchild.'

'You remember how she held her stomach before she died? You must remember that.'

'What I must do is remember to ask Fairchild what he thinks of you,' I go on.

'You lost your temper because she wouldn't take you back. That's what happened, isn't it? She told you to stay away, that you'd blown it, that she never wanted to see you again.'

'It's a lonely city, isn't it, Barnes?'

Sara looks at me with the faintest pout. She's patient, all right, but I don't lose games like these. She snaps her notebook shut and stands.

'I think I've got everything I need.'

11

We're taking the stairs two at a time, back in the dark, mind aflame like a swarm of fireflies. Fairchild injured somewhere above, one of the Roses dead, a new shade of red for the City Hall roof. All change. Here we go, do-si-do, pick your partner and follow me.

Shinji's a spry one. Give a runt lamb a second chance and they gain a sudden spring in their legs. I'm struggling to stay on the turncoat's heels. We're approaching the thirtieth floor, and my rusty old blood starts boiling again. Hell, I'm alive tonight.

'Boy,' I call down the stairs. He stops in his tracks, looks up. 'Give me that damn key.'

'Dag,' Jiko says. She's coming down behind me, panting. 'Forget it, let's go. The police will be here soon.'

She's right about that, and they'll bring lights and handcuffs with them. But I keep my eyes fixed on the boy.

'The key,' I say again.

The boy scans the staircase. He's two flights below, would be hard to catch from up here. I wonder how well I can aim in the dark. I'm about to reach for Old Trusty when the boy pulls the key from his shoe and dangles it in the air. For a second I think he's gonna drop it down the stairwell, but he places it on the step and nods, like that makes us even. Without a word he disappears into the darkness. Kosuke's little carrier pigeon, soaring into the night.

'We need to get out of here, Dag,' Jiko says again.

I pick up the key and turn to look at her. My eyes have adjusted to the dark, but hers look like they're seeing it for the first time. There's a Rose on the roof with a red cocktail for a head, and I'm not the only wanted criminal in the building anymore.

'Let's keep moving,' I say.

We're passing thirty-third and I've only got a few seconds to decide. In fifteen minutes, Sonaya will light up like a midnight carousel; apartment windows, street lamps, headlights of hurtling police bikes. Drones and drinkers and druggies slinking back onto the streets and the realm of the Rivers. Moths soused by the neon glare, ready for the night to really begin.

Down to thirty and my time's up. Now or never. There it is, a locked door with a room full of answers on the other side. One woman's death, my freedom, right there on those computers. All I need is time.

'Dag,' Jiko says. A plea and a caution all in one syllable.

I know what she's done for me, and I know what it means. Before we were even; now we're much more than that. I glance at the door and back at Jiko.

'Sorry, girl,' I say. Dag The Scum. 'My night's not over yet.'

I test the keycard and it works. A flash of green and a short little beep, a click of the lock. I push the door open and take a final look at the girl with red hair.

'I won't be long,' I say. 'Wait for me, then we'll get out of here—together.'

Tears well in her eyes under the shadow of death. She killed for a man who's cast her aside like a doll in the attic. My night might not be over, but hers is. She shoots me a furious and broken look, then continues down the staircase. I call after her but it's no use. Curiosity has beaten me, the old dog, and the night's gone all to hell.

#

On the other side of the door is an office lined with desks and dented filing cabinets. Computers and printers and copiers, even oldskool phones with number wheels and bulky receivers; it's like technology never went away.

I introduce my blood-splattered boots to the grey-scale carpet and glance at the vast windows; the city's still black, but the belly moon's making a break from the clouds. No drones in sight. A vast black ocean and I'm taking to the waves alone, board under my arm. This is it; a clear run.

I head straight for the glass office at the back of the room. The door is unlocked so I stroll on in and boot up the computer. Nice flashy desk with a swivel chair; I help myself to a seat.

Apparently old Bernd has friends in high places. He's the city's leading correspondent for Europe, but he's more Sonayan than German now. He's armed me with a dissertation of instructions and passwords and I get to work logging into the database.

It's been a good few years since I've seen a keyboard and it takes me a blasted eternity to locate the correct keys. *Loading.* I'm sure computers used to be faster than this. I enter the date of Ume's death. A whole stream of surveillance footage captured by drones appears on-screen. I try the first one. *Loading.* Whatever happened to high speed processors? I fast forward through the video but all I see are panoramas of the Rivers: lingering shots of addicts with their hands in their pockets and amblers with their heads down; people ducking into basement bars or standing at noodle holes, chewing on worms from paper containers and staring at the ground with dead eyes. The second one is more of the same. I scan through each video but find no trace of Ume, dead or alive. I'm running out of time and all I've gained so far tonight are a few extra enemies and another bundle of guilt to lug on my back.

Then I see her. Ume Uchida. Dark skin and darker hair; after a quick zoom, I'm treated to her wide mermaid eyes and her shawl of cherry blossom tattoos. She's standing alone in a quiet corner near the edge of the Rivers. I recognise the dumpsters and drab walls that towered over me and Fairchild a few days ago. This is where it happened.

Two men enter the shot: one tall and brawny, dressed in black, completely bald; the other has long hair and a stump of an arm. The bald man approaches Ume while the amputee turns away; Ume's backed up against a wall. This is it, the evidence I've been searching for. Baldie pulls out a gun and empties the clip into Ume. I capture some screen grabs. Enough, maybe, to clear my name. I click Print. *Loading.* Fucking hell. I rap my fingers on the desk. *Error: Printer Offline.* I curse and slam my fist on the keyboard. Maybe life *is* better without all this junk.

I examine the printer and press a few buttons. It beeps and flashes like a bright little kid waking up from a nap. The fucking cheek of it. I'm about to return to the computer to hit Print again when the lights blink outside. Time flies when you're fixated on pixels. Earth Hour is finished. Congratulations, sheep of Sonaya, you survived the long winter. The cops could burst in any second but I can't walk away, not now, not when I'm so close. If I can just print these pictures I might finally find a way to secure my freedom. But things just aren't going my way tonight.

Sirens. Sirens so loud my tattoos nearly fall off my face. Red lights flash on the ceiling like goddamn disco balls. The computer screen goes black and restarts itself; security shutdown. This is officially a break-in, with two lifeless bodies and only me at the scene of the crime. The stealth mission is over. Time to clear out.

I head for the stairs. Then I remember the electricity's back on, so I make for the lift instead.

Thirty floors at high speed, it's enough to make a man's ear pop. These lifts are the fanciest I've ever seen; not even

Kosuke has lifts with security monitors inside. I look at the screen and stare at a still of the lobby; empty from what I can see. I might have a clean getaway after all. Floor ten, nine, eight. Then I see movement. I focus on the screen: at least one figure is skulking in the darkness. Six, five, four.

Drones, Roses, dogs in uniform; what next? I crouch down, one knee on the floor, one hand on Old Trusty. An old cat primed to pounce.

Three, two, one. Doors opening.

#

I step out of the lift and the doors slide shut behind me. A breeze from the doors I smashed through earlier caresses my skin. I inch forward, my big bold boots moving cautiously for once. Someone's here, and they're waiting for me.

I look at the door, straight ahead. Twenty paces, maybe. I could run for it. Maybe it's all I *can* do. Why didn't I take Jiko's gun? I glance to the left. To the right. Now's my chance. The whip crack of a starter pistol. Run.

The old legs are chugging along like the wheels of a locomotive; old and rusty and nowhere near fast enough. Somewhere behind me the shadows shift; I can sense it more than I can see or hear it. I veer to the left, to the right. I'm like a damn cartoon, but I'll do what it takes to stay alive.

There are no gunshots. No knives whistling through the air. Only the figure, lurking behind me in the pregnant darkness. I reach the door and launch myself through the broken glass. I'm finally out and the streets are calling me to safety, but that ugly sin of my heart is baring its teeth again. Curiosity rips across my chest like a lion's claws, and who am I to resist? I stop dead in the doorway, turn to the darkness, and yield to my feline friend.

For a moment I think it was all in my head. There was no one there; all the double-crossing and darkness have turned me into a paranoid wreck. But then I see the silky silhouette of a woman.

'Who the hell are you?' I ask.

The figure slowly steps forward, immune to the double-time rhythm of this manic night. My pulse should be pounding but it feels like it's drowning instead, her footsteps soothing the beat of my heart. I still can't see her face.

'Just a latecomer to the party' comes the reply.

Her face finally appears in the glow of moonlight. Sara Barnes. My relief must be palpable.

'You look like you've enjoyed yourself tonight,' she says. 'How was your first Earth Hour?'

I consider my evening. Fooled by a thirteen-year-old, watched a brain fly out of its skull, probably became even more wanted than I was before.

'Wonderful,' I say. 'The hell are you doing here, Barnes?'

She looks me up and down with those mercury eyes.

'I've got to make a living,' she says. 'And you seem to be in all the best stories, Dag. What happened up there?'

'I'd love to stay and chat,' I say, looking over my shoulder at the street and the shimmering Pulse. Sirens blare in the distance and streetlights shine like miniature clones of the moon. A motorbike flies past and suddenly I feel vulnerable out in the open. 'But now isn't exactly the best time.'

Sara motions to the darkness behind her. 'Taking care of business?'

'Just trying to clear my name.'

'You're wanted for the murder of Ume Uchida,' she says. 'If you wanna clear your name, I can help you. I'm not a government puppet; if *we* print your story, our readers will believe it.'

'People in Sonaya believe what the government tells them to believe,' I say. 'Try and print something to contradict them and you'll be on the next ferry to Hokkaido. You wanna do something useful, then get up to the roof and get Fairchild some help.' The sound of sirens grows louder until two police motorbikes speed around the corner and head straight towards us. The Pulse is awakening. 'So long, Barnes. Watch out for the tigers.'

12

I rock up to Ganzo's place early and there's no one around when the bell above the door announces my arrival. My boots hit the wonky stairs and each footstep sounds like a dog being squashed under the tyres of a haul truck. Paper lanterns swing from the slanted ceiling and cast an amber glow on the long oak bar and the faded leather cushioning of the bar stools. The walls look like they're being held together by the ancient newspaper cuttings that cover their surface. The remainder of the room is occupied by a tattered corner sofa and stained round tables. It's the calm between the dinner rush and the indomitable flood of drunks, the best time to wet your lips in the Rivers.

'What are you drinking, Dag?'

Ganzo's standing behind the bar just the way I left him before I went away; straight back and hands folded across his considerable midriff, like a wind-up toy that's been waiting eleven years to be wound. He's got the face of a pug dog and puffy cheeks you'd never squeeze unless you were fast on your feet and swift up stairs. His small button eyes and slow doleful movements make him look like a panda that's been dumped in a pen with nothing but bamboo. He's wearing his customary white coat and matching sushi hat, and he spreads his big bare hands on the counter as I sit down in front of him. He's always refused to wear gloves; fish don't like plastic, apparently.

'You got wine?'

Ganzo smiles and wrinkles his goatee. A sushi bar usually means cold beer or hot sake, but Ganzo's a flexible guy. He reaches under the bar. 'White or red?'

'What are they?'

'Riesling or Merlot.'

'Give me the Merlot.'

'Glass or bottle?'

I look around. I'm taking a risk by being here; I must have half the city after me by now, but I hate being cooped up. Eleven years in The Heights has that effect. Anyway, this is the best part of the city to hide in, especially if you've got blood on your hands. I wish it was just on my hands; I'm up to my knees in the stuff. 'Let's take down a bottle. It's a night for burning demons and throats.'

'You're the boss,' Ganzo says. He takes down two glasses and pours a splash for me to taste. I'm not one for ceremonies; I throw it down my throat and big surprise, it tastes like wine. Pour on, panda. We clink glasses.

'What's the latest from the front?' I ask.

Ganzo knows the city's secrets better than most; he's got two keen ears and a bar full of big mouths that keep talking until dawn. This is one of the few haunts in the Rivers that caters to the rich; the suits and wild kids that live off their parents' dodgy dealings.

'Earth Hour was a success,' he says. 'For the hyenas anyway. They pulled some big players into The Heights. Your little adventure with the Roses was the least of their worries.'

'Good old Nishi,' I say.

Ganzo twirls his glass. Sticks his nose in and inhales.

'What can you smell?'

Ganzo's an aficionado.

'Wine,' he says. He keeps things simple for me. 'She's favourite to stay in office after the elections. The brainwashed masses are lapping it up.'

I nod. It's all the same to me; as long as I'm not back in a cell. Ganzo tops me up.

'Something to eat?' he asks.

'Salmon sushimi. As much as you can spare.'

'I can't spare much.'

'Then leave it. I'll eat the wine.'

Ganzo washes his hands and prepares his knives. Good man. We go way back, friends since we were kids with shitty scooters, smoking and drinking in deserted alleys. I always told him he was too soft for business, especially in Sonaya. He's only kept this place afloat because he pays off the gangs; that and he's twice the size of any man in this city.

I sip my wine and watch the big man at work. Something mystic comes over him when he's wielding his knives and carving his fish. His pupils dilate and he disappears into his own little world. A true genius, the knives an extension of his bamboo soul. He slices the salmon like an artist.

'Where's the biker girl?' he asks.

'How the hell should I know?' I give him a level stare. He's still too soft. 'Go to hell.'

Ganzo smiles and slides a teal porcelain plate towards me, salmon with a side of soy and wasabi. Immaculate work, as always. I stir the wasabi into the soy sauce and gently bathe a strip of salmon before gulping it down. Ganzo watches me eat. I cleanse my palette with the wine.

'How's the wine?'

'Damn fine.'

I'm drowning my sorrows *and* enjoying myself; not many people can do both at the same time, but I'm special. I haven't been out much lately.

'Enjoy it,' Ganzo says. 'I don't know how much longer it'll last.'

I look up at him.

'I haven't paid everyone off,' he explains. 'Now that you're acquainted with the Roses, *you* better watch out, too. They're the big boys in the Rivers now, and big boys want money from small boys and their businesses. A bar without booze is a bar without punters, and the Roses know it.'

'So?'

'So every month the cost of keeping the cops from asking about my alcohol licence gets higher. Of course, the Roses don't squeal to the cops; there's nothing to gain from that. They just demolish the place and sell what's left to the highest bidder. And I've had enough. I'm not paying them off anymore.'

I look at my free wine.

'I'll pay you back, Ganzo.'

Ganzo shakes his head. 'It's not about the money. I'm just tired of the threats. Tired of being bullied. You remember how it was in military?'

How can I forget? I did okay at school so I only served three months, but they were the most boring three months of my life. Out in the sticks with a bunch of dreary men in uniform. At least in The Heights I had my cell and my solitude. I didn't have anyone screaming down my throat as soon as I woke up.

'You remember that day, don't you, Dag?'

I don't need to ask which one he's talking about. I've been thinking about it non-stop since I saw the surveillance video. 'Hell yeah, I remember it.'

'Every man has to make a stand some day, and when that day finally comes, it's the making of him. *That* was my day, when Tsubasa found out just how much of a man I am.'

I smile just thinking about it. Ganzo flunked his finals, so he was forced to sign up for the full two years, and the big pug was the sergeants' favourite toy. My own conscription was almost finished and I was ready to get the hell out of there and return to my city and my women and my life. We were only eighteen and even though I couldn't grow a beard; I thought I was the base hot shot. In and out in three months and then off to study for the forces, gladly leaving the pigs behind to drag their rifles through miles of mud.

'You were a damn podger back then,' I say. 'When I first saw you I thought you were a balloon, that someone had drawn eyes and a nose on.'

Ganzo smiles. He's still a big guy, but at least now there's more in his chest and a little less in his gut.

'A regular punching bag.'

'And if it weren't for you that never would have changed,' he says.

I dismiss the notion with a wave of the hand. All I did was teach him how to take care of himself, use the clout in his stomach to throw the bullies on theirs. Before then I don't think he'd ever clapped a mozzie out of the air. I didn't realise I'd opened a box, though.

'Tsubasa never saw it coming,' I say into my wine glass.

'I'm not proud of it, but a line has to be drawn somewhere.'

'You didn't draw a line, Ganzo, you carved a ravine through the damn earth.'

The poor bastard in the bunk above him had pissed his bed and it was still dripping down onto Ganzo's mattress when we lined up for inspection. Ganzo was good about it and kept his cool, but Tsubasa picked the wrong day to take the wrong side. The bedwetter was a poker pal of his, so he blamed Ganzo and ordered him to clean up. For a second, I thought Ganzo would just roll over and do as he was told, but then something in his face changed. He grabbed Tsubasa by his only arm and twisted it around his back, threw him onto his bunk, and pressed his face into the piss-stained sheets.

'I'm no bed-wetter,' Ganzo said to him. 'You hear me?'

He did it with such ease that every single fucker in uniform finally realised what he was capable of. I've never seen him do anything like that since; I guess he no longer needs to.

'Maybe it's time I took another stand,' Ganzo says, staring me straight in the face. I can see it in his eyes:

pandas might be cuddly, but they're still fucking bears. When the Roses come back, Ganzo will be a good man to have beside me.

The bell at the top of the stairs rings. It's a kid, but not the one I'd hoped for. Another one of Kosuke's carrier pigeons; better late than never. It's only been a few days since she visited my attic, but the shaven-headed girl doesn't react when she sees me. She just saunters in like she's a regular customer. 'Your stairs are crooked,' she says.

Me and Ganzo look at each other.

The girl extends a hand with a scrap of paper tucked in her fist. I reach for the note and she pulls it away with a playful smile.

'It's dangerous around here,' she says.

'Kosuke pays his pigeons well enough,' I tell her.

She climbs onto the stool beside me and starts eyeing the fillets of fish on the counter and the bottles behind the bar, like she's thinking of ordering something.

'What's good here?' she asks me.

These pigeons get more bullish by the day. I fish a couple of coins out of my pocket and slide them across the bar. She scoops up the money and hands me Kosuke's note.

'Get this little pigeon something to eat,' I tell Ganzo as I unroll the letter. 'Stick around,' I add to her, 'I might need you to donkey a reply.'

'I'm no pigeon,' the girl says. 'I'm a dove.' I stare at her. Kosuke needs to warn his kids that messengers are always the first to die. 'The only difference between the two is the colour of the feathers,' the girl continues. 'Pigeons are dirty, right? A nuisance. But doves are a symbol of purity and peace. It's all down to perception.'

I look at her, then at Ganzo. 'Get this little pigeon some food,' I ask Ganzo again. 'Maybe you can shut it up.'

I leave the pigeon with Ganzo as I take the letter to the corner of the room and sit on the red leather sofa. Kosuke's writing is a damn mess. Rich folks with pagers have all forgotten how to write, but I'm used to his chaotic scrawl by now. *Tsubasa's down in The Warren at nights. Shouldn't be hard to find. Best, K.*

I slip the note into my pocket and watch the pigeon pile into her sushi. She asks Ganzo for wine, but he answers with silence. I stand and return to my seat at the bar.

'I need you to take a message to Kosuke,' I tell the girl.

She hops down from the stool and holds out her hand. I shake my head; I like my words to travel the old-fashioned way.

'Tell him to get me that other little pigeon. The one with the rose on his neck.'

13

The bikers are out in force tonight. It's always like this in the build-up to Independence Day. Anyone with a political bone in their body gets riled up; the politicians don't listen, so they take to the streets. Since the incident with the Roses, I've been lying low at Jiko's to take the spotlight off Nakata's joint. Blonde and Purple took the rest of the herd out as soon as the sun sank into the city quagmire, but I managed to convince the redhead to set me on my way for the night.

'How's the apartment?' she asks.

It's the first time she's spoken to me since I dumped her for a date with the surveillance videos. I turned up at her door unannounced with a hangdog look and a hip flask full of Ganzo's best sake, and she waved me in without a word. If looks could kill, she would have doubled her murder tally. Since then she's been out burning tyre tracks onto Sonayan tarmac, leaving me alone with discarded bras and an open window overlooking the sewers.

'A palace,' I say. Dag The Grateful Lodger.

We've ventured down to The Warren: an underground bazaar buried beneath the southern sector of the Rivers next to the coast. It's a twisted network of chalk tunnels that snake off in all directions like raindrops tracing crooked paths down grimy windows. The larger caverns are lit by millions of fairy lights, and if you look close enough you can see fleas riding rats as they skirt the twisted walls. The remaining tunnels are at the mercy of shimmering candles and paper lanterns that glow red and yellow through the passageways and cast gaunt shadows on suspicious prowling figures. Rotten timber barricades separate the caves into an array of alcoves, each patrolled by wrinkled crones selling greasy noodles and sushi that will give you a bellyache.

The Warren used to be a refuge for smugglers when meat and cigarettes were made illegal. At first it was easy for the bootleggers to remain hidden; cops just wanted smokes or mutton to secure their silence, but when the government discovered The Warren, they swiftly shut down the illegal trading operation and opened up the tunnels for small-time vendors; a place for earthworms to sell their wares. Despite their efforts, smuggling's back on the rise, and people tend to watch the wall when the gentlemen goes by. As long as you avoid the food down here, you can get by all right. Jiko comes here for the sake and I'm glad she has that to distract her.

'You must be mad at me,' I say.

'I must have missed the part where you apologised,' Jiko hits back.

She's wearing a short leather jacket that she's zipped halfway up her neck, which somehow makes her look even moodier than normal. I don't find much comfort in her expression so I scan our surroundings instead.

We're holed up in a chalk-walled grotto with warped wooden furniture that a gentle breeze could demolish. A hump-backed woman with curly grey hair clatters around in the corner, sizzling vegetable pancakes on a hot plate whilst chewing her wrinkled lips. Her husband's sitting next to her with cloudy red eyes and a bottle of soju, eyeballing the customers and sipping his drink. A group of teenagers are huddled around the closest table, dressed in matching navy jackets buttoned up to the collar; students from the university. Three boys and a girl; the girl is blushing from all the attention and Jiko's staring at her with unbridled contempt. The other tables are occupied with clumsy elbows and stumbling shot glasses; chopsticks falling to the floor every time a rabble of drunks slam their glasses onto the table. A long-haired punk with a goatee is strumming on a guitar in the cavern next door, crooning old English folk songs. His voice is shit, but hell, it's better than silence.

'I'll find another way to pay you back,' I say. Anything but apologies; once you start, you're weakened forever. 'Anyway, I haven't seen your face flash up on the wanted wall of the police station yet. My mug's looking pretty lonely up there.'

'I've got a hunch the Roses are hushing it up,' Jiko says. 'I haven't heard anything about the guy I killed. They'll probably just bump me off on the quiet, same as they did with Ume.'

'And you're not exactly the hardest person to find,' I say. 'Why not duck into old Fumiko's cocoon, get one of her girls to transform you?'

Jiko shakes her head stubbornly. 'I'll have nothing to do with that woman—apart from her death. Mark my words, Dag. As soon as we pay the Roses back for Ume, I'm gonna finish that old vulture.'

I shrug and pour her a good shot of sake; she sinks it like water and stares at the lanterns.

'I wish I was here when it was all going on,' she says. 'Those must have been some damn fine days.'

'All kids think the past is romantic,' I say, gouging at the greasy leek pancake with my chopsticks. 'But all I remember is men in uniform hiding in corners with pistols cocked and ready. Sirens and screams bellowing from one side of The Warren to the other.'

Now that I think about it, it was romantic as hell.

Jiko's got too many grudges to keep me on her loathing list and she's got a good mouth on her too; pays attention to the news, takes an interest in politics. I feel like her dad; I just nod along and drink, trying to keep up.

'We've been messed up ever since Japan let us go,' she says. 'The only way we're gonna be saved is if they rope us back in. That's why Independence Day's so important.'

I smile and top up our drinks. Jiko snatches her glass from my hand before the last drop's even settled. She throws it down her throat like a sailor, grimaces like an old man. My favourite drinking buddy.

'When Japan come for us,' she says, smacking her lips, 'it'll all get sorted.'

I nod and toss another sake shot onto my tongue. From what I remember, things across the pond weren't that rosy, either.

The cook's red-faced husband starts slurring insults at the table of kids next to us. His wife slaps him on the back and takes his soju bottle away. He keeps staring at the kids, but they just drink and ignore him.

'It's a damn shame you don't go to school,' I say to Jiko.

Jiko's face shifts again, showing me how well she can flex her jaw. She snatches the bottle and pours for herself, doesn't blink as she downs the sake, scrutinising me like a panther. Only the richest kids in Sonaya sent to Japan or Korea to study. The poor ones end up in greasy kitchens down in the Rivers—if they're lucky. There's only one university in Sonaya and it doesn't look too smart in the dim light of day. Still, a lot of money changes hands just for a place at SNU.

'You don't have a chance now,' I say. 'You know that, don't you? You've got blood on your hands. It doesn't matter if it's the cops who want you locked up or the Roses who want you dead, you can't stay here now, Jiko.'

When she doesn't reply, I feel the need to shove my point down her drunken throat.

'I don't want you to turn into someone like me, that's all I'm saying. Holed up like a rat, forever in hiding. What's next? You got a plan?' Now I really do sound like her father. 'Gonna keep burning rubber until your bangs turn grey?'

All I get in response is a stroppy teenage glare as I shove a rogue leek in my mouth.

'You're angry, and that's good,' I say, pointing my chopsticks at her. 'But you can set your hair on fire all you like, rev that engine like a beast from hell all summer long, but you're still just a kid. And I don't wanna see you standing on corners in the pleasure quarter, or worse still, dead like Ume.'

Jiko keeps her pixie eyes fixed on mine, flames still flickering deep inside, and I wanna make sure that fire keeps burning.

'You should get out of here while you can. I can get you some money, get you to Japan or Korea. Promise me you'll think about it.'

Jiko briefly drags her eyes away before they're back with me. There's life in them yet, and it's damn fine to see.

'I'm Sonayan,' she says, grabbing the bottle. 'I promise nothing.' She fills our glasses to the brim. 'But I never say never. Only a fool says never.'

I catch the attention of the curly-haired crone and she drops another bottle on the table.

'I've gotta go, Dag,' Jiko says, her cheeks almost the same shade of crimson as her hair.

'You're gonna leave an old man to drink alone?'

The truth is, I could use some help with what's coming next, but right now Jiko's too much of a loose cannon. I don't trust her not to pull the trigger before my target's answers fly.

'Bosozoku gotta ride,' she says, standing up. 'I won't be back 'til late, don't wait up.'

I watch her leave and seize the bottle of sake. One more for courage, and then the hunt begins.

#

I settle up and swagger out. The booze has loosened my bones and I'm feeling mighty fine. When you're on a sake buzz and loose in The Warren, it's easy to forget that people are after you. You're not the prey anymore, you're a predator. And every wolf loves a warren.

I follow my nose to the dangerous end of The Warren. The old folk hawking vegetables are replaced by grim faces lurking in tunnels with hands twitching in tattered pockets. My head is down, my eyes primed. Two left turns and a right. The lanterns and loitering bodies diminish; the tunnels narrow and darken. The ceiling is slowly sucked to the floor as the walls close in, the air heavy with the stench of salt. I'm getting closer to the coast.

Whispers fly like gusts of putrid wind, footsteps ricochet off walls. A high-pitched cackle trails and the hairs on my neck stiffen. Bear-like shadows shrink and grow at a junction up ahead, candles flicker beneath an unfelt breeze. A girl in rags sprouts from the shadows, a bundled baby asleep in her arms. She pleads in a language I can't understand, and I can only reply by dropping a coin into her palm.

I continue on, back to the hunt. I'm right where I should be, and there's a silhouette ahead that's just the right shape. If I had a bow and arrow I'd line up the shot. But I rock on instead, with some added swing in my step.

The figure disappears. I veer to the right but find nothing, so I double back and immediately sense movement off to my left. I follow my instinct and find myself deeper in the bowels of The Warren than ever before. Everything goes quiet. The tunnel slopes further down into wallowing darkness. I wish I had a flare.

I'm humble enough to admit that I'm lost, and my sake buzz is fading fast.

'Tsubasa!' I call into the darkness.

My own voice bounces off the walls. It's a tame imitation.

I can barely see my hands in front of my face. I drop to my haunches and listen. Any sound will do. A small sign of life. A cockroach scurries past my foot.

The hunt is over, and all I'm going home with is an empty bag and a bitch of a hangover. I'm not even sure if I can find my way out.

I try to retrace my steps. As long as I'm moving upwards I figure I'm on the right track. I see glimmers of light and hear distant echoes, both fading as fast as they appeared, lost to the scratching of a thousand rats.

Then out of nowhere the sudden chill of silver at my throat. A sneak attack from a master stealthman.

'You better have something smart to say, pal, or you'll say nothing at all.'

I hold out my hands, the steel pressed hard against my Dag's apple; A stale, musky odour fills my nostrils; filthy flesh and worse breath. I smile. I've found what I was looking for.

'I'm unarmed,' I say. 'Apart from the knife itching my ankle. I'd be careful with her, though, she's a tad sharper than yours.'

He removes Old Trusty from its sheath and shoves me forward so I fall to my knees. I turn around to face my assailant and there's just enough light for a decent look at him. He's got lank dark hair with streaks of grey, and stubble so coarse I feel the friction burn just looking at. His eyes are bleak crescents that have lost all ambition, their colour long faded, like a mahogany table that's been waxed beyond beauty. One stump of an arm hangs at his side. I like people with body parts missing; feel like I'm on their level.

'Taking an arm off's a bit much for a handsome tax score, isn't it?'

I'm only messing. Everyone knows what it means when a guy over forty only has one arm: a bygone punishment for ditching military service. That and an extended sentence in fatigues, teaching spotty boys how to load a gun and lay down mines, ignoring the fact that nuclear bombs made it all worthless.

'Daganae Kawasaki,' he says.

He inches forward, his gaze slight and sceptical, as always.

'You must be confusing me with someone else,' I say. 'Daganae Kawasaki's a wanted man with half the city after him. I'm just a lost fool with one ear and sake up to his gullet.'

Tsubasa tilts his head to one side.

'Fool is right,' he says. His voice is hoarse, as if his stubble also lines his throat and scratches each word on its way out. 'Why are you here? I thought I'd seen the last of you in The Heights.'

'I know about Ume.'

Tsubasa glances to his left and makes a point of looking casual. 'Who?'

I'd forgotten how much I enjoyed disliking this guy.

'My friend Kawasaki. He's been framed for murder, and I've come to clear his name.'

Tsubasa shakes his head. 'Sorry, pal. The only way to do that is to join the other side. Cross no man's land, take a few bullets. There's only ever one winner, and it's the guy with two arms and two ears.'

'I saw the drone footage,' I say. 'The night Ume died, you were there. You stood there and let it happen.'

He stares at me for a solid minute, before slinging the hobo pack off his shoulders. He drops it to the floor and pulls the zip wide open. It's full of plastic rectangles. Pagers.

'Bit risky, isn't it?' I say. 'Working for the government *and* the black market boys?'

'Not when the government's bankrolling you. There are some places the drones can't reach, know what I mean? The big wigs like to have ears on as many walls as possible. If I wanted, I could have the dogs down here in five minutes, and you'd be back in The Heights in ten.'

I eye the bag of pagers warily.

'You know I didn't kill her, Tsubasa.'

'It doesn't matter who killed her, pal, not anymore. All that matters is who *they* want to have killed her. I just do what I can to make sure that's not me, and I suggest you do the same.'

This isn't getting me anywhere. I cut to the chase.

'Who was it? Who wanted Ume dead?'

Tsubasa zips up his bag and leans against the wall, slowly scratching at his silver stubble.

'I thought you already knew where I get my orders from, pal. It's your old friend, Goichi Fujii. Said this Ume girl was causing him problems, wanted her gone. Promised he'd make my life outside The Heights better if I helped him out. But I'm no murderer, never have been. All I did was hook him up with the owners of the streets.'

'The Roses.'

Tusbasa nods, slings his bag over his shoulder. So Baldie's one of Silver Beard's boys.

'What kind of problems was Ume causing Fujii?'

Tsubasa shrugs. 'Slaves at the foot of the pyramid don't ask questions of the pharaohs, Kawasaki. But you don't need to be a genius to work it out. The power players are in it together, aren't they? Ume burned down one of Fumiko's places, so the old vulture got Fujii to sort it out for her.'

I think back to my first encounter with Ume in the Heights, that look in her eyes, a yearning to reveal more. But maybe I got it all wrong. Maybe there was nothing more to tell and all this happened because of her vendetta against Fumiko.

'I suggest you don't come looking for me again, pal,' Tsubasa says, tossing Old Trusty to the ground and turning to leave. 'Next time there won't be a warning.'

'I met with Ganzo the other day,' I say. 'We were reminiscing about our military days. Some good memories.'

Tsubasa stops in his tracks. He turns around, his eyes piercing the dark, tainted and tired. 'You should know better than anyone, pal,' he says.

'I should know what?'

'How a single mistake can affect the course of an entire life. I often wonder what things would've been like, if I hadn't deserted. If I'd just done my service like everyone else, served my two years and returned to my life.'

'Cowardice isn't a sin that people consider too fondly. Or forget.'

'Cowardice isn't even the start of it.'

Tsubasa sounds old; I sometimes forget we're not kids anymore. He might be missing an arm but he doesn't look too bad for someone who's seen half a century.

'You probably never knew my parents, did you, Kawasaki? They weren't like us. They were good people. Simple. They were old, and I was about all they had when we got shipped off to Broken Hill. That was when Tokyo pushed for heavy industry and we lost our farm to make way for those rusting giraffes out there. Everyone calls it Sonaya's Golden Age, but that's not how I remember it.

'Then the Koreas started going at it again, and I was in the first conscription for service. Just when I'd found steady work—thought I could finally take care of the folks, keep them going for a few more years. I knew if I left they wouldn't be there when I got back. So yeah. I ducked out, went missing when the dog tags came round in their deafening trucks.

'But they caught me anyway, and I lost an arm for it. My parents died within a year of my enlistment. When I came out, I had nothing and no one. Just one arm and the mark of a coward.'

He stares at me. 'If you're looking for help, pal, I got none to give.'

He turns and sets off into the darkness.

'You might not have been a coward back then,' I bellow at his back, 'but you are now.' He stops but doesn't turn. 'You stood by and watched an innocent woman get killed just to save yourself. That's a coward in my book.'

He remains fixed to the spot for a moment longer, waiting for more, but I don't offer it to him. I'm done. Finally he moves on and disappears into the dark tunnels of the underground.

14

4 MONTHS TO RELEASE

I don't get a lot of visitors. It's not that people don't wanna see me. It's just that The Heights isn't the kind of place a person wants to spend their free time. If you like to see folk with death in their eyes or listen to screams bouncing off stone walls, then come on in. Hell, bring a friend, we'll make a day of it. But there's more to The Heights than the hurt. There's something about the air. Something in the light. You spend a couple of hours in here and you can't see the sun even though you're looking right at it. You inhale through your nose and a piece of your soul breaks free and escapes through your mouth. *I* wouldn't visit me, and I'm my own biggest fan.

Kosuke's the exception. The old man's got so much money he could buy a new soul if his own went missing. He's been visiting me once or twice a year ever since I was incarcerated. Every time he arrives, I expect him to have aged, but the passing years have been kind to him. The hair on his head is thicker because he's transplanted the fuzz from his chubby thighs, and the bags under his eyes have smoothed after surgery, but apart from that he's hardly changed. I still don't know which eye to look at when we talk, and that's how I know he's the same old man who saved me.

He enters through the mirrored door and I'm leaning back in my chair on the other side of the glass screen when he lands in his seat. Usually someone like me can't use the private rooms, but Kosuke's a special case; every time he signs in the warden gets a new watch. Today the old man's wearing a bright silk shirt that's bursting at his belly, and his cufflinks are crass sparkling Ks. He doesn't say anything and we just look each other up and down to assess how much the other has changed. Kosuke goes first.

'You need a haircut.'

I shake my head. 'I'm going for a new look.'

'You look like a mermaid. As if it wasn't going to be hard enough already for me to find you a job when you get out.'

'All that money,' I say, 'and you still haven't found a personal trainer. At least go under the knife and cut that bag of fat out of your stomach.'

Kosuke looks down and smiles for the first time.

'I wouldn't want to double my taxes,' he says.

'With that face, you couldn't double them if you spent a week in a cocoon. How you been, old man?'

'A hell of a lot better than you, but I don't suppose that's saying much.'

'Do they miss me out there?'

'They don't even remember you existed. Things have changed a lot since you left.'

'So I hear. Maybe it's for the best.'

We sit in silence as Kosuke squirms in his chair like a dog that's too fat for its bed. 'I'll do what I can for you when you finally get out,' he says.

'Don't worry yourself. I'm a big boy now and you've done enough already.'

Kosuke stares at me like a grandfather gazing at a hole in his grandchild's clothes.

'You remember when your pops died?'

'Remember it? I can still smell the vomit on his chest.'

'Nasty way to go,' Kosuke says, shaking his second chin.

'I promised your mother I'd look after you. Swore on my life. And now look at you, rotting away like a scarecrow scorched by the sun. To this day I blame myself.'

'You should,' I say. Kosuke furrows his brow. I wave it away with a hand. 'You didn't owe my mother anything, Kosuke. Never have. I'm my own man and I'm the only reason I'm here. Let it go, old man.'

Kosuke examines the rings on his sausage fingers with concern.

'She was one hell of a woman, Dag, your mum. Maybe you were too young to appreciate her.'

'I remember her well enough.'

'You remember her with the rage of a fourteen-year-old boy. You're well past that now, Dag. A man has to take responsibility for his mistakes. If you still think of your father as some kind of hero, then you're thinking all wrong. He was a fool, same as you. It wasn't your mother who tore your family apart.'

I exhale loudly. 'Everyone deserves a second chance. He never got one.'

'I've known a lot of criminals, Dag, and most of them think like that. Get your heart broken and then we'll see if you're so quick to offer that second chance of yours.'

I shrug. 'He didn't kill anyone.'

Kosuke's good eye rolls in exasperation. The other one remains fixed on the table, like he's looking right through it to study the shine of his shoes. I direct my gaze at the second one; it's easier to get along with.

'He cheated on your mother—with a common whore. That's your father, Dag. That's the guy you look up to.'

I lean back in my chair and admire my reflection in the ceiling. 'This coming from his best friend.'

Kosuke exhales like a tired bull; his nose hairs flutter and his fat cheeks flush.

'Listen,' I say. 'I know what happened. That was another life, another family, another Dag. If you think I care about any of that, you're wrong. And I know you loved her, too. I can see it in your eye.'

Kosuke's lack of a reaction is enough of an affirmative.

'I bet you wanted us to be a happy family after my dad died. Thought you could scooch on in and raise me as your own.'

'Your father was my closest friend, Dag.' His tone is sharp; I'm surprised it doesn't slice the screen that separates us. 'That's why I took you under my wing when you ran away from your mother and sulked like a spoilt little shit. Yes, I wanted her to stay—admit it. All it would have taken was one word from you and she would have. But you refused to even see her. She was too good to you.'

I bite my lip and examine the mirrors. I wonder if the guards are interested in kitchen sink drama.

'I don't suppose you've heard from her.'

Kosuke shakes his head. Silence bounces off the mirrors for a few moments. This is why I prefer to leave the past in the past.

'Your assessment's coming soon,' Kosuke says eventually. His voice is devoid of emotion. 'Do you have a plan?' He sees me glance at the walls. 'Don't worry, I made sure the guard took his lunch.'

I shrug. 'Why would I have a plan? I'll just smile and they'll give me a ten like always.'

'With that hair and those lines on your face you might have dropped a few points, but you could do with losing some more. I'm sure you remember Tsubasa. Tsubasa Ono.'

'One arm too few and one grievance too many. How could I forget? He's down on thirty-six, serving time for armed robbery. Must be the only one-armed robber in the history of Sonaya. What's he got to do with me?'

'You might need some help losing those points, and if you need help in here, you're going to need a plover.'

'Any chance of getting him onside?'

'I'll see what I can do. Until then, I'd steer clear of

him and keep your eyes and ears open. Plovers will do anything to get out early.'

He taps a hairy finger on the table.

'I best be getting back, Dag,' he says.

'Sure.'

He stands up and considers the mirrors as if they were the walls of his childhood home.

'Kosuke,' I say, rising to my feet. I want to say something but I can't get the words straight in my head. Something about my father, something about regrets. I wish you *had* been my father; maybe that's what I'm trying to say. If you had been my father, maybe I wouldn't be here. But every sentence I string together in my head doesn't sound right, doesn't fit with the cold glare of the mirrors and the thick air in the room, so I just stand still and say nothing, like the scarecrow Kosuke thinks I am.

He looks at me like he's reading my mind. He nods and leaves.

See you on the outside, old man.

15

The clouds burst open, and if there's one thing better than Sonaya at night, it's Sonaya at night in the rain. The neon glows brighter and the ground shines. Puddles gather on the doorsteps of singing rooms and broken umbrellas drown in alleys like spiders with fractured legs. The monsoon season's well and truly begun, and that's fine by me. Every evening the charcoal heavens sing their hymns and Sonaya sparkles in the night. It's enough to make a person thirsty.

Fairchild's got two black eyes behind his glasses and a bandage on his nose, but that doesn't stop him from smiling. His bony arm is wrapped round my neck and he's wearing the ugliest pink and palm-leaf shirt I've ever seen, which can only mean one thing: he's celebrating.

We're on the third floor of a run-down building that leans over the southern alleys at the edge of the pleasure quarter. Window seat, looking out through smeared windows at the rain and the way it hits the puddles. Fairchild and Stones are having what they call a one-night stand; they choose a building and hit every floor in one night. They chucked down some buckwheat noodles in the restaurant on the ground floor and washed it down with some soju in a crooked bar on fifth. By the time I joined them they were already half-cut; I doubt they'll make it to any further, but they're intoxicated and insistent.

We're in an old-school tea joint, which I guess you could call traditional. The wooden beams are powdered with dust and the ceramic bowls cracked with age. The wallpaper's a peeling mess of Korean calligraphy that gradually fades into obscurity. An incense stick puffs away on the windowsill, and it almost masks the smell of rotten wood which hits you square in the face as soon as you step inside. The only light in the room comes from a ripped paper lantern and the spluttering neon outside.

'So let me get this straight,' Stones slurs. 'You just left him alone on the roof, half-dead, while the drones circled?' I nod. 'And you're alright with that?' he asks Fairchild.

'Best friend a guy could have,' Fairchild says, smiling.

'You're alive, aren't you?' I say. 'And the police couldn't care less. So I'd say you got off pretty well.'

'They swept it under the carpet like it never happened,' Fairchild says. 'The Roses must have some good contacts. The cops didn't even wanna know, said they had bigger fish to fry, never even mentioned the guy that was killed right next to me.'

He sits back with a wry smile, as if it were his own genius that got him out of it.

'What are you drinking anyway?' I ask.

On the table are two old teapots that look like they've been battered by baseball bats. Fairchild picks them up and swings them in front of my face. 'Yuja, ginseng.'

I point to the yuja and present my crooked bowl. Fairchild pours my drink and I give it a taste. The bitter-sweet tang of citrus caresses my tongue but there's a kick in the throat I wasn't expecting.

'The lady of the house added a little something extra in there for us,' Fairchild says, nodding to the thick-jawed woman behind the warped wooden screen.

'She's a sweet sweet lady,' Stones adds. Then, suddenly raising his voice, 'A dame, queen of tea!' He rears his bowl and spills ginseng over the rutted table. Fairchild and Stones howl like buffoons; damn ex-pats can't even hold their tea. I call across the room for some coffee; at least one of us has to keep a clear head for what's to come.

'How'd they get you anyway?' I ask Fairchild. 'The Roses, I mean. How'd they find you and knock you out and everything?'

Fairchild swigs from his bowl and smiles at the shower outside. A mangy crow's perched on the windowsill outside, hammering its bent beak on the glass. Morse code for 'Get me out of this fucking rain.'

'I was stumbling home from a bar, I think,' Fairchild says, watching the bird. 'I don't remember too well. Anyway, next thing I know, Sara Barnes is standing over me and I'm covered in blood, head pounding so hard I can't tell if it's the booze I sank or the beating I took.'

Stones laughs and I look at Fairchild. He doesn't seem to care that he almost died. Maybe this was how I was too, before The Heights; a lonely drunk wandering aimlessly from bar to bar, never knowing how or where I was gonna wake up, *if* I woke up at all.

'She seems mighty interested in you, Barnes, I mean,' Stones says, nodding to me.

'Course she is,' I say. 'She's a journalist and I'm a damn firework with a brain.'

Stones and Fairchild yap away like hungry terriers. The crow turns its head to reveal a hideously mangled eye, wreathed in clotted blood. The boys don't notice; they're too busy downing dopey tea. It's only when the crow starts pecking at the window again that Stones slams a closed fist onto the glass. The crow flinches and disappears into the downpour as the old lady brings me my coffee. I've barely tasted it when the boys become antsy. It's like a pub crawl for an ADHD meet.

'Ready for round four?' Fairchild asks, clapping his hands together.

The boys neck their drinks and stand. We settle up with

the silent, hard-faced woman at the counter and Stones suddenly goes in for a hug. I drag him away and we duck through the beaded curtain. We make for the stairs and he almost tumbles down the first flight, so I grab him by the arm and guide him along.

We hear the racket from the basement before we get there. Fairchild barges the door open and we're assaulted by the sound of crooning teens and crashing tambourines. We're in a long, dimly lit corridor of splintered doors, disco lights painted on the peeling walls through tiny stained windows. Half-naked girls lean against the doors and as we stumble along one of them offers us her company; she's got sallow cheeks and sunken eyes with as much sparkle as the beer-stained carpet; Fairchild starts ogling so I slap him away and only pay for an hour in the room. She shrugs and shows us to the third door on the right.

The room reeks of rotten vomit, and shabby sofas line the surrounding walls as a giant screen broadcasts grainy ads for Sonayan brothels. Large glass windows above the sofa offer depressing views into adjacent rooms, another hand extended for the sad schmucks of Sonaya. No friends? No problem. Just look into the next room and pretend you're not alone.

In the room to our left two teenage girls in tiny skirts are having the time of their lives. One of them's belting out a ballad with both hands on the mic. The other one's close behind with a bottle of beer in one hand and a tambourine in the other; slamming it against her thigh way out of time. The room to our right is empty, but strobe lights flash and flicker all the same.

Stones takes to the mic and sings some old rock song I've never even heard before, something about summer nights in the city. The disco ball starts spinning and spitting strobe rainbows around the room, the lyrics flashing up on screen in front of the call-girl ads. A middle-aged woman enters our room with a tray full of beer, enough for a birthday party. Fairchild cracks them open and passes them round; Stones grabs his beer and gets up on the table, knocking a bottle to the floor so it smashes to pieces. But he just keeps on singing. The girls next door point and laugh and it only spurs him on.

I take a seat on the other side of the sofa and suck on my beer. I've got a lot of talents, but singing isn't one of them. Fairchild takes the next song and Stones collapses beside me in a sweat. He downs half his bottle and wraps an arm around me. 'God damn it I love this city,' he says. 'You know, I can't even tell Aimi just how much I love it or she'd up and leave me.' He raises his bottle to the window and toasts the girls; they smile back and butcher their duet.

'Where's Aimi tonight?'

'At home with her books, same place I should be.' He finishes his beer and reaches for another. 'She was a model once, did you know that? Met her when she was waitressing at a party on the strip, most beautiful sight I'd ever seen.'

Seems like people no longer need an invitation to talk - especially about themselves. Even though you don't ask for it, you still have to sit there and listen. Stones gets all misty-eyed.

'She grew up poor as hell, hardly had two grains of rice to rub together. I think she expected me to whisk her away. She keeps talking about going to Europe, finding a pretty place by the sea. Somewhere I can write and she can - well, she can do whatever she wants, can't she? Open a café or something, you know?'

I just nod and sip my beer. 'She seems like a keeper.'

'She is - she is, Dag. Far too good for the fool sitting next to you.'

Fairchild finishes his song and downs his drink. He stumbles outside and I know why long before he returns with two girls and a schoolboy grin. I can't even bring myself to roll my eyes. They're both in their thirties and caked in make-up. One of them sits on Fairchild's lap while he scans for his next song; the other one makes a beeline for me but I brush her off onto Stones. With all the commotion going on, none of them notice the man in the room to our right, sitting on the sofa beneath the strobe lights, staring right at us.

#

One of the women gets up to sing and I take her place beside Stones. I place my hand on the back of his neck so he turns my way. 'Go home, Stones. Before you do something stupid.'

Look anyone in the eyes long enough and they believe everything you say. Stones gets all misty-eyed again and pats me on the chest. He stumbles out of the room without a word. Writers are all the same once you get to know them; they're all messed up inside and sometimes they just need to be up to their eyebrows in ethanol to realise it. Fairchild falls into the vacant seat beside me and I tell him Stones has gone home to his wife.

'I thought he would, he's gone soft.' He raises his voice to be heard over the music. 'Let's you and me finish this one-night stand alone.' Presenting his bottle, we clink and watch the women sing; the girls next door have gone.

'He's got a good heart really,' Fairchild says, leaning back and swigging his beer. 'Too many addictions, maybe, but the main two are Aimi and this city. He could quit all the rest, he just hasn't realised it yet.'

Now that Stones has left, Fairchild's calmer. It's the Fairchild I know from The Heights. Sure, he might be drunk and have that distracted energy behind his eyes, but look at him now and you might believe he was once a respectable guy with a reputable job. Just.

The music takes a depressing turn and no one is singing or slapping tambourines. The women silently watch the lyrics light up the screen.

'And you?' I say.

'Me what?'

I hold my hands out to signal the room. 'Look at us, Fairchild. We're not kids anymore. Stones has Aimi and his writing, at least. I've got a life to rebuild, even if I've only got ashes to build it with. But you, you can do whatever you want, go wherever you want. Where *are* you going, Fairchild?'

His lips form an awkward smile that looks like it's held together with plastic and paperclips.

'I'm gonna get it all back,' he says.

'Yeah? And how do you plan on doing that?'

Fairchild rubs his fingers against his thumbs, like a kid that's been playing with glue. 'I'm still working on it.'

'Anything I should know about?'

'It wouldn't help you if you did,' he says, twisting and turning to avoid making eye contact. Eventually he looks to the room on our right.

'Fuck me. What's Tsubasa doing here?'

#

Tsubasa is staring at the walls like he expects the glass to shatter around us. His greying hair is tied back in a bun and the strobe lights flicker across his dour face.

'Why'd we have to meet here?' he asks.

'Because it's a great place not to be heard,' I say. 'Take ten,' I add to the women. They glower at me and slink back out to the corridor. Fairchild looks at me like I've just faked an orgasm for him. Sorry bud, I'm on another kind of one-night stand.

'Different atmosphere from the last time we were all together,' I say.

'I didn't come for a reunion, pal,' Tsubasa says. 'What do you want?'

'I wanna know how far you're willing to go into the

crocodile's mouth,' I say. 'Seems I've got myself in a web and I need some help slicing my way out.'

Tsubasa glares at me with his empty grey eyes.

'Someone's trying to frame me for murder,' I go on. 'And I need proof to clear my name.'

Fairchild's looking at me with more clarity and focus than I've ever seen in those pinball eyes of his. Tsubasa's studying his big upturned hand.

'What's in it for me?' he asks. 'Why would I risk my position for you?'

'Because I'd owe you a favour. And I'd keep the girls off your back.'

'Which girls?'

'The bikers are pretty sore about Ume. They're not gonna switch their ignitions off until everyone involved in her death is appropriately dealt with. And from the looks in their eyes, I'd take them seriously. Especially the redhead.'

Tsubasa turns his hand over like he's conferring with his flesh.

'I'll think about it,' he says, glaring at me between heavy eyelids, like he's been asleep for the last twenty years. Welcome to the new world, plover man. Step out of that crocodile's mouth and discover your wings and the world beyond.

He stands and moves to the door in that weird, lopsided way he does.

'Not staying for the one-night stand?' I say to his back.

Without replying he exits the room. In twenty minutes he could be back with a squad of cops and a wad of fresh cash in his pocket. In the Sonayan safari I'm the elephant's tusks, and I've just offered them up to a truck of hungry hunters.

'That was stupid,' Fairchild says.

He's probably right.

'He'll sell you out before sunrise. If this Fujii guy really wants you, he's got you now.'

I get up and finish my beer. 'So long, Fairchild,' I say as I open the door onto the dim corridor. The women storm back into the room and sit either side of Fairchild. 'Finish your one-night stand alone and see how you feel about yourself in the morning.'

#

I reach the end of the corridor and burst through the metal doors. Most of the basements in the pleasure quarter are connected and the tunnels can take you pretty far if you know how to navigate. I walk through passages shrouded in smoke. Past storerooms, padlocked gates, singing rooms, endless empty corridors of stone. An old man hobbles past me, teetering on a walking stick and whispering to himself. A trio of ragged boys run after him; one of them flips me the middle finger once he's safely out of reach. The ground shudders and shakes and for a split second I think it's an earthquake, but it's just the Pipe, rattling through the underground somewhere beneath me.

Pretty soon I'm in Fumiko's cocoon near The Cross. She's sitting in a chair at the bottom of the staircase that falls from street level, a black shawl over her stooped shoulders. Her eyes are closed, hands crumpled over her cane.

'I didn't think bats slept at night,' I say, approaching her slowly.

Fumiko opens her eyes and cracks a wrinkled smile. 'Kawasaki,' she says, showing me her gums and rogue rusty teeth. 'I didn't hear you waltz down the stairs.'

'I was in one of your singing rooms across the way.'

'You finished already? You know you can have the girls all night. You after something? Another transformation, perhaps?'

'For now, I just want you.'

She warbles like a dying turkey, which I assume is a laugh. 'I thought you'd never ask.' Forcing herself to her feet, she leads me to the closest room on the left. It's exactly the same as the previous cocoon I was in; black, mirrored, halfway between a bankrupt barber shop and a twisted tattoo parlour. This time I let her take the seat in front of the mirror as I silently stand behind her.

'I don't look as young as I used to,' she says, raising her tired eyes to face her reflection. 'You should've seen me when I was younger, Kawasaki. I would've been just your type.'

'I wanna know if Ume died because of you,' I say.

Fumiko's expression doesn't change and I can't tell if her eyes are open or closed. 'What does it matter to you, Kawasaki? Did you have something going on with her?'

I don't answer. I just try and study her wrinkled face, but it's like trying to decipher a riddle of dead worms.

'I hear you've made friends with the Bosozoku,' Fumiko adds. 'I suppose they've told you we've got history.'

'They've mentioned it.'

The folds in Fumiko's ancient neck crease and ripple as she laughs.

'It might surprise you, Kawasaki,' she croaks. 'But I wasn't too different from those girls when I started out. You know what they were doing before I helped them? Sleeping on the streets, or five to a room in goshitels. Shoplifting, pickpocketing. Barely surviving. At least I gave them *something*,' she continues slowly, nodding to herself. 'I put a roof over their heads, gave them money for food. It's more than they had when they came. It's more than *I* had.'

A sudden scream erupts from a nearby room. Fumiko turns her head to one side. 'Don't worry,' she says, 'it's just a girl getting a nose more suited to her face.' She refocuses on the mirror and bows to herself again. 'They got out eventually, those girls, but I wasn't as lucky as them. There was no escape in those days. And I know what they think— that I'm the worst poison in the city. That I'm worse than all the drunken suits who come paying for it. Truth is, I'm a victim. Same as them.'

'I wouldn't know about any of that,' I say. 'But if I tell them you were responsible for Ume's death, I wouldn't fancy your chances.'

'Su-young, the blonde,' Fumiko says, ignoring me, 'I've known her since she was eight. Bo-min since she was twelve - and Jiko, too. Ume, well, you might not believe it, but she loved me once. Maybe not towards the end, but she did once. Like I was her mother.'

I stand mutely and watch Fumiko converse with herself in the mirror. I might as well not even be here.

'Maybe I should have had her killed when she burned my brothel down, but I didn't. Those bikers will be the end of me, Kawasaki, I know that, but I'm not going to be the one to stop them.'

She jerks her eyes open, as if she's trying to bring me into focus.

'Daganae Kawasaki,' she says softly. 'It's a shame you got locked up when you did, you never got the chance to settle down.'

'Maybe I prefer it this way,' I reply as I move towards the door. Looks like neither of us are emerging from this cocoon transformed.

'Your father must have felt the same,' Fumiko says before I can leave. 'The fact that he had a doting wife and kid didn't stop him from knocking on my door all those times.'

There's a crack in her face that morphs into a smirk. I suppress the urge to snap her neck. So this old sack of skin is the woman who broke my family apart.

'Remember,' she says, exhaling and closing her eyes. 'The only people who get what they want are the people who pay. The rest of us are victims. You and me included, Kawasaki.'

I slam the door shut behind me, leaving Fumiko to stare at her reflection.

16

I meet Sara Barnes outside her basement apartment near The Cross. She's leaning against a wall beneath a bright neon sign that paints blue hues on her forehead and nose. She's wearing three-quarter length black jeans and a white vest that reveals her collarbone. Her hands are deep in her pockets and as I approach and tip my new hat she barely bats an eyelash.

'You look less like a journalist every time I see you,' I say.

'And you look more and more like a cartoon. What's next, a fake moustache?'

I've adopted a new look since the extra spotlights fixed their sights on me: a brown fedora with a wide brim, pulled down over my eyes. I'm growing the beard out, too. Gotta keep playing the game.

'A moustache isn't a bad idea. Maybe next month.'

We follow the great pulsing vein of Isorimu; The Busy Stream. It's Friday night and that means everyone's drinking. Drinking to celebrate, drinking to drown, drinking because it's the only thing to do. The place is bustling. You could pick any one of these alleys and you'd find more action in five minutes than you would in an entire night in Tokyo. On nights like tonight, Sonaya's the place to be. A fedora-wearing flamingo and a black ex-pat; we're hardly regular faces in the crowd, but the crowds are kind tonight. Drones patrol the skies above, but we're flowing like liquid particles through the manic migration of the sheep.

We reach the food quarter: a labyrinth of old moles with food carts tussling for space in the endless alleys south of The Pulse. Wizened hags bark for custom and thrust steaming plates in passing faces. Silent couples and lonesome suits loiter at the stalls like pigs at a trough, chewing on oily onion pancakes, fish cakes soaked in salty broth, stews of tofu and bean sprouts and kimchi that could start a fire if kissed with a match. It's cheap shit; tasty, but not for us. Tonight, dinner's on me.

We elbow our way through the throng, absorbing stale smells that cling to our clothes like fetid sweat, and head down a flight of stairs squeezed between two ancient taverns; watering holes for the old guard. We duck into another nook and emerge at The Log; a damp basement with a curved stone ceiling and walls soaked with smoke. Plastic tables are crammed together like pigs in a pen; I came here with Ganzo once and he took up half the room.

Log is what we call meat substitute—meat analogue—and The Log was the first place that started cooking it well; something in the sauce and the lick of charcoal make it taste almost real. Some folk say it's *too* real. All I know is that a lot of stray cats roam the Rivers, and strangled meows are common melodies of the night. But no one round here asks too many questions.

I know the owner from years back when he was a silver fox with a damn fine jaw. Used to be a ten like me until he lost his job. Shaved his head, grew a beard too big for his face; now he makes a respectable living hunched over a cauldron of coal, flipping forkfuls of log for the luckless.

'Susumu,' I say, claiming the last empty table right in the heat of the action.

'Daganae,' he barks, a hint of a smile flashing in the forest of his beard. His face is crimson and sweaty from the heat of the coal and he's far from a ten today. But tens are brothers—forever. 'Take a seat, you scoundrel.' His voice is so gruff it sounds like a threat.

'I will,' I say, before piling up a plate of sides: lettuce leaves, soy bean and pepper sauce, steamed eggplants and spinach. We squeeze into our seats and I pour out glasses of cheap beer. We clink our glasses and toast.

'You seem in good spirits,' Sara says, watching me wet my lips. 'You found something out I should know about?'

'What people know and don't know is beyond me. Maybe I'm just getting used to that.'

She fixes me with a cool stare. 'You're planning something.'

I take another sip. There's log on the way and a beer in my hand. Flames roar from Susumu's grill of soy nuggets and they stain his forehead a deeper shade of red. The fire smells damn fine. 'I'm always planning something. It's the only way I can make sense of this circus I'm stuck in.'

'Did you find out what happened to Ume?'

I unleash my chopsticks on the spinach and chew it over. 'I know everything and nothing all at the same time. I know where she died. I know who pulled the trigger. I know who wanted her dead, and I know who organised it. As for why, I've got nothing but a theory.'

Sara leans in and waits for me to spill.

'I don't like to show all my cards at once,' I explain.

She frowns and cautiously sips at her beer as Susumu arrives with the hot grate of the grill in his gloved hand. It's stacked with smoking chunks of log, black grill lines tattooed on their flesh for flavour. He tilts the grate and slides the log onto the plate in the middle of our table. We watch it sizzle and smoke between us.

'Winning the fight, Dag?' Susumu growls, spooning barbecue sauce over the log.

'Never lose,' I say, rearing my chopsticks in gratitude. 'Have a drink on me.' He fires me a one-fingered salute and returns to his grill.

'You don't seem too concerned about being one of the most wanted men on the island,' Sara says.

I pinch a piece of log with my chopsticks and drag it through the sauce. 'You worried about me?' I ask. I blow the smoke off the log and drop it in my mouth. It tastes damn good, almost like the real thing. 'Or do you just want a story?'

Sara positions a leaf of lettuce in her palm, plunges a piece of log in the middle and tops it with spinach. She wraps it all into a neat little ball and stuffs it into her mouth.

'There are always stories,' she says whilst chewing.

'You're right. You can still see my face plastered on the side of the police station, and that's not all. Fujii, the sergeant, he's got more than the cops and drones to work with, he's got the Roses, too. And if the Roses also want me knocked off it'd be easy enough, they've shown that already. There's also a guy with one arm who could buy a second one if he decides to sell me out.'

'Tsubasa.'

'Tsubasa. And then there's Fairchild.'

'Fairchild? You think he's in on it?'

'I got him and Tsubasa together last night and I can read faces well enough to know they're not working together. Yet.'

Sara leans back in her chair and smiles. 'I guess you're right, then. You *do* know everything and nothing. Maybe you've got a guardian angel who wants to protect you.'

I've been thinking exactly the same. But something's still bothering me. Something's still missing. The missing piece of the puzzle.

'But you know,' Sara adds, 'this doesn't have to be so hard.'

I look at her closely, chopsticks hanging limply between her fingers, eyes as cool as ever, maybe more so. I'm not sure I like it.

'This doesn't have to be a story about a man sneaking

around in the backstreets, searching for answers. This story could be big—*huge*. We could blow it up. Like I told you before, if you're innocent, I can help you prove it. But… if you don't want me to,' she adds with a shrug, 'that's fine, too. But back in The Heights when I asked you if you remembered what happened. That was what Ume wanted to talk to you about, wasn't it? Dag, have you never considered that the missing pieces to this are all in your head?'

I take a long sip of beer and watch Susumu slog over his grill. The flames flicker free and wild as plumes of smoke engulf his face. I remember my hands on the smoking gun. I remember the blood. I remember running.

A couple at the table beside us leave and a new rabble replaces them as fast as Susumu pockets the money and wipes the table clean.

'It can't be easy always being hounded,' Sara says. 'Especially for something you didn't do. It must be a lonely life.'

I shovel lettuce into my mouth and resist the urge to laugh.

'Maybe that's what you see in me,' I say. I chase my chewing with a mouthful of beer. 'Expats and criminals have a lot in common.'

Sara's eyes rediscover their edge; barriers up, lasers ready to fire. I finish my beer and fill us up.

'I get the feeling you've got a lot of secrets,' I say.

'You're one to talk.'

I pin her in place with my stare. 'Let's hear it then. Gruesome deaths in the family, abusive boyfriends, abandonment.'

Sara shakes her head and glares at me, trying to figure out if I'm poking fun at her. 'Nothing as dramatic as that. My parents are normal people. Only one long-term relationship.'

'How did it end?'

'He was too dull for me. Too straight on the line.

Had everything planned out—for the both of us—for the rest of our lives. The kind of guy who doesn't count on lightning striking,'

'And you need lightning.'

'At least I need to know that it *might* strike.'

I drink my beer and behave.

'And no one abandoned me. I'm the one who left, remember? I volunteered for this assignment. In fact, I jumped at it. Sonaya has a hell of a reputation. The history, independence. The roaring thirties when the expats and artists poured in. Like Paris back in the day. Then there's all the policies; no one can agree if it's ingenious or insane. Tokyo's rebellious little sister, that's what they say.'

'And?'

'Let's just say I'm in no rush to go home.'

I study her face. I'm good with interrogations. 'Fifty percent bullshit,' I say.

The smile means she's impressed. 'But which fifty percent…you'll never know. Eat up. It's about time I delivered what I lured you out for.'

#

I lace Susumu's palm with money and we leave him and the smoke behind. The moon is masked by cloud and we're at the mercy of the purple neon parade of Isorimu. My brain is buzzing from the beer as music seeps from bars that line the street, drunken howls from unseen windows. Scooters cut smoking trails through the parades of pedestrians, engulfing high-heeled girls in toxic clouds of exhaust fumes. A dance hall is spilling out wasted teens, and half of them expel their dinners over the doorstep.

It's all a façade: these lights, this music, this street. The fancy clothes and coats of makeup, the smiles. Like a sewer draped in fairy lights, the reality isn't hard to see. Behind the teenage punks straddling idle motorbikes sits a middle-aged man beside a cardboard box bursting with blankets. A pack of runt kids skip through the crowd like they're on their way to a country picnic, but watch them close and you'll catch them pick the pockets of drunken suits. Later they'll find an empty alleyway to shit in before curling up in a hole somewhere to sleep.

Sara couldn't look more different from everyone else, yet she also fits in like a grain of rice in a bowl of porridge. It's in the way she walks, the cat-like roll in her shoulders, the cool turning of her head when something catches her attention. She cuts a swathe through the crowd unnoticed, moving through them like a ghost they can sense but never see. She walks ahead of me, turning only now, her lingering eyes black beacons in the night.

'So what is it you have for me?' I ask.

She's taking me north to Broken Hill, where the edge of the Rivers merges with a stream of shanty houses that crawl into Sonaya's ceiling. The road dries out and gradually distorts into cracked concrete veins that burrow into the hillside like gnarled tunnels, littered with loose wires. We pass rows of ramshackle huts built on top of each other, roofs of corrugated iron that blunt the moonlight. Broken Hill is the Rivers without the flaring neon, without the mask, and that doesn't leave you with much. Most of the people here are the forgotten old folk; there's no such thing as a happy retirement in Sonaya.

Crushed beer cans congregate in sloping alleys amid dark and silent houses, and the sour stench of sewage assaults our nostrils in episodic bursts. As we climb, the views improve and the smells worsen. I pause to catch my breath and gaze at the grid below. A cool summer breeze blows down from the summit, carrying with it the brackish scent of the sea. Neon blares from afar, multicoloured lights chequering the windows of the high-rises along the Pulse. The half-moon's hovering above the scrapers on the strip and I can scarcely see the lights reflected on the water. Onwards.

'You can pay me back for this later,' Sara says, suddenly stopping as we reach the playground.

I look around. 'Pay you back for what? Why the hell have you brought me here?'

Anyone who drags me from my neon and takes me for an evening hike is no friend of mine. Sara points to the spot beside the crumbling church where couples come at night to kiss and confess. I squint and scan, and finally I see him, elbows perched on the rusted railings, staring out to my Sonaya.

'How did you know he'd be here?'

'This is where I come to think. I found him here last night, promised him a reward if he returned this evening.' And with that she turns and sets off towards the city of lights we left behind.

'Don't forget, Dag.' She glances over her shoulder. 'We could make this *big*.'

#

I ghost through the skeletal playground and cautiously step over syringes abandoned by the broken swings. A gaunt-faced couple are sifting through a heap of trash piled against the shit-stained slide. If they can pry enough plastic from all the filth, they might just enjoy a decent meal. They watch me pass with scheming stares, plotting to strip my corpse for scraps. I've had enough of this goddamn hill.

I'm slowly approaching the lookout point, and just as I'm stepping over the mangled gate, the old geezer crushes a beer can under his boot. That's when I catch the sight of two gleaming eyes watching me from afar. The boy's seen me, and just like that he spins away and disappears between shacks.

I'm no athlete, but when I give chase, I chase to catch. I run through a blur of rickety houses, dingy squats, dim shoebox rooms stuffed with unsmiling faces. Drunken screams, babies crying, music scratching from old radios. A naked clothesline catches me around the neck, but I recover quickly. I'm gaining on the little punk.

He slinks into a narrow lane between leaning shanties, and I join the cast of shadows. I press my back against the wall and listen. I can hear his ragged breath. Inching forward, I glimpse the sorry state of his clothes. A carrier pigeon indeed, and his feathers need a clean. A pack of dogs howl as I break cover.

I'm so close I can almost touch him, until he sparks to life and clambers up a rusty pipe onto a tin roof. I sigh and follow, less nimbly, but well enough. Now we're leaping across rooftops like mad dancers from a musical, a disjointed soundtrack accompanying our act; the hollering of angry residents and the rhythmic slamming of boots against corrugated iron. The kid stumbles and falls and I take my chance, tackle him with full force and pin his arms to the roof, digging my knee into his chest. I stare at his face, scan him up and down, and smile.

'The fuck are you doing here, Shinji?'

I'm still pissed about Earth Hour; I don't like being double-crossed.

'Where you been? You back with the Roses?' I look around, half expecting the shadows to glisten with guns.

'I'm done with them.' He sounds angry and bitter, and I like it. The tattoo on his neck is still there, a stark reminder of his deception.

'Where have you been?' I ask. 'Are the cops after you?'

'No one's after me. Just been busy, that's all. Let go of me!'

I search his pockets and find nothing but some scrunched notes and a bag of powdered milk. The diet of the streets isn't what it used to be. The owner of the roof we're on isn't happy about our reunion and yells up at us. I let the kid loose and we jump down to face the old terrier and his shaking fist.

'Found a pigeon on your roof,' I tell him, leading Shinji away by the scruff of his neck.

Once we're out of sight, I pin him against a wall, his head inches from a cracked pipe that's leaking muddy liquid down the wall.

'Tell me what you're doing here, or I'll rip your ear off and use it for my own.'

All I receive in reply is a flash of rancid teeth and a barrage of exotic expletives. Sullen eyes and a sack full of bitter bones, that's all this kid is.

We stand in silence, catching our breaths and listening to a pair of hissing cats somewhere down below.

'You look like a fucking cowboy,' Shinji says, looking at my fedora.

Damn kid. I *am* a cowboy. A pirate and a criminal too. Take your pick, as long as he's the villain.

'You better watch it doesn't fall off,' he continues. 'Hats are meant for heads with two ears.'

The kid's mouth makes me glad I've only got one ear. I loosen my grip and he glances over his shoulder at the uneven row of shacks crawling up the hillside. There's enough wax in his ear to make a fine dinner candle.

'You got friends around here?' I ask. 'Family?'

'Family?' he says, like I've asked about rainbows and pots of gold. 'I'm a seven-nineteen.'

That's news to me, but I try to look unfazed.

'You planning some kind of birthday party then?' I say. 'You want a present? I'm not your father, boy, and I wouldn't give you one even if I was.'

Damn July nineteens; another one of the government's stupid incentives to increase the population. A national holiday: October nineteenth, Family Day. They want everyone to stay at home and fuck. Let your patriotism explode, they urge. Women who give birth nine months later receive big bonuses, and births on Independence Day are awarded a fortune. Bad news all round.

The kid exhales long and hard. He looks over his shoulder again but there's nothing there.

'What happened to the money your parents got, then?' I ask. Like I need to.

'They shot it straight into their veins,' Shinji says. 'I've been on the streets since I was six.'

Nice sob story kid, but I'm no nun. He looks like he's about to say more, but he bites his lips and falls silent. Fine by me.

The nightly downpour starts. I feel a few thin drops slide down the bridge of my broken nose.

'There's been a lot of births this week,' the kid says at last.

'Course there have,' I say. The big day's right around the corner, and that means it's lambing season in Sonaya. 'Broken Hill's full of junkies like your folks trying to make an easy buck.'

'Go to hell,' the kid says.

I take my hand to the scruff of his neck. This runt pup owes me his life, but I don't want it. 'Listen. Just tell me what you're up to. The truth this time.'

He grits his teeth, angry as hell. The clouds burst above and rain hammers down atop a sea of tin roofs; a sound that makes you want to crawl inside and curl up. Instead, I'm out in the open, watching raindrops seep from my fedora, a shimmering wall of water between me and the invisible cloud of Shinji's halitosis.

'I'm on a job for Kosuke,' he finally reveals, before cracking me in the shin and shaking himself loose. He spits at my boots and legs it down the hill.

I watch him go and stand there listening to the rain, marvelling at how it intensifies the putrid smell of waste that runs down the hillside in a stream. A squat woman shuffles past in search of shelter from the crying sky. My socks are already soaking and I'm a long way from home.

Second chances are all well and good, but this damn kid; he's running clean out. The dove told me that Kosuke hadn't heard from Shinji in a week.

17

I ride The Pipe through the worst part of the Rivers, heading east with a gang of pigeon kids sprawled across the priority seats. I lean against the doors at the other end of the car and watch them closely. They're conspiring to rob me; I can see it in their faces. Even the oldest kid in the group is still in single digits. They must be the children of The Pied Piper, an old homeless cat with a little lair in the last car. He employs the littluns to run errands and carry out pocket jobs for him while he sits in silence buried beneath stained blankets. Harmless old coot, really. The real gangs could finish him in a heartbeat if he was worth it, but his squabs mostly empty the pockets of unconscious skunks. It's like gang warfare for pre-schoolers. I eyeball them hard until they get up and move to the next car.

I step off the train and Fairchild's already at the top of the stairs by the exit. He's chewing on a cocktail stick and staring blankly at the alleys in front of him. His curls are glistening in the rain and the bruises behind his glasses are gradually fading from purple into brown.

'My brother,' he says when he sees me. There's that old glint in his eyes. 'Ready to bring the house down?'

'I'm ready to stop dancing in the dark,' I say.

'Good enough. Let's go.'

We take off into the dark arteries of the east Rivers.

Back in the day, there were bustling markets in the squares through the week, but now they're sad affairs and only on Sundays. A solitary cyclist appears behind us; a girl in school uniform, her bike twice as old as her. She's holding a polka dot umbrella in one hand and the handlebar in the other. As she approaches the bike veers from left to right, her face contorted with concentration as the wheels cut through a parade of puddles. We stand aside to let her pass.

'You ever find out who they were looking for?' Fairchild asks. We're both watching the girl disappear amid the downpour. 'The girl the Roses were after?'

I shake my head and we turn into a narrow lane of PC rooms. Most of the neon signs are broken and all that remains are a few rogue characters blinking on the walls: a couple of Kanji swirls, a few licks of Hangul. Fractured fragments of different worlds, flickering like fireflies at death's door.

I don't venture out this way often; there are too many dodgy businesses and not nearly enough watering holes. Second-rate plastic surgeries are sandwiched between crummy estate agents flogging squalid cells in the goshitels. Pawn shops with cracked windows and cobwebs, and late-night pharmacies with too many regular customers. A mangled mongrel with three legs bares its teeth from the doorstep of an ancient boarding house. Fairchild splashes through the puddles in his stupid wicker shoes like he doesn't even notice; he's either got too much on his mind or not enough. It's hard to tell.

'What about Tsubasa?' he asks. 'Has he given you an answer?'

'Not a word.'

'Strange. If he wasn't going to help you, I would've thought he'd have cashed you in to Goichi.'

'I was thinking the same.'

Fairchild glances sideways at me, but I keep my eyes forward. 'How was the rest of your one-night stand?'

'It lasted two nights,' Fairchild replies, a hint of a smile stretching his lips. 'I hear you had a romantic meal with Barnes. You sold her your story yet?'

'If I knew what it was, I'd have sold it years ago.'

We turn a corner and enter a nook between two shabby apartment blocks. An open dumpster spills fetid smells of rotting food into the heavy air. A towering black door is encased in the wall opposite; the balcony above drops a curtain of rain before it. We pass through the deluge and Fairchild raps his knuckles against the door. An ugly brute twice my size appears in the doorway; he's got a boxer's nose and a head like a gnarled potato. Fairchild slips him a wink and a fistful of notes with a sly shake of the hand, and we're ushered in without a word or anything that resembles a smile.

The doorman watches us from the top of the stairs, his shoulders holding up the walls as we descend down a steep flight of stairs. Fairchild pushes the door open at the bottom and we're in.

We enter a room with a low ceiling and long walls of black and green swirls. Mercury-vapour lamps hang above two dozen tables manned by penguin-suited croupiers. A bar stretches along the back wall, stools all empty, as a smoke machine purrs in the corner, puffing out scented clouds of smoke that make the women look twice as good and the men twice as shady.

'Let's play,' Fairchild says. He cracks his knuckles and makes a beeline for Stones, who's nursing champagne on one of the roulette tables. Stones motions for me to join them, but I only nod from across the room and stay where I am. I wanna take a turn about the room and get my bearings. There's a big crowd at the craps table, a bunch of noisy youths with gold watches and glistening chains around their necks. In the corner there's a game of poker going down that looks about as fun as my dad's funeral. I lean on the bar and show the back of my head to the

barman, a round-faced man with gorilla arms and cropped
hair. He gives me a scotch on the rocks and I hold it in my
palm as I soak in the room. I find my target, but I'm in
no rush to pounce. The scotch warms my throat as I listen
to the speakers seep jazz. I wait for my glass to be refilled
before making my move.

'Evening, ladies and gentlemen,' I say, taking the empty
stool between Kosuke and Sara. Blackjack. A girl with a
face that gleams like plastic drapes her pale skinny arms
around Kosuke's neck like a human necklace. Sara's alone,
looking all hard and serious, but she nods at the table
when I sit down beside her. She's in a silver sequin dress
that looks too damn fine for somewhere so far from the
golden lights of the strip. A silver pin in her hair catches the
light whenever she moves her head.

'Didn't think you'd make it, old boy,' Kosuke says as the
croupier swaps my crumpled notes for chips. 'What's with
the beard? You gone hipster?'

'Chameleons always change.'

'Chameleons should look in the mirror once in a while,'
Kosuke says, caressing the arm of the girl. 'I hear you're
mixed up with the Roses now, as if you didn't have enough
people on your back. What's that about?'

I shrug and slide a chip into the middle of the table.

'Apparently they're after someone,' I say. 'A girl. They
seemed to think I might know where she is.'

Kosuke frowns at the chip I've sent into battle. 'A girl?
Any idea who?'

I shake my head.

He fixes his good eye on me while the croupier deals.
'You're not a chameleon, Dag. You're a bloody mosquito
bumbling around spider webs. And if you get too close,
you're going to get stuck for good.'

Tell me about it.

Sara's flying through her chips. She flicks them into the
middle of the table like a child throwing breadcrumbs to
ducks.

'How's the story coming, Barnes?' I ask.

'Better than you'd think,' she says, cool as ice.

'Barnes has a good nose for a story,' Kosuke says approvingly. 'That's why she doesn't let you out of her sight.'

'I don't see it,' I say. 'Journalists have big mouths and never shut up. But this one,' I say, turning to meet Sara's cool stare, 'she's playing the long game.'

'And what's that supposed to mean?' Sara asks, turning to the croupier. 'Hit me.'

The croupier flips an eight and crashes Sara's bet.

'I'm not sure yet,' I say, 'But your pen's been mighty still for someone who sees so much. Don't you think so, old man?' I ask Kosuke.

He just crumples his nose and looks at the spread of cards on the table.

'What did you want to see me about, anyway?' the old man asks. 'You know it's not easy for me to get out, and you've hardly got the keys to the city yourself. You'd better spit it out before the cops show up and shut down the party. And they *will* show up, Dag. They'll show up because you're here. I'll grease their hands, of course, but even I don't have enough butter to stop them from locking you up again.'

'Not enough butter, that's good,' I say.

'Fujii will be out of hospital soon and that's not going to help you any.'

I nod to the croupier and she hands me some fresh chips. 'I need to find him first. Fujii. Fumiko, Tsubasa, they're all just lowly pawns, same as me. They don't know anything I don't already know.'

It's hard to read the old man's face. Whatever expression he's wearing, it's ugly. He tells the girl behind him to take a break and she plants a silicon kiss on his blotched cheek before waltzing off to the bar.

'Forget about him, Dag. He's in power, and you're not. A mouse doesn't run towards a cat.'

'He killed Ume and pinned it on me. That's plenty reason

for me not to forget. I've done my time, Kosuke, and I'm not going back to The Heights, not for something I didn't do. Are you any closer on getting that video?'

'What video?'

'The one that proves it was the Roses that killed Ume.'

Kosuke laughs. 'There's no chance of us getting back in there now, not after your little Earth Hour adventure. They've doubled security already. Not even Bernd can get at those computers.' His smile disappears when he notices my expression. 'Listen, I'm working on it, all right? I've helped you escape once already—'

'—At your party,' I cut in. 'When you knew I was being set up.'

'And I've been helping you ever since,' Kosuke continues, ignoring me. 'Have a little patience, won't you? I'm doing everything I can.'

The croupier knocks me bust and Sara follows suit.

'I've just got a feeling there's more to all this,' I say. 'Something Ume said to me in The Heights.'

Sara's looking at me hard but Kosuke's still focused on the cards.

'I wouldn't think too hard on what *that* girl said. From what I hear she was a junkie, and mad as a hatter, too.'

'Whatever she might have been, she wasn't mad,' I say. 'She had something to say, and whatever it was, Fujii didn't want her to talk. I think…'

I can't get it out. I feel stupid for even considering it.

'What do you think, Dag?' Kosuke asks, but he doesn't sound convinced about wanting to hear it.

'I think there's more to that night. The night Hana died. No matter how I spin it, I keep coming back to that night.'

Sara keeps her gaze fixed on my face, and now I'm the one who can't meet anyone's eyes. Kosuke drops his interest in the game and turns to face me.

'Dag,' he says. 'I've known you a long time. And I know how important it is for you to keep that glimmer of hope alive. The hope that it wasn't your fault. But it's done, Dag. You killed her.' I look up at the croupier but she's well trained and doesn't bat an eyelid. 'Eleven years staring at stone should have been enough for you to come to terms with that.'

He turns and orders another drink from a passing waiter. Sara's eyes are still stuck to my face but she remains silent.

I take a long hit on my drink. I'm tired. I'm tired of throwing balls against walls and watching them bounce straight back. No one cares, no one wants to know.

'I think I'm done for the night,' I say. Kosuke must catch the edge in my voice because he gets up from his seat. He grabs my arm and pulls me over to the bar.

'Listen, I'll find out what the Ume business was all about,' he whispers. 'Trust me, Dag. I promised your mother I'd look out for you, and I will. But give me time. You have to be fucking sure if you're going to take on Fujii. Get it wrong, and it'll be the end of me too, you understand? Now I'm still on his leash, Dag, like a fat dog, and he wants you bad. He wants you more than anything else, and from what I can gather he's getting closer and closer.' He peers over his shoulder at the rest of the room. 'You've made a lot of friends since you got out, Dag. Can you trust them all?'

I look right into his wonky eye. 'The only person I trust is myself.'

'Good, because Fujii seems to think he's got the inside track on you, and that means you've got to be extra careful. Once he's got you in cuffs, it'll be too late. Take a good look at the people you're slamming shots with, Dag. It seems to me Fujii's bankrolling someone to enjoy your company.'

I glance back to our table, and Sara coolly averts her gaze when we lock eyes. Across the room, Fairchild kills a drink and blows good luck over his dice. Stones is at his shoulder, egging him on and having a ball.

'Get out of here, Dag,' Kosuke says. 'You've been under the lights too long for one night.'

It's like he's said the magic words. The doors burst open and three men in blue barge in, guns up and ready to fire.

18

3 MONTHS TO RELEASE

I'm back at the honsool. The soju's stinging my throat when I hear the girl arrive. I consider ignoring her altogether. I could sit here like a deaf mannequin and pour shots into my hollow body until I pass into black or my time runs out. I'm not obliged to talk, and if she doesn't like it she can ring the bell and find someone else. No biggie to me.

'Hi,' she says. Sounds like she's in her late teens or early twenties. The younger ones aren't as interesting; fewer tales to tell, less disappointment in their voices. They say exactly what they think and feel and make it all too easy. It's like reading a book with pictures on every page when you want riddles in every damn sentence.

I don't answer. I'll let her work for it. Tonight, I'm a cat's cradle tied up in knots.

'You have a name?'

No, I don't. Tonight I'm a mannequin, soon to be an unmarked grave.

'Well, this is going to be fun.'

She's definitely young. Sarcastic and ready to give up already.

She knocks on the wall between us.

I smile. She's impatient. I like it. I knock back and we slide the partition open.

I was right; she's only a kid. Her face is small and narrow, surrounded by a wild rag of wiry black hair. Her big brandy-coloured eyes sit under heavy knitted brows that are close to joining forces, and her nose might be cute if I couldn't see her brain through her nostrils. She doesn't look happy to see me. I can't imagine her ever looking happy.

'I've been waiting six months for this,' she says with bite. 'If you're gonna be a prick, I'll get up and leave right now. I know plenty of pricks already. But I might be more interesting than you expect.'

Ho. Yeah you are. Meeting Ume here wasn't an accident, and I can see from the girl's unblinking eyes that this is no accident either.

'I'm Dag.'

'Yeah, I know. Stupid name,' she spits. Alright, I get it. She's sore at me for being difficult. It's not like she can sing from a branch like a bluebird; in The Heights, you sing and you're shot down with a rifle. 'How long you got left?' she asks, reading through the script like she's eager for an early lunch.

'Three months.'

'Really?' She doesn't even try to hide her boredom. 'You must be due for your assessment soon? You're assessed before your release, right?'

I take a nice slow swig. 'That's right. Next month.'

'So how does it work? I've never been on a panel. You see the women who rate you?'

I shake my head. I try to tell her with my eyes to play it cool, but she doesn't give a damn. Whoever's hired her must be paying her a lot. Not many people would give up their honsool visit for a gig like this.

'One-way mirrors,' I reply. 'I won't see anything but my own pretty face.'

The girl pours herself a shot and flashes me a smile. I've seen better teeth.

'That's a shame,' she says. 'If only you could see your panel, you might find someone worth talking to.'

She holds my gaze for far too long. I get the picture, but I've no clue where I'm supposed to hang it.

'Never been on a panel myself,' she continues. 'But I know a girl who's been called up. Red hair, pretty, name of Jiko. We used to ride together, before they locked me up.'

I wait for her to run out of cue cards.

'You done?' I say.

She smiles and shrugs her small shoulders. She's done. Her message has been delivered loud and clear; as subtle as a storm.

'Then shut up and drink,' I say, and her smile fades as fast as it appeared.

#

'You could shave off your eyebrows,' Fairchild suggests.

I shake my head. 'This isn't a frat party. You can't just pull an ugly face and get a low rating. They *add* points to your score if you try any stupid shit like that.'

'Then what do you want me to do?'

I've been having second thoughts. Maybe Kosuke and Sara were right; it's gonna be hard enough for me to find a job with my record. And if my assessment turns out to be half as exciting as I imagine, it might be worth making an effort.

I look around the mess hall. A guard strolls by, and his cold stare lingers on me and Fairchild before sliding to the next table. I lower my voice and lean in; the mess hall's one of the few places in The Heights where your every word doesn't end up on tape.

'We need to make it look real, and I'm not talking about a bad haircut. You're gonna break my nose.'

Fairchild scoffs and sizes me up like I've just asked him for a fight.

'What the hell is that gonna do? It'll just be bruised and swollen for a few days.'

'Not if you do it right. A crooked nose might be worth a lot of money.'

He examines my face like he's imagining how it will look on me. Then he looks down at the rectangle of tofu in front of him. Neither one is pretty.

'And that's not all,' I say. 'When I get out, I'll be an ex-con. I'll never work again unless I drop a lot of points.'

'So we break your nose,' Fairchild says, rubbing his temples. 'What else are we gonna do? Chop your head off?'

I shrug and glance up at the translucent ceiling. A couple of uniforms hover above us, legs shoulders' width apart, hands behind their backs. They're so close I can make out the sizes marked on the soles of their boots. Nine and eleven. They're staring down at me with big unblinking eyes. Nine whispers something out of the side of his mouth but Eleven doesn't respond. I pinch a square of tofu between my chopsticks and salute them before shoving it in my mouth. They don't react and eventually walk on.

'We have to be careful,' I tell Fairchild. 'Whisper the wrong word to the wrong person and suddenly you've got three years added to your sentence—and you can forget about visiting the honsool bar again.'

'Not many guys in here would take that risk,' Fairchild says, shaking his head. 'No one wants to spend more time in here than they—'. He cuts himself short when Tsubasa places his hand on the back of my chair. His silver stubble is longer than usual; long enough to comb the fleas from a dog.

'I just wanted to offer my congratulations,' he says, his voice glazed with gravel as always. 'I'm getting out soon, and it seems you are, too. I never thought you'd make it.'

He holds out his only hand and Fairchild and I share a look. There are no guards nearby, but Nine and Eleven are returning slowly above us. I take Tsubasa's hand and flinch at the feel of his dry, calloused skin, but there's something else, something unexpected against my palm. Looks like Kosuke came through after all. I'm a master of discretion, and subtly drop it in my pants as I pretend to adjust them. Nine and Eleven are back, fixing us with their empty eyes. The three of us glare back at them, until I look back at Tsubasa.

'Go fuck yourself,' I say, and Fairchild almost chokes on his rice.

Tsubasa's bleak eyes study my face like he's trying to memorize every perfect inch of it. When he's finally finished, he glances at the guards stationed above our heads. You can say whatever you want to a man who's about to be released; he won't do anything to risk another day in The Heights. 'Always a pleasure, pal,' Tsubasa says, and turns to walk away.

#

I have to wait three days for a chance to use my new toy: a tiny piece of plastic that could be the key to my new life. It's shaving day in The Heights, so we're supplied with razors to take into the shower cubicles. I don't give a damn whether I shave or not, unlike the rest of the prigs in here. Most of them think you're scum unless your skin is as smooth and soft as the long legs they imagine wrapped around their heads. Mostly I decline the donated razor, but today's a day for a close one.

I strip off at the showers and the guard gives me a once over to make sure I'm not carrying anything. He's a squat guy with low-hanging eyes, and if he ever had a chin, then it got bored of being there. He nods and hands me my razor before moving onto the next schmuck in line.

I step into the small stall and close the half-door they give us. It's hardly privacy, but enough to get busy with your hands and not worry about witnesses. We're usually given five minutes for a shower, but on shaving day we're granted an extra three. I don't have long, so I get straight to work and pull the plastic present from Tsubasa out of my jungle of hair; the guards never think to check my mane. The razors they provide are cheap and easy to break, and that's where Tsubasa's little gift comes in.

It doesn't take long. I shave as fast as I can, just for show, and when I'm sure the guard's out of sight, I snap off the metal blade, hide it in my hair, and replace it with the plastic blade that Tsubasa gave me. I've still got minutes to spare, so I lather up and sing as I scrub, just to keep things breezy. The guy in the stall next to me bangs on the wall but he doesn't do it hard enough to shut me up.

When the water shuts off, I exit the stall and wait for the guard to take my razor. His droopy wet eyes have slipped even further to the floor since the shower started.

'Did I miss a spot?' I ask as he takes my razor in his pudgy hands. I show him my chin, but he barely looks; it probably hurts to look at a jawline in such fine shape.

'You're good,' he says. It's enough of a distraction. He passes one perfunctory glance over my remodelled razor and sends me away. I smile and head back to my cell, singing as I stride away.

\#

Afternoon is our best chance. After the lunch count, when we're allowed more of a free reign. A lot of the guys on sixty-third aren't allowed to leave the floor, but good behaviour has a lot of advantages in The Heights. I meet Fairchild on the rooftop gym. We chat shit and cycle the generators, staring at the grey sky of Sonaya through the mesh cage that surrounds us. There are hints of blue behind the haze of cloud, but the air is heavy and thick. Even the guards eye up the sky like they're expecting fat chunks to fall down and flatten us.

Fairchild gets to work and stirs up a fuss with another

prisoner. It starts off small, believable, just an argument about who's next on the pull up bars. Happens all the time. But then it escalates. A couple of the bigger boys with boulder stomachs step up, and before you know it the skinny guys with tattoo sleeves have joined in. Pretty soon half the guys on the roof are involved, and the women pile up and push their noses through the fence that separates us to chide and choose sides.

Within seconds all hell breaks loose. Dozens of guards swarm the roof and dive into the brawling mass of inmates, trying to separate scuffles and restore order. I break away and Fairchild's right on my tail. We run back to sixty-third and even point the guards in the right direction as we pass on the stairs. In a flash we're back in my cell with no guards in sight. It's just us: me, Fairchild, and a cell with a conveniently broken camera. The guy in charge of surveillance will be sporting a new gold chain tomorrow; either that or he'll enjoy a date with one of Kosuke's swans this weekend.

Fairchild's nervous. I can see it in his eyes. It's not easy to punch a friend in the face, even if they ask you to. I remind him we won't have long until the guards return, and he takes a deep breath before sending a fist flying at my face. He hits me so hard I stumble and blink stars. It only takes a few seconds for blood to start streaming from my nose.

'Again,' I say.

Fairchild winces but does what I ask. The second hit is even harder than the first and I crash against the wall. I asked him to break my nose, and from the pain pulsing through my face he's done a good job and smashed it to pieces.

'Nice,' I say, spitting blood on the floor. 'Now finish it.'

I fish the blade out of my hair and hand it to him.

'Which one?' he asks, looking rattled by the sight of so much blood.

'Which one what?'

'Which ear? Right or left?'

I glare at him like he's asked for my preference in unicorns or fairies.

'Just cut one of the fucking things off,' I say, and lean against the wall.

Fairchild frantically scans the cell and the open door. The racket outside is fierce but there's no one around. Yet. We won't have long.

'Hurry it up.'

'You sure about this?'

'Cut my fucking ear off or I'll have that blade across your throat.'

Fairchild nods weakly. He's sweating and shaking and his hands are unsteady. He presses the blade against my flesh and hesitates. I close my eyes.

'Do it, God damn it!'

Fairchild tries to steady his shallow breathing. I open my eyes and see him grit his teeth, take a deep breath.

The pain is more intense than I could've imagined. Eleven years in The Heights and you think you're some kind of hard man, think you can endure anything. Truth is, you're safer from physical pain in here than anywhere else. I barely manage to suppress a scream as blood pours down the side of my face, the pain surging through my body as I crush my fingers into my palm, and I know we've only just started.

'Fuck, do it quick!' I say.

Fairchild's face is a white-green mess and he looks like he might pass out before he can finish the job. I squeeze his arm and look him right in his bottle-green eyes.

'Listen to me, Fairchild. You do this for me and we're brothers. You hear me?'

His lower lip quivers and the sickly shade of his cheeks remains, but I see the resolve flare in his eyes, like the sharpening of a knife.

A second later I see his fist flying towards my face again,

and when my head slams against the cold stone everything goes dark.

#

I wake up in the hospital wing wrapped in bloody bandages, and my head's pounding worse than a morning after a honsool visit.

'What the hell happened, Kawasaki?'

It's the warden of the sixties. Half-bald, half-decent suit, half as likely to talk down to you as some of the others. Rooted wrinkles run in parallel lines from his receding hairline to his burly black eyebrows, and his bulbous nose is flanked by flushed cheeks. He's straight-laced, has a wife and a kid, and he likes me more than most because he knows I'm good for a decent conversation. He's sitting in a chair next to my bed in his standard grey suit, examining my face and looking me over.

'No idea,' I say, and gently touch my plastered nose.

'Broken in two places,' he says. 'Misaligned.'

Nice; Fairchild did all right. I feel around for my ear and find nothing. It's not there. Beneath the bandages there's nothing, just the smooth and flat skin beneath layers of gauze. There's no going back now; I act surprised.

'Where's my ear?' I ask, running my fingers up and down the side of my head.

'It's gone,' he says. 'We're still trying to find out what happened, but as usual, no one saw anything. We found a razor blade beside your unconscious body. Do you know anything about that?'

I shake my head.

'Your assessment's coming up, isn't it?'

'You suggesting I cut my own fucking ear off?' I try to look as incredulous as I can. 'I was a fucking ten! It was the only thing I had going for me!'

'All right, Dag, calm down.'

Yes, I will. Calm as a summer dusk.

The warden sticks around for a few more minutes, but there's not much left to say. No eye witnesses, no suspects, just a victim with a bad memory. I tell him I'll be all right, that I just need time to get used to my new look. And I guess it's true. I was a ten for a hell of a long time, and now I've got a busted nose and a lonely ear; a definite loss of points and a slide down the scale. Exactly what I wanted.

19

Damn I love a good chase. It gets the heart pounding like nothing else, and that's something you usually have to pay for. When I was a young pup, earning my badges, I dodged the chase as much as I could. Hell, I'd do anything to avoid drumming my pulse over sixty; sweating like a Merc in the slow lane. My dad would preach about fight or flight, and I always took the easy option because I thought it kept you alive longer. Later, I realised it meant you were never alive at all.

The old ticker's thumping so hard I can feel it throbbing in my chest and pulsing through my veins right out of my boots. I fly out the back door of the casino and dash down the alleyway, swing like a maypole braid around the corner and duck left into the shadow alleys. Corner shops and kitchens with blacked-out windows, restaurants and bars without diners or drinkers. I hole up in a slender space between two buildings and wait beneath a wheezing air conditioning unit that looks ready to drop off the wall. A couple of cops slingshot past like a pair of clowns, and a drone hangs in the air up ahead like a spider waiting for its web to tremble. I watch it closely until it leans to one side and speeds off.

Then there's a whistle—a human whistle—followed by a human face; Sara Barnes resplendent in silver.

'There's another cop coming up close behind,' she says. 'You got a safe place?'

'I did until you showed up,' I throw back. 'Let's move.'

We slip out and head west towards the heart of the Rivers; to the lights, the action, and the greater despair. Another drone appears over the rooftops and we duck into the nearest alcove. We're squeezed in face to face, her body pressed up against mine and her lioness eyes a few inches from my broken nose. We're breathing heavily; her breath hot and seasoned with whisky. She looks down to my chest and watches my lungs throw their weight at my ribs. When she speaks, it's barely a whisper.

'Try anything and I'll take your last ear and shove it somewhere not even your mother would be able to find.'

I watch her eyebrows form a dark valley over her eyes and let it go. The drone's gone, so I slide out of the alcove, my breath coming back to me slow. Sirens blare somewhere over our shoulders but we continue on towards the heart. We walk in silence, scrutinising every shadow. Sara's basement isn't too far and I've half a mind to ask if I'm staying the night, but I know all I'll get in reply is another threat to swallow.

'I think you're in the clear,' she says.

We're south of the Cross and it's quiet. I lean against a broken sake vending machine and scan the street. Further down a dreadlocked youth in a leather jacket is balancing on his haunches; when he sees me watching, he stands and moves off in the opposite direction. Two kids speed past on scooters, dragging tails of smoke behind them. A young woman is passed out on the doorstep of a kitchen with shuttered windows. The sky is free of machines, but there's an ugly smell in the air that tells my bones I'm still being stalked.

I pull Sara into a smoking nook behind an old tofu stew joint. We're surrounded by heaps of bagged-up food waste, and the clatter of the kitchen filters through the steamy barred-up window: the clanking of pots and pans, whistling exhalations of kettles, the shrill complaints of overworked staff. Sara queries my actions with her eyes but I shake my head and point my ear towards the street. Someone's on our tail. Someone stealthier than a drone and quicker than a cop. Sara soon senses it too. We're shoulder to shoulder, holed up with nowhere to go, watching the darkness and waiting for deliverance. I flex my fingers like I'm fixing to tickle the ivories. Trusty's itching my ankle and I'm set to scratch. What's another crime to my name? I'm halfway to hell already and there's no stopping gravity.

Then he appears, his face as white as the clouds above Hokkaido.

#

There's a wriggling bundle in his arms and white fear in his eyes, a perfect polar to the relief in mine. I exhale and whistle quietly at my boots, but Sara's on the boy in a flash, gripping his shoulders and scrutinising his face. As if the little limpet needed any encouragement.

'Shinji…where on earth did you find a baby?'

Damn it. Somebody wake me up.

Sara takes the tiny bundle out of the kid's arms. Shinji's eyes are loaded with red veins and I don't like the way they're looking at me. I don't need this. Not tonight. Sara's rocking the baby in her arms like we're in a fucking nursery rhyme.

'My mum,' Shinji finally answers.

I didn't know the kid still had a mum.

'She tried for the seven-nineteen again, Dag,' he says. 'Born last week. A little girl. My sister.'

Born a few days before Independence? The kid should have swiped the reward money and left the baby behind, then maybe I might've understood, but instead he's stood in a shady backstreet, shaking and staring at me like I'm Mother Teresa. What the hell does he want me to do?

'I saw her, Dag. My mum, that night on Broken Hill. I went to see her. She's in a bad way, coked half to death. The baby's starving, look.'

Christ. Who knew this little skunk had a heart? He's not as similar to me as I thought.

'Dag,' Sara says, holding the infant out towards me. 'Look.'

I look at the baby's tiny red face, wrinkled like Kosuke's neck and just as ugly. The thing needs a doctor, not a criminal on the run.

'So take it to the hospital,' I say, stepping out of the nook. I scan the street and return to the boy. 'We don't need your drama tonight. Go back to your hole and find some suit with heavy pockets. Get that mite some food, and if she survives the night, I might pay you a visit.'

Sara shoots me those sharp eyes. What does she expect? I'm not running a damn orphanage.

I set off in the direction of Sara's apartment, past the homeless girl asleep on her blanket of used syringes. I feel Sara and Shinji's eyes boring into the back of my skull and stop dead in my tracks. I sigh and turn around. 'Fine. Come on, then,' I say. Damn softies; they'll be the death of me.

We work our way through the evening parade around Isorimu. A man, a woman, a kid, and a newborn baby. Happy fucking families. The woman's got a hard face that looks like it's never been given permission to smile. The kid's got too many morals and dried tears on his cheek. The baby's half-dead and I don't give it much of a chance. The man's me, and I'm hardly a princess. We pass through the night like a family picnic gone wrong.

Sara's basement apartment is beneath an old locksmiths that I've never seen open. There's nothing else on this street except for a couple of red-brick love motels and a three-storey makgeoli bar with dim lights and dark windows. We fly down the stairs and Sara's about to unlock her door when we realise it's already ajar. She holds up a hand to command silence, shakes her head as I reach down for Trusty. 'Sorry,' she mouths, and ushers us away like a teenage girl shooing her secret lover through a bedroom window. Shinji and I trudge back up the stairs, abandoned. We watch Sara enter her apartment alone and close the door behind her. So much for her help.

'What the hell do we do now?' Shinji asks. The baby's wriggling in his arms and he's freaking out. A rabble of suits fall out of the makgeoli bar and you can smell the sour rice wine on their collective breath as they bow and shake hands.

'Just hold it a second,' I whisper. I'm not done yet. I don't mind being dumped, but I like to know who I'm losing out to. I slip back down the stairs, slide past the door, and lean up against the wall to see if I can hear anything. I do. Sara's talking to someone—a man—a voice I don't recognise. I sidle up to a window which has been loosely boarded up and find a small hole to peek through. It doesn't take me long to spot Sara, standing in the centre of the room with her arms crossed over her chest. The man opposite her is wearing an immaculate black suit with velvet lapels and a thin black tie fresh out of the box. I've seen him before. He's as bald as the baby in Shinji's arms, and he might be as much of a nuisance.

Shinji's calling to me from the top of the stairs in a loud whisper, and when I look up at him I see the desperate fear on his face. He signals over his shoulder. What is it? Sirens? Drones? I can't see or hear anything, but I figure I'd better follow the kid's lead. I take one last look at Sara and her egghead friend then pile back up the stairs.

'What is it?'

'Police bikes are circling. What's going on? Who's down there?'

I'm about to spill but stop myself. Shinji might look like a wastrel mouse now, but I still don't trust him as far as his sister can run. Kosuke's right; I can't trust anyone.

'Just another guy I've lost out to,' I say.

Shinji scrunches up his face in confusion, but I don't elaborate and leave it for him to chew on.

'Where do we go now?' he asks.

Good question. There's only one place I can think of.

'We can crash at Jiko's tonight.'

We're on the move again, only this time I'm pounding the pavement with a baby in my arms. I don't wanna think what Jiko will say. I've had all the drama I can stomach for one night.

It feels like Sonaya's one big chess board and I've been stuck in my square while the other pieces have been moving into position. I don't know who the two sides are, and I don't know how to get to the queen. I didn't even know I was one of the pieces, but it looks like checkmate is closing in, and all I've got to show is a runt baby in my arms and a mismatched army of pawns who are neither black nor white.

I better hunker down and get some sleep. Tomorrow I'll find out which players are on my team.

20

Shinji's baby sister hasn't slept a wink and she's been crying and screaming every single night. I'm not ready to be tied down yet, but I've done my bit; borrowed money off Nakata and supplied Shinji with formula for the tiny thing. We tried to get her into a hospital, but they don't take in any old raff off the streets, dying or not. Doctors need money, same as everyone else, so I'm waiting for Kosuke to sort us out. Communication's harder than ever.

Jiko's place is a decent size, but she hasn't got many maternal instincts. Most nights we've left Shinji alone with the noisy little mite; Jiko's been out riding her bike while I've been searching for empty bars to drink my nights away in peace. Ganzo's, Nakata's, new holes down in the Rivers and The Warren that I've never tried before. As long as I don't stay in one place too long and keep my fedora pulled down, I'll be fine.

I drink long and hard and avoid returning to the crying baby. Every time it opens that hole in its face and wails like a banshee I expect the hunters of Sonaya to burst into the apartment. Jiko's pad stinks of soiled nappies and newborn vomit.

I'm not surprised when the place gets raided. As soon as the cops find out someone has a link to me they might as well have a siren on their head. They arrived when Shinji was alone with the baby, asked him what he knew about me. Kid brushed them off okay, but they promised to return, so Shinji packed up their things and left.

I can't risk putting Jiko and Shinji in any more danger; kidnap and blackmail are the dogs' solutions to unanswered questions, and it's only a matter of time before they're either locked up or killed on the quiet. I'm struggling to stay sober, but I still manage to move the kids into a goshitel in the Rivers. They'll be safe there until things quieten down. I need Kosuke to help me out, but he's had even more cops on his back since casino night.

The wine bar's quieter than ever. I come looking for Jiko, but there's no one here except for the dove. She's perched on a stool with a full glass of white in front of her, and when she sees me coming, she pushes it away. Like a toddler with chocolate-smeared lips.

'How old do you think you are?' I say, picking up the glass. I swirl it around and stick my misshapen nose inside like I know what I'm doing. I sink a throatful and examine the glass. 'What do you think of it?'

The dove looks at me and shrugs. 'I don't like it.'

'Good, it's bad for you. Where are the girls?' She's wearing her usual baggy getup and that familiar look in her eyes, like a house cat that's crawled into a lion's den and doesn't give a shit what the lion thinks about it.

'They've already gone. Said they had a score to settle.'

'What score? With who?'

'The Roses. Jiko said they're gonna get revenge for Ume.'

Damn it. Maybe she's not as smart as I thought. I sit on the stool beside the dove and together we stare at the bottles behind the bar. The place is lit by the usual brigade of burning candles, which combine to cast a soft bronze glow on the back of the dove's neck. The bar is completely quiet except for the subtle sounds emerging from somewhere behind the dove's closed lips; she's humming along to a tune I can't hear.

'You done running jobs for old man Kosuke, then?' I ask.

She reaches for the wine glass out of habit and pauses. 'He likes to rotate his carriers. Anyway, I prefer holding fort for the girls. They let me do what I want.'

'Where are you sleeping?'

'I'm sharing with one of the girls upstairs. They're out all night, anyway.'

She finally grips the glass and doesn't let my gaze stop her. She gulps the wine with wide open eyes and I have to grab her wrist to slow her down. Wincing, she swallows and slams the glass down on the counter. She looks around the room with satisfaction, like she owns the place and is happy with the night's take.

'What's your story anyway?' I say.

The dove looks at me like I've just spoken Latin. She gives me a smile that transforms her face; she's got a full set of gleaming white teeth and dimples deep enough to dive in.

The door swings open and two girls enter the bar. Blonde is first down the stairs, blood splattered all over her crop top and the mugunghwa blossoms that spiral down her arm. Her little leather shorts offer me a generous view of the discoloured bruises on her skinny legs. Purple follows close behind with a shiner on her neck the same colour as her hair.

'The hell happened to you two?'

'Roses,' Purple says. She seems to be moving okay but Blonde groans as she collapses into the booth in the far corner.

'Just a little scuffle,' Blonde says. 'A few of us raided their pachinko joint up west, but the big boys weren't home.' Her face breaks into a pained smile. 'We burst in on our bikes, you shoulda seen their faces.'

I try to imagine their motorbikes charging through a bustling arcade.

'We faced off out the back, hand to hand, and it was going alright until their backup arrived.'

'How did you get away?'

Blonde massages her ribs. 'Jiko. She pulled a gun on them.'

Damn, I need to get that gun back. Stupid trigger-happy kids. 'She kill anyone?'

Blonde shakes her head. 'The other girls split and the Roses slipped back into their hole…but Jiko's gone after their boss—the one with the beard. She got one of the Roses to talk, spill where he is.'

'You're a god-damn stupid bunch of girls, you know that?' I say. 'A bunch of angry kittens. They'll put an end to you all.' Blonde doesn't reply and Purple just stares at me. 'You got a first-aid kit in here? Bring me something to clean these cuts.'

Purple slips behind the bar and returns with a stained cloth and a bowl of steaming water. I examine the wounds on Blonde's body and have second thoughts—I don't want a reputation as a lecherous old man. 'Dove,' I say, 'clean her up.'

Purple returns to the bar and pulls down a dusty bottle of red. She pours three drinks and considers a fourth.

'You want some, dove?' she asks the girl. I'm glad the name's caught on. The dove shakes her head and starts dabbing the wet towel on Blonde's bruised cheek.

'What's it gonna take for you to quit all this?' I say. 'You girls got a death wish, is that it?'

'It's Su-young,' Blonde says.

'Sure it is,' I say. She offers no more and downs her drink. I remember Fumiko mentioning the name. Korean names aren't uncommon; descendants of refugees from the First Korean War. 'What happened to your family?'

Blonde shrugs. 'They were ordinary people,' she says. 'They got by, working the land, you know? We had a decent patch out east, in our family for three generations. Wasn't a bad life out there for a kid. Fresh air, forests, rivers, endless open land and corn fields to play in.'

I sip my wine. It can't have been easy being Korean while they squabbled over this island like kids fighting over a doll. Rich fishing grounds and endless natural gas: pretty damn vital needs for two countries trying to survive after the war. In the end, of course, Korea struck deals while Sonaya slipped under Japanese rule. By that time, though, the people of Sonaya weren't Japanese or Korean. They were Sonayan—and proud of it, no matter which flag flew above their heads.

Blonde holds out her glass for a refill as the dove rinses the bloodied cloth in the bowl. She watches Blonde like she's expecting her to burst into song.

'Then one day some suit arrives from the city, tells us we're being bought out. My parents refused, of course, despite the dough on offer. When you live off the land like that, there's not a lot you want for. Your home is everything, you know?'

I watch the dove dab Blonde's bruises with the wet towel. She doesn't flinch.

'For a few weeks nothing happened, but then one morning I woke up to a silent house. I knew something was wrong, so I got up and searched the rooms. Everyone was dead. My mother, my father, even my grandmother. Dead in their beds. Can you imagine waking up to that when you're seven years old?'

I can't look at her, so I watch Purple empty the bowl of bloody water into the sink.

'What's a kid meant to do in a situation like that? I was all alone, scared shitless. No family or friends or anywhere to find help. I stole a ride on a freight train to the city, and I haven't been back since. Slept rough for a while, then hooked up with some girls my age. We swindled and stole to survive until Fumiko took us in. I worked the Homework Clubs for five years before she forced me to move up. I was fifteen the first time. Fifteen years old.'

We neck our drinks and avoid eye contact. Even the dove takes a blast from the bottle.

'They're all the same, in it together,' Blonde says. 'Fumiko, the government, the Roses.' She counts them out on her fingers. 'Girls like me are nothing but objects to them, pieces of flesh to fuck and fuck over, and as long as the money keeps coming in, nothing's gonna change. Ume was the only one brave enough to stand up to them, and now she's dead.'

'The Roses were just following orders,' I say.

'The Roses are the government's firefighters, and me and the girls are the Rivers' biggest flames. And I tell you what, Dag, we're gonna bloody explode before they extinguish us. You think we're dumb, good on you. You strut around like a pampered dog with no problems or worries because you haven't seen what we've seen. You got cops after you? Poor thing. I'd take the cops on my tail any day of the week if I could only forget.'

Purple drains her glass and slips her riding gloves back on. She examines her arms, maybe to check her tattoos haven't been scratched.

'If you're not gonna join us, fine,' Blonde goes on. 'Stay here and keep an eye on the bar, but I guarantee you, this place will burn—with or without you.'

#

We lock up the basement and I send Blonde to Nakata's to recover. Safer, maybe. I jump on the back of Purple's violet bike and we shoot through the Rivers like an explosion of light. The alleys are quiet with weekend hangovers so we're quick to reach the west of the Rivers, beyond the pink glow of the pleasure quarter and the monolithic shadow of The Heights.

Purple's quiet. She's quiet even when we stop and watch the other bikes pass. It suits me fine. I'm not much of a talker myself.

We're out of the Rivers and streaking along the harbour road, the wind licking the hole on the side of my head as I swallow the streets like a starved addict. The tarmac's black and smooth beneath us and the engine purrs with pleasure. Soon we're onto the strip, candied by neon lights, the hotels glowing in the darkness of night.

'Where are they?' I ask Purple.

She doesn't answer, and suddenly she seems a hell of a lot cooler. She pulls the bike up at the side of the road next to The Imperial and we get off and scan the strip. The promenade is painted pink by the hotel's lights, and empty except for the scooters that blaze up and down the ocean road. Purple looks at me and then at the flaming red bike next to hers. Jiko's here all right.

'There,' Purple says, signalling the building next to the neon-fronted hotel—the biggest bathhouse in the city, a four-storey relic bedecked in swinging lanterns. The small square windows are flanked by wooden shutters and sit beneath crooked little roofs with missing tiles. If it weren't for the garish fluorescent sign emblazoned over the entrance it might look like something from a bygone era.

'Any idea how this is gonna go down?' I ask Purple. She looks at the bathhouse like she's expecting Jiko to burst through one of second-floor windows. Without answering, she strides towards the bathhouse and disappears through the doors. I follow her inside.

The lobby maintains the ryokan façade of the exterior; tatami mats and sliding panels of translucent paper, and piles of zabuton pillows stacked in each corner. The whole place smells faintly clinical, of freshly laundered towels and unvarnished wood, fresh from the forests of Hokkaido.

The staff at reception are wrapped in meticulously ironed yukata and look like they know how to handle riff raff like us. A stern-looking guy is already heading our way as we canter in smelling of wine and gasoline. He's got the cheekbones of a model and the cold stare of a disapproving mother-in-law. Before he can sling us out, Purple pulls a wad of notes from her pocket and slams it on the reception desk. They stare at the money like it's a judge's gavel.

'Very well,' one of the women says in a sickly sweet Tokyo accent. She flashes a smile but the crooked curl of her upper lip can't disguise her disdain.

We're escorted to the elevators by a young woman in white robes. I'm surprised by how calm and collected Purple appears as she assesses our surroundings; I love having a sidekick who knows what she's doing. Once we're inside the lift and the doors close we both glance up at the camera in the corner above us.

We exit the lift on the third floor and a bellgirl appears to usher us to another desk. The air smells like soap and chlorine and the girl behind the counter looks like she's scrubbed her face with both. She hands us a pile of towels that are so damn soft I've half a mind to bury my face in the fabric and disappear for the night. Our porcelain-faced guide points at the plastic curtains either side of the lockers—men to the left, women to the right. We ignore her instructions and head straight for the red-headed girl stood in the middle.

'What are you doing here?' Jiko asks.

If she was involved in the earlier fight then she came out of it well. Her fiery hair's tied back in an unruly bun and her face is flushed, but I can't see a scratch. She's in her trademark black leather trousers and vest that reveals the rays of her Rising Sun.

'You're a woman down,' I say. 'I'm here to make sure you don't get yourself killed.'

Jiko flashes me a glimpse of the gun tucked into her trousers. 'Then you're just in time. I won't have long once I'm inside.'

Purple tightens the velcro fastenings on her riding gloves. 'What's the plan?'

Jiko glances at the porcelain doll on reception; she feigns disinterest and busies herself with a pile of paperwork. Jiko lowers her voice.

'Shower Silver Beard with bullets and then burn rubber before the police get wind.'

THIS RAGGED, WASTREL THING

I stare at the scorching coals in her eyes. She's wired and restless; has been ever since I met her, and probably long before. Maybe this is about Ume. Maybe it's about Shinji and his baby sister. Maybe it's about the Rose she killed on the rooftop of City Hall. Or maybe she doesn't even know what it's about.

'No,' Jiko replies, so loudly the receptionist glances over. She leans into my good ear. 'He's the leader, Dag, and he's going to die tonight.'

'Just give me one shot,' I whisper back. 'If I'm not out in five minutes, follow me in and finish it.'

Jiko chews her bottom lip and looks at Purple. 'Five minutes.'

I strip off in the changing room and wrap the towel around my waist. I might as well do this properly. I enter a high-ceilinged cavern of marble, where a group of guys are huddled together in a steaming circular pool, their pink man-boobs bobbing on the surface of the water. A smaller pool to the side is empty. There's no one else around and no sign of the Roses. I nod at the guys in the pool and they nod back.

The sound of my naked feet slapping the wet tiles echoes through the spa. I pass through a beaded curtain at the far end of the room and find myself under the open sky. The surrounding walls are high, so there's no view save for the black city ceiling, which only shows stars if you stare long and hard. In front of me sit four more pools, blanketed by clouds of hot steam. Through the rising mist Silver Beard reclines, alone and exposed. I stand there for a second, watching the back of his head until he turns around. He doesn't look surprised.

'I was wondering when we would meet again,' he says. 'We didn't leave things on the best of terms last time.'

I approach slowly, cautious of my calm surroundings. There's no one else around; it's just me, him, and the pools of steaming water. I lose the towel and join him in the pool, positioning myself directly opposite him, the simmering water up to my neck. It's almost hot enough to singe the hairs on my chest.

'I didn't think this kind of place would be your cup of tea, Kawasaki,' Silver Beard says, his eyes closed and a peaceful expression plastered on his face, like a corpse prepped for a final viewing. Without his suit he looks smaller, almost frail. His skinny arms are sheathed in shaggy skin, and grey wispy hairs cover his wrinkly chest. 'Peaceful, isn't it? And not a bar in sight. I don't suppose it's a coincidence you're here.'

'Jiko,' I say. 'She's waiting right outside, and she's itching to blow your brains out.'

'Ah, the redhead,' Silver Beard says, smiling, his eyes still closed. 'She has quite the temper, doesn't she? You know, it's not common for someone to kill one of my men and get away with it, Kawasaki.'

Beads of sweat trickle down my forehead. 'You were holding us at gunpoint. Can you blame her?'

He shakes his head and opens his eyes slowly. 'Thankfully we have friends who sit in some pretty important offices, and they don't seem too concerned about what happened on that rooftop. But that doesn't mean the redhead will escape punishment. Those leather-clad girls are a nuisance for everyone. They've been on the police's radar for quite some time, even before Ume started her war with Fumiko. I'd venture to guess that once you're back behind bars, the Bosozoku girls are next on their list.'

Pins and needles begin to slowly spread from my legs to the rest of my body. I hear high-pitched laughter from over the wall to our left; the women's section must be busy tonight.

'And you?' I say. 'You're happy to forgive?'

Silver Beard blinks and raises an eyebrow. 'I'm sure our business with those girls isn't done yet. I hear there was a scuffle tonight. I hope there were no casualties?'

'For once it seems like your boys were unarmed. Just a playground scrap from the sounds of it.'

'Wonderful. You know, we don't go out looking for trouble, Kawasaki. We don't pull the trigger until we're paid to, and no one's offered us enough to get rid of those bikers...*yet*. The raids on the Homework Clubs are becoming far too frequent and Fumiko is a wily enough business woman to know when to take action. I have a suspicion she's simply waiting for the most opportune moment.'

'She won't do anything to those girls,' I say. 'That old turtle's got a withered heart in there somewhere, believe it or not.'

This time Silver Beard's eyebrows almost disappear into his hair. Maybe I bought Fumiko's story too easily. I flex my fingers and ball fists beneath the water; they've almost lost all feeling. The girls over the wall sound like they're having one hell of a time.

'So when can we expect our guests to arrive?' Silver Beard asks. 'I'm afraid I'm not presently in the best position to defend myself.'

As if they were eavesdropping at the door, Jiko and Purple burst out to join us, Jiko gripping her gun and Purple following close behind with the usual moody look set on her face. They stop dead in their tracks at the sight of us soaking in the pool. I raise a hand in greeting.

'Get out,' Jiko commands. 'Dag, out of the way. Time's up.'

Silver Beard doesn't turn around to acknowledge their arrival. He peers at me patiently.

'At least let me get some clothes on,' I say to Jiko. I start to stand up and the girls look away, but Jiko aims the barrel of her gun at the back of Silver Beard's head. I walk over to the wooden bench and wrap a towel around my waist before throwing another one to Silver Beard. He steps out of the water and follows suit.

'Get down on your knees,' Jiko commands.

Silver Beard does as he's told, introducing his bony knees to the cracked tiles beside the pool. He's graceful about it all, and even appears slightly amused. 'If I may…' he says amiably, looking up at the girls, 'what is this about? It was you who murdered one of my men, not the other way around. His name was Daishin Hane.' With his beady black eyes, Silver Beard examines Jiko's rigid face. 'He had a loving wife and two young children, a girl and a boy, both now fatherless. They rely on us for support. He was good at his job.'

Jiko's mouth opens minutely but no sound slips out. Another shriek of laughter erupts from over the wall. Silver Beard's flat expression doesn't falter.

Jiko gathers herself. 'You killed Ume.'

'Did I?' He answers with a trained tone of mock-surprise.

Jiko doesn't blink. I let Silver Beard continue his little performance.

'Now,' he says, lifting a finger in the air. 'I *do* remember her death—tragic, I'm sure. However, despite what you may have heard, I am not the kind of gentleman who abides getting dirty hands.'

'One of the Roses killed her,' Jiko says.

'Yes, yes, that might be correct,' Silver Beard maintains the same tone, like a lawyer on the stand. 'But my men require a reason to kill, and a more significant reason than money alone. We do not kill merely to satisfy whims, little girl.'

Jiko cocks her gun. 'Ume was innocent.'

For the first time Silver Beard's face tightens, and the smile vanishes. 'I would hardly call Ume innocent. Let us not forget that she torched a building. She was lucky no one died. Regardless, it was Sergeant Fujii who ordered the hit, and my men were merely the hired hands. When your flesh is scratched, do you blame the claw, or the cat? If you have a problem, I suggest you take it up with the sergeant.'

I move towards Jiko and hold out my hand for the gun. We stare at each other, and I can see fear in her eyes. She doesn't want to pull the trigger any more than I want her to. Finally, she hands me the gun, and I put it right back in position, pointing it square at Silver Beard's grey-streaked chest.

'Tell me,' I say. 'Why did Fujii want Ume dead?'

The smile returns to his face. 'Maybe Ume knew something he didn't want other people to find out. What that might have been, I have no idea, so don't bother asking. However, if it's true that Ume arranged a meeting with you in The Heights, *you* might know more about it than anyone.'

Sirens blare from the strip below and we pause to listen to the familiar Sonayan soundtrack.

'So there you have it,' Silver Beard says, sounding mildly bored. 'I'm done. Are you going to kill me now, Kawasaki, or are you going to let these girls do it?'

The sirens whir weakly at street level now; I'd guess at least one cop has come to check things out.

'We need to move,' Purple says. She glances over her shoulder at the entrance to the large marble room. Jiko looks at me but I can't draw my gaze from Silver Beard.

'I've got one more question,' I say.

Silver Beard holds out his hands in cordial invitation.

'That night on the rooftop, you said you were after someone. A girl. Who is it?'

Silver Beard blinks and tilts his head to one side. When he eventually answers, the words are carefully chosen, his answer measured for his audience.

'That was a mistake.'

I can't say what I'm thinking, but Silver Beard guesses accurately.

'Hana's still dead, if that's what you were thinking. You can't bring people back to life, Kawasaki. The permanence of mortality didn't change while you were in The Heights, so I suggest you forget about her. Forget about the whole thing.' He looks at each of us in turn. 'Now, how does this night end?'

I glance at Jiko and Purple. We can still make it out of here if we leave now.

'We have enough blood on our hands as it is.' I empty the chamber of the gun and toss the bullets over Silver Beard's head and into the pool. 'We better get out of here fast,' I say to the girls. 'Before they realise who we are.'

As I make to leave, Jiko presses a hand to my chest. 'I can't just let him go, Dag.' Her eyes are pleading and desperate, no longer filled with anger or fear. 'Ume.'

'I'd wager there's at least one cop downstairs,' I say, handing her the hollow gun. 'Now's not the time to finish your little turf war. Call it a temporary truce.'

She stares hard at me, and I touch her hand, try to make her understand. She doesn't need another notch on her belt, especially not one as well-connected as Silver Beard. Not yet anyway. Not until we know more.

Jiko grits her teeth and spits on the floor. Purple copies her, glowering at me. They turn on their heels and head for the exit beyond the beaded curtain. The three of us disappear and leave Silver Beard behind, still breathing and alive, down on his knees, smiling.

21

This mountain of concrete squalor brings back bad memories. I used to live in a dump like this when I was a teen running jobs for Kosuke. Think of an apartment block and then imagine everything that could go wrong: that's a goshitel. They became popular during the boom when floods of people arrived in Sonaya looking for work. Now they're homes for the lower working class, the forgotten souls who survive on scraps. Half the population of Sonaya, then.

Twenty floors, sixteen rooms on each, though calling them 'rooms' might be a stretch—'cells' would be more accurate. Six foot square cubicles with nothing but crumbling walls, rotting floorboards, and maybe a tiny splintered window for the lucky ones. Corridors so narrow you can't even open your door if the one opposite beat you to it. A few years ago there was a fire in the biggest goshitel down in the Rivers, and two hundred people died because they couldn't get out fast enough. Damn death traps in emergencies, and they're not much better on the good days. Forget air-conditioning and cleaning staff; think cockroaches in the basement kitchen and faeces on the floor of the shared bathrooms. Goshitels are the last bastion of the city's deprived and desperate.

The air reeks of body odour, misery, and loneliness. People die in goshitels all the time, and sometimes they don't discover the bodies for weeks. Forgotten old folk neglected by family, single mothers with sobbing kids, penniless graduates struggling to survive, aching addicts and their solitary suffering. Bloodied syringes and soggy condoms litter the corridors between piles of empty bottles. Depression in concrete form. I'd prefer to stay away, but I've got work to do.

I set Shinji and his sister up in one of the cells, Jiko in the cell next door. It's just temporary, I told them. I'm not proud of it, but what choice do I have?

When I arrive, the building manager is holed up in his tiny office, his suspicious eyes staring at me through bullet-proof glass. His blotched cheeks hang like deflated balloons around cracked, bleeding lips. I slip an envelope through the grill and after he's counted the contents his chubby hand waves me in without a word. As long as his pockets are full he doesn't give a shit who comes in or out, dead or alive.

I take the stairs and immediately the stench of the bathrooms hits me in the face. The floor is wet and the flickering lights cast shades of grimy yellow. As I make my way up I pass an old lady on the stairway with the pale, beady face of an eagle chick. She clutches the bannister and stretches one crooked leg in the air like an arthritic ballerina. Next is a bony teen in glasses with his door wide open, sitting on his bed, staring at the blaring box beneath the window. I pause at the sight of his empty eyes as a loud burst of anime fades swiftly into bullshit propaganda. A middle-aged man is enclosed by crumpled clothes and stacks of tarnished comic books, engrossed in a game on his ancient computer and caring for his avatar more than himself. A scrawny woman attempts to quiet her wailing kids. The youngest squirms in her arms, doing his best impression of a fire engine falling into a ravine, while the elder child stares at me with all the expression of a kitchen sink. It's enough to make you want to tear down the walls and set everyone free. But then what happens? There's nowhere else to go.

When I finally reach the ninth floor there's no need to knock—Shinji's door is open. He's sitting on the filthy lino floor and staring at the shadows. When he sees me in the doorway something flickers in his eyes, but he quickly snuffs it out and pulls himself together. I look him up and down as I lean on the door frame. His eyes are bursting from their sockets and he looks thinner than usual, even the rose on his neck is wilting. He spins his shabby baseball cap on one finger while I stare fixedly at the scar on his head.

'Here he comes,' he says. 'The Robin Hood of the Rivers.'

I squeeze into the room and wince at the spoiled milk stench, turning my face away so the kid can't see. If the walls have ears then they've never heard of a colour called white, only the bloody blotches of crushed mosquitoes. A solitary mattress splattered with mould sits among strewn baby clothes. Oh, and the baby's there, too, s prawled on its back, squinting.

'You doing okay?' I ask.

Shinji looks at me weakly, the fight in his eyes extinguished. I want to put my arm around him and tell him everything will be okay, but I've never been good at that kind of thing.

'You got enough food?'

Shinji shrugs. 'Enough for the baby.'

I dig into my pockets and hand him some money, enough to tide them over until tomorrow. He stares at the crisp currency.

'You been to see your mum?'

'Why? She won't have noticed we're missing,' Shinji says. 'We were only ever extra mouths to feed, and she barely fed herself; 'cept through her veins, of course.'

Shinji crouches over his sister and begins to change her nappy, so I stare at the ceiling and try to breathe through my mouth.

'I remember the first time I ran away. My mum's boyfriend wanted me to go out picking pockets for drug money. I refused, and the guy didn't like it.' Shinji indicates the scar on his head. 'I had nowhere to go so I slept in the streets, out in the cold. It was hell, but what got me through it was the thought of causing her pain. You know, hoping she was worried about me. I thought I'd return like a hero, mum would throw her arms around me and promise to change. Quit the gear, quit treating me like a dog. When I *did* go back, the only thing different was that the boyfriend was gone. Dead, my mum said, but she didn't seem to care. She didn't even notice I'd been gone.'

I'm touched that the kid's sharing his troubled childhood with me, but all I can think about is how goddamn long it takes to change a nappy. I don't know how something so small can drop so much shit.

'I tried to get her to quit the junk. I mean, I didn't know what it was back then, but I could see what it was doing to her. But I was just a kid and she wouldn't listen to me. I couldn't do anything, so I left home a few months later. This time for good. Once in a while I go back, just to check on her, you know. I hate her, and I hate myself for it, but what can I do? She's my mum. Every time I go back, I stupidly hope things will be different, hope she'll treat me like a mother treats a son. But it's always the same. She barely even recognises me now.'

'Who's the baby's father?' I ask.

'Eiko,' Shinji says. 'I'm calling her Eiko.'

'Who's Eiko's father?'

Shinji fastens the fresh nappy and tickles his sister. He's a pro already. 'No idea. I'm not even sure she remembers—or cares. She got what she wanted. She got the money.' He looks up at me. 'As soon as I found out she was pregnant, I knew I had to do something. Pigeon jobs don't bring in enough money to support a child. I want Eiko to have a better childhood than I did.'

'That's why you joined the Roses,' I say.

'I swore to myself I'd protect her. And here we are.' He

picks up his sister and cradles her against his chest. 'Hardly better than that shack on Broken Hill.'

'I told you I'd help you,' I say.

His brow creases. 'Help? You've stuck us in a cage. This isn't help, Dag, this is stowing us away so you don't have to think about us. You know...' he hesitates and shakes his head.

'Go on. Say it.'

'We don't have to live like this,' he says, staring at me, the fire in his eyes flaring again. 'I could sell you out in a second. You know that, right? It would solve all our problems.'

'I need you to trust me,' I say.

He replies with a hollow smile. We both know trust isn't worth shit in Sonaya, and now Shinji's trusting for two.

'Just tell me,' I say. Back to business. 'Have the Roses come back for you yet?'

His eyes shiver in their sockets—he doesn't know whether to tell me the truth or not. It's all the answer I need.

22

TWO MONTHS TO RELEASE

They say you should get a good night's sleep before a test, but this might be the exception. I haven't slept for a week. A broken nose and a missing ear is all good, but a week without sleep can add five years to a face. Dry patchy skin and pus-filled pimples, heavy black bags beneath my eyes; by the time assessment day arrives I'm a goddamn zombie. Only problem is, my big day is gonna be bigger than they expect, and I'll need my wits about me.

A half-dozen of us were rounded up after morning roll call. I recognise a few faces but they're nothing special. My cell is on the highest floor, and that means I'm top dog in this ragged-ass crew. As they tie our hands behind our backs, I look around at each of the gathered men. Damn, they're a sorry bunch. I've worked overtime to make myself look despicable, but these droopy-eyed bugs will trump me without even trying. Why did I stop at one ear?

They started tying prisoners' hands before they introduced one-way mirrors for assessments. You had to feel sorry for the girls who got roped in for the panels in those days. They said it wasn't ethical for prisoners to be rated anonymously, so back then you could see the face of each jury member. The problem was that locked-up men don't have a great deal of self-control—faced with a parade of dolled-up women, the prisoners' hands went missing down their pants, and that wasn't the only issue. You don't need to be a genius to figure out what happened when newly-released convicts caught up with girls who gave them undesirable ratings. Now it's all one-way mirrors and anonymity—for most people, anyway.

There's a whole floor in The Heights dedicated to assessments and officialdom, with clean, white walls like the hospital wing. We're frog-marched down the corridor in our khaki jumpsuits like a chain gang on its way to the railroad. Several security guards stand sentry beside unmarked doors. I nod at each of them as we pass; I know, boys, my eyes tell them, you're only doing your job. We're marched into a big room, told to sit down and wait. There are seven of us and only four chairs. Without incident the biggest men claim the seats, while the others fall to their haunches or lean against the wall. I snag myself a seat; no ear, no arguments. This new look is working fine for me so far.

'I hear there's a stunner on the panel,' I reveal to the room, dipping my toe in the water.

'How'd ya hear that?' asks one of the smaller inmates slumped on the floor. He's the youngest one here, with a flat nose and a chain of tattoos choking his neck. I spot a few flowers among the inked motifs, but if he's in The Heights then they can't be roses.

'How'd you hear anything with that measly ear?' asks another. He's got a face like a locked-up bulldog lusting for air. A couple of guffaws resonate in response.

'Maybe I've got someone on the outside,' I say. I'm freestyling here; that's how I work best. 'Maybe I've put money in the right hands.'

'You should have saved your money for the cocoons,' the bulldog says. He looks around for a reaction but this time there's nothing but nervous smiles. Even these lowly skunks know who I am.

We sit around inhaling stale air as I examine my brothers and wonder what's waiting for them on the outside. The young one will probably stride back into the tattooed arms of his gang, but unless one of his tulips morphs into a rose, he'll be back here within a year. The bulldog might return to a loving wife and doting kids and a fancy suite on the strip. And I might grow a new ear.

Eventually a podgy guard enters the room and casts his eyes over us. I peer at the ID tag pinned to his man-boob, and the four-digit number marks him out as Kosuke's final gift. The man I've been waiting for.

'Electrics have been playing up today,' he mumbles. The other inmates look at each other; not too fast on the uptake. 'Security won't be compromised, though, so don't try anything stupid.'

I search their blank faces. I tried to tell them, but if you can't take a hint, you can't take a hint. We can't go spelling things out in hieroglyphics.

The guard orders us to get to our feet. It's showtime. We're released from the room and escorted back through the corridor to another set of sealed doors. I have to admit it; the nerves are getting to me. There are no butterflies in my stomach, only ravenous roaches burrowing through my bowels.

One by one we enter. Here it is. The famous mirror. The line-up. It's been a while. I missed my last assessments; prisoners in The Heights don't require a rating, so they wait until we're due for release. We line up against the back wall, but there's only a couple of feet between us and the one-way mirror. The panel girls will get a close look at our sorry mugs, that's for sure.

'Face forward,' the guard barks, before exiting and closing the door behind him. A second later his voice echoes over the intercom. 'Heads down,' he commands. We do as we're told. 'Heads up. Left. Right. Good. Await further instruction.'

We stand there like lemons, stare at our ugly reflections and wait for the next round of the hokey cokey. I squint to avoid the bright lights on the ceiling. My eyes will need to adjust quickly, and I'm determined to be ready. Then comes the first instruction.

'Smile,' the intercom orders. 'No teeth. Hold it.'

We smile; a line of gurning clowns. We're frozen for what seems like forever before the next instruction booms. 'Now with teeth.'

It's hard to offer a natural smile when you're lined up next to men who smell like they've not bathed for a decade, but I do my best.

'Number four, what the hell is that? Make it natural or we'll make you a ten.'

I steal a glance to my left as number four rearranges his expression into something less pained. The guards have been doing this a long time; there's no faking it.

This one lasts even longer. I struggle to hold my smile as I wonder what kind of score I'm heading for. I can see the dimples in my reflection; some things you just can't chop off.

Then it happens. The lights fizzle above us and the bulbs explode. We're thrown into darkness. I rush forward and push my face up against the glass. The wonderful thing about one-way mirrors is that it's all just a trick of the light. Take out the light and we're even. I cup my hands around my eyes and get a good look. The goons beside me don't realise what's going on, and neither do the girls on the other side of the glass. All except one.

She steps forward and stands directly in front of me. Despite the darkness, I can make out her basic features. Thin eyes like a fox, a button nose, and punk feathered hair. Dyed hair. So this is Jiko.

I can see her lips moving but the words are lost on me. She can hear me all right, but all I get are frantic hand gestures and exaggerated lip movements. It's not long before the other dregs realise what's happening and charge

THIS RAGGED, WASTREL THING

at the glass to plead with the girls. Pandemonium erupts. I better make this quick.

'Give me a two and as soon as I'm out I'll pay you back,' I say. 'I give you my word. In your report just say you were freaked out by my ear.'

I turn my head so she can see for herself, nothing but a hole and a tunnel of worms. My eyes are adjusting to the dark and Jiko's coming in clearer by the second. She's young, pretty, acres of attitude. Twenty years ago she would've been just my type.

She points to her chest. *My turn.* I watch her mime a cloud above her head...then glasses on her face. I'm not in any doubt who she's talking about, even before she mouths his name, slow and clear. *Dustin Fairchild.* What the hell has this punk girl got to do with Fairchild?

Now she's pointing at me and shaking her head, but I don't understand her. This is one hell of a desperate game of charades. She stops and sighs, inhales deeply, and tries again. I stare fixedly at her lips as she mouths the words that might change everything. *Don't trust him.*

The lights flicker and switch on before I can question her. I fall back to the wall with the others. We stand to attention and try to look innocent, like teenagers caught in the act. The bulldog clears his throat and bows his head like he's just walked into church, while kid tulip looks up at the lights like he's stunned by their sudden presence. Like the l ast sixty seconds never happened.

'Apologies for the electrical issues,' the guard announces over the intercom.

Don't worry about it, bud. We're assured this has never happened before, that it was the first—and last—time, which I doubt. The guard on the other side of the wall might be about to retire early. Either that or he'll be part of next month's line-up, grinning grotesquely into the glass.

#

I thought I would have peace of mind once the assessment was done. Ten years of being a good boy in The Heights concluded with a whirlwind of action to see me off. I've done everything I can to ensure I've got a chance on the outside. In the space of a few weeks I've deformed my face and bribed my panel, and I've done it while making regular visits to the sake hole on the top floor. I don't know if anyone's written a book on riding The Heights like a champ, but I sure fucking should.

Ever since my encounter with Jiko, bees have been swarming inside my head like it's a damn hive handing out honey on the house. Dustin Fairchild. Guys like me don't do friends, but if I had to trust anyone in this monolith with my life, it would've been him. I might have even put my life on the line for him. Maybe.

A few months in here might as well be a few lifetimes. When you see a man locked up, you see the flesh beneath the feathers. Stripped raw like a newborn rat, wrinkled pink skin and eyes scrunched shut, scrambling for light. When Fairchild first arrived, I saw straight through him. Sure, he had swagger, American confidence, but there was more to it than that. I saw the fear behind his glasses. He was no different from the rest of us, or more specifically, me. The day he cut off my ear was the day I knew what I'd long suspected: we were in it together.

So some girl I've never met before tells me I can't trust the only person I've chosen to trust. That he's playing me? Playing me for what? I run through every possibility in my head. If he wanted me dead, he could've slit my throat after he knocked me out. If he wanted me to rot in The Heights it would only take a word to the big boys in uniform; I've regularly bent my bars and Fairchild's been there every time. The only thing I can think is that he's setting me up for something once I'm outside. But why? So I end up back in here? It doesn't make sense. I try to shake it off, snap the suspicions away like flies from my mane.

I'm being steered to my cell by my own private escort and we pass through the meeting room, where visiting hours are coming to a close; long rows of cons facing morose mothers or sullen lovers. And there he is, my right-hand man, glaring at a bald guy in a slick navy suit and skinny grey tie. Fairchild is hunched forward with his elbows fixed on the table, gesticulating with nervous hands. I can't hear what he's saying but by the look of them it's clearly not a friendly catch-up. The other guy is hardly moving, a straight stick up his ass, watching Fairchild like a tiger studying its prey. I try to slow things down, linger, but I'm pushed straight through.

Okay. So Fairchild's got friends on the outside, that's nothing special. He's been in Sonaya a couple of years and friends come and go. Could be a dealer sorting out drugs for his release party, or maybe a loan shark from some gang. Wouldn't surprise me if Fairchild's involved in such circles; addicts are always the easiest prey. It wouldn't matter if only he'd told me about it. Maybe then I could forget Jiko's warning.

23

Shinji's alone again, sitting on the floor and shoving clothes into a hobo sack.

'Where is it?' I ask. He knows I'm talking about Eiko. It's easy enough to seem heartless; just mix up your personal pronouns.

'With Jiko on the roof.'

I nod. The kid's pouting like a catfish and I'm not surprised. He doesn't look at me and I don't bother with small talk, I just leave him with his bad mood and head on up to the roof. The staircase is empty and dark, the bulbs long blown, and the door to the roof is ajar, propped open with a brick. Sonaya might be short of fresh air, but I swear I swallow a sweet lungful when I step out under the open sky.

There's an old man leaning against an air vent with a bottle of sake at his feet, his small wrinkled head poking through his jacket like a curious turtle. He's arranging his mattress for the evening when he peers up at me. It's not uncommon for residents to sleep on rooftops during Sonayan summers—if there's a goshitel with air-con then I've never heard of it.

'I know your face,' the old man says.

'Want an autograph?'

'This is no place for a wanted man,' he says, fixing his crafty little eyes on me. 'People here would cut off their noses for a wad of cash, and the price on your head could buy this whole building.'

He takes a long swig from his bottle but his eyes don't leave my face. I pass him a note with a few zeros emblazoned above the face of a Japanese man that no one remembers. Then I tell him where I'll shove the next one if he doesn't keep his tongue behind his crooked teeth.

I leave him to think about my threat and find Jiko crouching behind another air vent. Baby Eiko is splayed out in front of her, blankets and nappies and tissues creating a collage of a future I don't want any part of.

'Motherhood suits you,' I say.

Jiko turns around and slices straight through me with her blazing eyes.

'Don't you dare, Kawasaki,' she says, standing up. She's still wearing her outfit from the bathhouse; the same tattoo peeking out of her shirt and the same menacing look on her face, only this time it's aimed at me. She's only been here a few days, but it's enough. I remember what it's like to live in a place like this, how it sucks your soul from your skin.

'Dag, this isn't my baby. I don't care how you get yourself in these messes, but I don't want a part of it anymore. You hear me? I'm out.'

I glance at the baby. The little cherub's looking healthier. Not great, but better. Her face has filled out and colour's returned to her cheeks. Her brown eyes are alive again but they don't find much to like about me, and suddenly she's bawling pretty loud. Jiko huffs and I shrug in response.

Sonaya's no place for babies. Sonaya's a place for surly men with bloodshot eyes and leathery skin. Babies can't take care of themselves, and to survive in this city that's rule number one. Anything else is a weakness. I look into Eiko's eyes and all I see is weakness; whoever holds this baby ends up with two fewer arms to fight with, and that just won't do.

'We need to get her out of here, Dag,' Jiko says, picking Eiko up with a wince and gently rocking her. I've never seen her so serious. Life's not all leather and sake anymore, and it's all my fault.

'I haven't slept since it happened,' she says, not looking at me or the baby or anything.

'Since what happened?'

'Don't pretend like you've forgotten, Dag,' she says. 'Earth Hour. I killed a man. I killed a man I didn't know — didn't know anything about. Some random guy, and I killed him, just like that. I can't stop thinking about it. The blood, his body dead on the roof.'

She turns away and stares out over the rooftops. The new moon smolders in a starless sky that looks emptier than ever.

I place a hand on her shoulder. 'You saved our lives that night. It was better him than me or Shinji.' She remains silent, so I lie. 'Don't worry, it'll pass.'

'I had to pawn my bike,' she says. Jiko's not the type to cry, but her eyes are glistening. So this is what it's like to know me.

'I'll get it back for you. I'll get it all back, I promise.'

What kind of world is this where I'm a father figure? This whole damn world's flipped upside down.

Jiko carries Eiko towards the wall and looks out over the Rivers. The dark has descended and Sonaya is stirring awake, lights igniting the alleys. Sonaya looks better at night with neon to paint over the cracks. A group of teens are conspiring on the corner with their heads down and their shirt collars up. A middle-aged woman attempts to steer her bicycle through them, but one of the kids kicks a leg out and she almost crashes to the ground trying to avoid him. A little further down the road, squeezed between a scooter garage and a shuttered coffee house, a smoky kiosk serves steaming noodles to bent-backed suits who slurp through fat greedy lips.

Jiko is trembling, tears streaming down her face, nothing but a kid condemned. I pull her and Eiko into my chest.

'Listen to me,' I say. 'I'm getting you out of here. Tonight.'

From the look in her eyes I can tell she doesn't believe me, but as I enclose them in my arms Eiko stops crying and the night falls silent.

'Something's gonna happen, Dag,' she says. 'Shinji's not himself. Something's wrong…I don't know what it is…but it feels like we're being set up.'

Good instincts, girl. We're all being set up. At least her wits are still working.

'You talked to him yesterday, didn't you?' she asks. 'Whatever you said, I don't think it worked. I don't know if…I don't know if you can trust him.'

I kiss Jiko on the forehead. I kiss the baby too. It's okay; there's no one up here to see. We stare at Sonaya in silence.

'Get us out of here,' she says.

#

We gather up the baby's things and head back inside, back into the stench of stewing life. Down one floor, then another.

'See you outside,' I say, leaving Jiko on the ninth floor. 'I'll get the boy.'

When I reach the kid's room it's empty. I call Shinji's name, but there's no answer. Heavy footsteps stride up the stairs and two men in black appear at the end of the corridor; padded pockets, loaded belts, eyes for one man only. One has a big bouldery face with slow black eyes simmering beneath bushy eyebrows. The other is taller but built just as heavily, a smattering of spots spread across his bulbous nose. Something tells me they haven't dropped by for a cup of tea.

'Evening, Kawasaki,' the first one says in a surprisingly soft voice. I don't recognise him or his friend, but I don't need to. He pulls down the collar of his vest to reveal a rose tattoo. Finally, the weeds are surfacing from the soil. It's about time we put this all to bed.

I throw the doors either side of me open and take cover behind them as the people in their rooms scream and the Roses lock and load their guns. I guess the truce is over; my bath with Silver Beard was bullshit.

'You want me dead or alive?' I call up the corridor.

'Why, alive, of course,' the first man replies. 'What fun can we have if you're dead?'

That kind of revenge, is it? The drag-it-out torture kind? That suits me fine; I love second chances.

A split second of silence passes before they start shooting. The doors almost do their job until a bullet cuts through the timber and grazes my leg. It's like I've written the script myself.

The shooting and screaming stop as the rooms empty out and everyone runs towards the stairs, the shooters standing aside to let them pass. Now it's just me and the tigers and these wonderful doors. I know how the next bit goes. The doors still open and splintered to shit in front of me, I flatten my body against the wall. Silent. Playing dead. That's what they do in the movies. I hear the Roses' slow, cautious approach, even the hand signals they exchange. Whatever this film is, I've seen it before. All I have to do is wait.

'We know you're there, Dag,' the first tiger says. He's ten feet away, breathing heavily. He cocks his gun and I hold my breath. I feel like a video game character with an extra life, and it's time for my special move. Wait for it. He's on the other side of the door now, three inches of wood separating me from the smoking barrel of his gun. I can almost hear the countdown in his head. Three. Two. One.

Smash.

I throw my full weight against the door and send him reeling backwards, showering the ceiling with bullets as he falls. I skid across the floor and kick the gun from his grip, smash him in the face with my other leg and take cover behind another door. The second tiger dusts the floor with wild pot shots as I take aim and nail a bullet into each of his legs. I turn back to the man on the floor and grant him the same courtesy, making his bushy eyebrows dance. They're both screaming in pain but what they should be is grateful. I don't wanna be a killer anymore; it doesn't help a man sleep at night.

I step over the wounded tigers, pick up the second gun and head back to the staircase. I can hear Jiko calling me from below, but I've got to play this right.

'Watch out, Dag,' Jiko calls. 'There's another one!'

I knew the alpha would arrive. Sure enough, I hear the advancing footsteps. It's like a damn funhouse in here.

I run up to eleventh. Room 1107. He's right where he should be, sitting on his tatami mat with his stumpy arm hanging loose at his side. Tsubasa.

'Heard shots flying,' he says. 'Thought it might've been you, pal. You get a hit?'

I look down at my bloody leg. 'Just a graze,' I say. 'You seen the boy?'

'Not a sign. Causing you trouble?'

I shake my head. 'Wouldn't have him any other way. You made the right choice. I know it wasn't easy to get hold of. And I know what you've risked.'

Tsubasa nods mutely. Every time I look at him all I can see are the ghosts of his parents on Broken Hill, waiting for their boy to come home. In this sorry pile of stones that too many people call home, he fits right in.

Footsteps sound in the corridor outside, and they're not subtle.

'Oh, Daganae,' the alpha calls. 'Where are you hiding now?'

I hand Tsubasa the guns. 'These will only weigh me down.' I shake his only hand and get ready. 'Wish me luck.'

#

206

A bald head and a hard face that looks like it's been carved out of limestone, shrew eyes with thin lines for eyebrows. Slick navy suit and skinny tie. Ume's killer in the flesh, a gun in one hand, the other tucked into his pocket.

'You've injured my boys, Daganae,' he says with mock-disappointment. He must have taken thesping lessons from Silver Beard. 'Had enough of killing, have you?' He tuts and shakes his head. 'Don't worry, I know what it's like. Nightmares are tough to shake, aren't they?'

A man after my own heart. He lowers his gun and slides it into his holster. Confident indeed.

'But I'm afraid we're not done just yet,' he says. 'There's a blood-debt to pay. Your little biker girl killed one of our men, Daganae, and it's time for someone to suffer the consequences.'

'I saved your boss's life,' I reply. 'Silver Beard wouldn't want me dead.'

'Oh, we won't kill you, Dag. Fujii's eager to take you out of the picture, but you've got an admirer who wants you all to themself. All *we* want is a little prize. An eye, perhaps, maybe an arm. Or better still, your other ear. We'll see. However, I can't guarantee the same mercy for the redhead.'

Oh happy days.

'If you come quietly, I promise to be lenient. Might even let you leave with both your legs.'

Enter Shinji. Cometh the hour, etcetera.

The bald man is quicker than he looks. In a flash he's wrestled Eiko from Shinji and thrown him to the floor.

'Well, look at this,' he says, peering down at the baby. 'You've got yourself a little family, Daganae. Shame your boy has sold you out again.'

I look at Shinji, who shuffles on the floor and avoids my eyes.

'Once a Rose, always a Rose,' the man says. 'We offered him everything you couldn't, Dag. Money, protection, a home. He couldn't wait to rat you out, tell us you were coming tonight. So much for family. And the best part is we got ourselves a two for one special, a one-eared mongrel and a biker girl.'

'You said you wouldn't hurt my sister,' Shinji cries from the floor.

The bald man glances back at Eiko. 'Well, that all depends on your man Kawasaki,' he says.

With his eyes now fixed on me, he grips his gun and casually spins it on his trigger finger, inches from Eiko's innocent face. 'It's funny how I get after too much coffee,' he says. 'Makes me jittery. You ever get like that, Dag? Like you can't control your fingers?'

I sigh and hold up my hands as the two injured tigers appear behind Shinji, limping and cursing. They're dragging Jiko behind them, her hands tied and her face bloodied. She spits expletives as she's thrown to the floor next to Shinji.

It's that time again. The time for miracles.

'Tsubasa,' I call to the corridor.

Silence.

The bald man laughs; a pity laugh, perhaps.

'No friends left, Dag?' he asks. 'That one-armed plover wouldn't be much use to you anyway. He belongs to Fujii, didn't you know?'

Time's up. I set off towards them, head hanging and hands raised, ready to face my fate.

'Let me say goodbye to the baby,' I say. That smile again.

I pluck Eiko from his arms and carefully adjust her blankets. She's looking at me with those large expectant eyes, and for the first time she smiles at me. What the hell did you do to deserve being born in this damn place? Reluctantly, I hand her back and step away.

'Tsubasa!' I call again.

Eventually he emerges from his room and glares at us from the other end of the corridor.

'What do we have here?' he asks in his gravelly drawl.

Two police officers appear from the room next door, a middle-aged man with a taught, serious face, and a young woman with an eager one. A small camera is mounted on her shoulder, a little red light flashing on its face, the loaded rifle beneath pointed in our direction. The smirk on Baldie's face slides away.

'That's your man,' Tsubasa says. 'Check the bundle.'

The bald man laughs with relief. 'It's just a baby, officers.'

The male officer approaches with a complete absence of expression, while his partner stares down the sight of her rifle. The man takes the baby from Baldie and reaches inside the blankets. He rummages around and finally removes something concealed in his fist. I already know what it is. A memory stick: the same one Tsubasa passed me five minutes earlier.

'It's here,' he says, revealing it to the camera.

'What the hell is that?' Baldie asks angrily.

'Our informant tipped us off,' the officer says. 'Said the evidence of Ume Uchida's murder, which was recently stolen from the system, would turn up here. Tonight.'

The female officer lowers her gun and grabs the stick from her partner. She stuffs it into a pocket and smiles. The light on her camera is still flashing and recording the whole party. 'Daizo Coda,' she says to Baldie, detaching a set of hand-cuffs from her belt. 'You're under arrest on suspicion of the murder Ume Uchida.'

Daizo Coda looks at Shinji. I knew I could count on him. I hold out my hands.

'Are we free to leave, officers?' I ask.

Tsubasa nods. 'These three are with me,' he says. ' The baby too.'

Good old Tsubasa; not a bad guy to have on your team.

The male officer nods. 'Free to leave,' he says.

I shake Tsubasa's hand and unfasten the ropes around Jiko's wrists. I'll make this up to her later. Shinji gets up and takes hold of his sister. They follow me down the stairs.

'Got the money?' I ask Shinji.

He pulls a fat wad of cash from his pocket. 'Roses pays well for snitches.'

'Enough for the hospital?' I ask.

'More than enough.'

More Dag-hunters taken care of and profit in pocket. Two birds and all that.

'You set all of this up?' Jiko asks.

'I told you to trust me,' I say. 'Shinji, get Eiko to a hospital.' I give half the money to the boy, the other half to Jiko. 'And you, find somewhere safe to stay. For all of you. And get that bike of yours back.'

Jiko flicks through the stack of notes. 'What are you going to do?'

I glance back at the goshitel.

'I owe someone a drink.'

24

I emerge from the Rivers and gaze at the glowing harbour, take a great gulp of air like I'm trying to swallow the sky and chew on its candied stars. Freedom sure tastes sweet.

I pause to watch the projection of the prime minister, addressing Sonaya from the pixilated wall of the National Bank. She has the kind of natural look people trust, one of the few elites who hasn't filled her face with plastic. She's changed a lot since I last saw her in person, but I guess that was a while ago. The fire in her eyes still blazes bright; I'd even call her attractive if it weren't for the coffee-stain birthmark on her cheek. Some say it adds personality, others sympathy, but for me it's only a reminder of a time I'd rather forget.

Her voice is husky, measured. She scrapes every *s* over her incisors and sounds smart and sophisticated. No wonder everyone's lapping her up. I can't listen for long, though; all that political stuff dries me out. There's corruption all the way through, like arteries clogged with fat, and we're just blind little mice taking whatever crumbs of cheese they throw us. Blind to the rest of the world. All we need now is a famine, and then we'd be like North Korea before the Second Korean War.

I pass the lighthouse and keep moving until I reach the Hunting Grounds, a long slab of concrete on the waterfront where people gather at night for liquid picnics. It seems like half the city's out to celebrate the end of monsoon season, and there are even a few stars blinking through the black. A carpet of newspapers blankets the concrete and groups huddle around upturned cardboard boxes weighed down with sake and soju and beer. Chopsticks hang from fingers while gossip blasts between mouthfuls of cheap food. The incoming tide stinks of shit but no one cares; sewage is Sonaya's nostalgic perfume.

'Daganae Kawasaki!'

A hundred eager eyes target me, but it doesn't matter anymore. That's my name, and this is my new face, Sonaya. There's no need for the fedora now. No need to hide. I went into a cocoon as a butterfly and I've come out as a damn peacock. Yo, Sonaya, check out my feathers and watch me fly. I could jig along the strip with bells on my shoes and castanets in my hands and all they'd be able to do is watch.

I spot Nakata by the water wearing baggy washed-out jeans and a plum-coloured top that matches the highlights in her hair. She's waving and calling me over so I nod and slowly thread my way through the muttering crowd. Outside of her bar she looks smaller, or it could be because she's standing next to Ganzo, who's spread like a washed-up whale that's given up trying to shuffle back in. He's still in his white chef jacket; I don't know if he owns any other clothes.

'You know it's summer when this place is packed,' Ganzo says as I claim a corner of newspaper and split my wooden chopsticks.

'Never seen it so busy,' Nakata says as she pours me a cup of soju.

'You should've seen it back in the day,' I say, toasting my friends and socking one down. 'We used to come here all the time when we were young bucks. Remember, Ganzo? The food trucks were stacked with barbecue chicken and skewers of pork. Beautiful girls with big dreams and bright futures. Long summer nights, drink and women; Sonaya was electric.'

Ganzo nods and chews on his squid. He scans the sea of youthful faces around us like he's trying to find the teenage versions of us.

'Any news from the powers that be?' I ask. 'The dogs in blue told me they'd be in touch, but I haven't heard a thing.'

'Baldie,' Ganzo replies, brandishing a strip of squid in question.

'Daizo Coda,' I say.

'Daizo Coda,' Ganzo repeats, nodding. 'They charged him for murder as soon as they reviewed the drone footage. I heard that as soon as they locked him up, he tried to share the blame like a kid sharing slices of cherry pie.'

'Fujii?'

'He's been officially suspended,' Ganzo says. 'But nobody knows where he is.'

'He's out of hospital?'

'News of the video must have spread pretty fast,' Nakata says. 'Fujii discharged himself soon after they arrested Coda, and no one's seen him since.'

'Fujii's greased a lot of palms,' I say. 'He'll buy his way out of it somehow.'

'When a video like that does the rounds,' Nakata says, 'even the cats at the top can't ignore it. A sergeant implicated in murder isn't good news, especially with the elections coming up. Fujii's money tree has run dry.'

'Kosuke thinks that once they've caught Fujii, you might get away with a slap on the wrist,' Ganzo says.

'Community service, maybe,' Nakata says. 'Anything more than that and there'll be too much publicity, and that's precisely what the government wants to avoid.'

'I stabbed a sergeant,' I say. It all sounds too good to be true.

'But that was after the sergeant set you up for murder,' Nakata says. 'It doesn't carry much weight anymore.'

Ganzo's button eyes disappear above his big panda smile. Nakata nods, daring me to believe it. When I left The Heights I was a free man for five days—that's only about fifteen minutes in Dag years. A drone sweeps over the moonlit picnic and I stare at it head on. Come and watch me dance, old boy, we're all friends now. Let's see if I can make freedom stick a little longer this time.

'Just in time for Independence Day,' I say. 'Any plans?'

'Same as always,' Nakata replies. 'Get ready for riots and parties, and probably both at the same time.'

I nod and drink. 'Sounds like the perfect night to take care of business.'

'What business?' Ganzo looks between me and Nakata. 'You're free now, Dag. It might be best to keep your head down for a while.'

The bean pancake's not half bad. I wolf it away and wash it down with soju.

'Dag,' Ganzo continues. 'I know what you're like, but it's all done with now. It's finished. Sometimes it's best to let things lie.'

I feel their eyes on me even though I don't look away from my food.

'Kosuke said you mentioned Hana,' Nakata says.

Blabbermouth Kosuke. 'Pour me another soju,' I reply.

'Hana's dead, Dag,' Ganzo says. 'Move on and live your life. You've been waiting long enough.'

I glare at him. 'Like you, you mean?'

He stops chewing and blinks slow, like his eyelids are forged from granite.

'Maybe you're right,' I say. 'Maybe I can find a little basement of my own, one like yours. Live like a woodlouse, rolling up whenever I get scared. Is that what I should do, Ganzo?'

'Dag,' Nakata says.

'And what about you, Nakata? Are you living? Or are you still hiding from your parents' ghosts?'

I don't know where this is coming from, but it's not finished coming yet. Nakata sighs and Ganzo stares at the squid like he's waiting for it to silence me.

'You know who I admire?' I blabber on. 'Ume and Jiko and all those biker girls. At least they're fighting for what they believe in. They haven't just given up.'

Never mix soju and sake; it makes a man wild. No one says anything. We all sit in silence and think about what a fucking prat I am. The party continues around us, oblivious. A group of girls are having a contest to see who can wear the shortest skirt; the boys beside them are trying to judge the winner.

'Given up,' Ganzo says at last, focusing on his chopsticks. We watch the big man as he carefully weighs his words. 'Maybe that means something different to you.'

'Ganzo—'

'I've wanted my own sushi bar ever since I can remember. Nothing too fancy, but somewhere with white walls, a conveyor belt. Three or four chefs slicing up fish behind me. A steady stream of customers. I thought if I could save enough money I might make it out one day, maybe to the mainland, Tokyo even. Maybe find someone to settle down with. That doesn't sound too bad, does it?'

I shake my head, but what I should do is hang it in shame.

'A few years ago, while you were locked up in your cell counting down the days, and I was stuck in my kitchen carving tuna every night, I realised it'd never happen. The money never added up, and it got harder and harder to stay afloat. That's when I stopped dreaming, and finally started living.'

He stops talking long enough to sink his soju. Licking his lips, he returns the paper cup to the makeshift table, and carries on.

'Sonaya kept spinning and nothing changed, nothing except the way I looked at things. I've got my own place, my fish, my knives. It's a hell of a lot better than most people. I don't see that as giving up. I see it as appreciating what I have.

'The problem with you is,' he says, finally looking up and aiming his chopsticks at me, 'you're always chasing something. The next bar, the next woman, the next piece of action. I thought you might've changed, or matured or something. I thought eleven years would be plenty of time for you to get over what happened, what you did. But you're exactly the same. You haven't changed one bit. You'll do anything to keep from moving on.

'You're a free man now, Dag. Hopefully soon you'll realise what it is you're looking for.'

Every second of the ensuing silence makes me feel more foolish.

'Sorry,' I say. I can't remember the last time I said the word. Maybe freedom doesn't agree with me after all. When you spend half your life searching for the sun and suddenly the sky bursts open bright and blue, it's hard to remember what the hell you're living for.

'Sorry, Ganzo. Sorry, Nakata.'

They nod and stare at the sea. Ganzo's right; who am I to accuse them of hiding? Nakata's coming out was the bravest thing I've ever seen. When have I ever done anything remotely as brave?

I look around at the crowds. Kids are leaving their rubbish on the ground for the midnight tide to wash away. The fishermen are huddled together on the groynes by the lighthouse; simple men in shabby baseball caps. They stare at the lapping waves and put off going back to their empty homes up on Broken Hill.

'At least you shouldn't have any trouble from the Roses,' I say to Ganzo. Let's get this picnic back on track. 'Silver Beard might still be around somewhere, but the rest of his crew will have to keep a low profile, for a while now at least. With Fujii out of the picture, whoever takes his place is gonna start a new auction for turf rights. The Rivers are about to be shaken up.'

Ganzo nods slowly. 'Maybe this is the start of it, then. A new beginning, peace at last.' Him and Nakata share a straining smile, daring each other to believe in better times, and I don't wanna be the one to burst their bubble. Sure, they might not be hiding, but they're living with their heads in the sand. Things have been brewing for a long time now, and whatever game's still going on, it's about to enter the final act. You can smell it in the air, like a storm crossing the ocean. Peace? Maybe in another life, panda.

#

The Arkansas is looking mighty fine under the bright blue lights of the jetty. Aimi's wearing a bikini under a turquoise sarong and Stones is in a white wife-beater and florid shorts like a teen on spring break. We're only a ten-minute walk from the Hunting Grounds, but it feels like a different country. Stones has put on some eighties Japanese city pop and the cocktails in our hands are rainbow-coloured and coated with sugar around the rims. All the ingredients are in place for a fun time, but there's something sour in the air I don't recognise.

Aimi hasn't blinked once since I came aboard and Stones' smiles are less convincing than his novels. I'm sat on deck like a kid stuck between divorced parents.

'You gonna take this thing out for a sail one of these days?' I say, just for someone to be saying something.

Stones glances at Aimi before answering, but she's clearly uninterested in playing house. 'For sure, Dag. We'll have a grand old trip, the lot of us. Fairchild and Kosuke and everyone. We'll take her out to one of the islands, I know a good spot for snorkelling, and we'll have a beach all to ourselves. Aimi can bring along a friend, we'll set you up.'

One of Aimi's eyebrows almost makes a crease in her Botoxed forehead.

'And when will that be?' she spits at Stones. She slams

her glass so hard on the table it's a wonder it doesn't smash to pieces and bring the mast down with it. 'You'll have to forgive my husband, Dag, he's full of empty promises. The sad part is, he actually believes them himself.' She throws him a scathing look and storms off below deck to clatter and crash in the kitchen.

'Don't mind her,' Stones whispers, his smile more strained than ever. 'She wants out of Sonaya, that's all. Has done for a while, but all these damn campaign promises are making things worse. Nishi's pledging a crackdown on drugs, and it's looking likely she'll be re-elected.'

'Aimi wants to get out of Sonaya because you *can* get out of Sonaya,' I say.

He stares at me blankly.

'You expats are all the same,' I say. 'You don't understand. You cruise into Sonaya and see all the neon and parties and drugs.'

'It's not just that—'

'No, but it's a big part of it. You're blind to the rest. You don't see the real Sonaya because you don't have to. You could sail this thing to Japan or Korea in the morning and board a plane to America in the afternoon. Blink and you're gone—you wouldn't feel a thing, like cutting a strand of hair with giant scissors. But Aimi grew up here. She knows what it's really like. More than you ever will.'

'She loves it here,' Stones says.

'*You* love it here. Aimi loves *you*, not Sonaya. She wants you to quit while you're ahead. She doesn't want you turning into Fairchild.'

'Fairchild's doin' fine,' Stones protests, waving me off.

'Sure he is,' I say, swirling my glass to make a whirlpool of my drink. 'Where do you think he is right now? In a book club? On a date in some fancy restaurant? Hell no. He's either sucking dust up his nose or selling me out to whoever the hell wants me.' I finish off my cocktail with one huge swig.

Stones sighs and moistens his bottom lip. He relieves me of my empty glass and places it on the table.

'I don't know what you've heard, Dag, but Fairchild isn't going to sell you out. He's a fizzing jumble of wires for sure, but he's no snitch. I know that much.'

'Yeah, well, we'll see about that. Things have been going my way a little too neatly these last few days, and it doesn't sit right with me. I feel like I'm waiting for a bomb to drop.' I stand up and shake his hand. 'Tell Aimi I said goodbye. And think about what I said. You've been here long enough to know this government keeps all of its worst promises. A little time away might not be such a bad idea.'

I step over the railing and head down the jetty in a diagonal shaft of moonlight.

'Dag,' Stones calls from the deck. I turn back to look at him. 'You might be right, you know. If a bomb *is* about to drop, get clear of the blast zone.'

I nod and salute my friend as I leave the harbour lights behind.

25

Independence Day. The day we cut the strings that Japan held us up with. Nobody knew that without strings we'd just be a rotting, lifeless doll. Woodworm destroying the whole thing from the inside. Self-destruction like nothing the world had ever seen. So here it is everyone: raise your glasses, clink them together and then slit your wrists. Cheers to us.

It was all for a good cause, of course. Ageing population, rising health problems, fucked up environment; all things that needed fixing, somehow. It's just a shame Tokyo rolled out their new policies on our little farming island first. We were what they called a 'Special Administrative Region' back then. Training wheels time, after Japan blew billions helping to end the Second Korean War and Sonaya's heavy industry push went all to hell.

Meat was the first thing to go. Later they banned cars and cigarettes, then the internet and mobile phones. A whole slew of crackpot policies followed. Admirable? Maybe. But it doesn't feel too good when your home becomes a rat cage and the big wigs from another city keep coming round with needles for their latest injections. It was only a matter of time before the guinea pig nation cut itself loose.

There'll be parades through the streets of Sonaya tonight, and by parades I mean protests, fires and drink. I'm fine with all three as long as the drink is good and the dogs in blue don't have the Kawasaki scent on their noses.

I try to let Ganzo's words dissolve into the more malleable lobes of my brain, but they just won't take. I sit in my dingy attic on my moth-eaten chair and try to let things lie; every secret, every lingering look, every suspicion of the past few weeks. I can let the police take care of Fujii, let Fairchild play his little games, let Sara conspire with all the baddest cats in town. Maybe it's time to leave Sonaya to the next generation. I can watch as Jiko and her girls scorch twisters into tarmac, as Shinji starts a racket of his own. I should sit back and settle in for the show, grow old and grey and leave the truth to fade away like a heat haze in the desert.

Forty-one isn't young. At forty-one a man should be settled. A steady job, a loving wife, a snotty kid bouncing on his knee. What do I have to show for my forty-one trips around the sun? An attic coated in dust and a group of acquaintances with more guilty faces than a police line-up. All I can do sitting here is roll around inside my brain of bad memories.

I fix myself a drink and stand at the window to watch the party fire up. A rowdy group spills out of the singing room opposite and they sway and stumble through the streets, singing to the sky. An army of motorbikes follow, and the sound of the engines echoes through the backstreets long after they're out of sight. The veins of the Rivers are starting to clog already, as bars overflow and troops of revellers march to the Pulse for fireworks and fights. Independence Day looks exactly the same as it did twelve years ago.

I can't be alone tonight. It's a hard thing to admit, but I can't shift the thought that I'll still be here in ten years, swathed in dust, lips wet with whisky, watching my tiny corner of the world sparkle and spin like a ferris wheel, while I run glorified pigeon jobs for pocket change.

Ganzo and Stones are right; I need to move on. I might have one ear, but I can still be respectable. In a couple of years I'll be slick in a suit, have a decent job, maybe even a family. That's the future I'll fight for. But I don't need to start tonight.

#

The streets are stirring but it doesn't feel like I'm invited to the party. Everyone's drunk and crowds are flooding the streets like swarms of frenzied insects. No fights, yet. It could be any old night in Sonaya, but I'm too damn sober and all alone.

The religious freaks are heading the rallies with painted placards and bitter chants. They want back in with Japan because they reckon prostitution and drugs don't exist there. They need a lesson in history, same as everyone else. Japan's where everything started, my dears.

The big ride's about to begin. I find Jiko, Purple, and Blonde in their usual alley behind Vino Isorimu. Hands deep in her leather pockets, Jiko's back in black. Hair red, cheeks red, her eyes flashing with fire. Not the girl I saw the other night at the goshitel; this is the Jiko I first met. The girl with a bike at her back and boiling blood in her veins.

'Jitsuko,' I say, trying to summon a smile.

She smirks and spits on the floor because her friends are watching.

'Got your bike back, I see.'

Jiko nods and slides her fingers along the fuel tank. 'Had a little scratch, but nothing I couldn't fix. A few days without her and the harbour road never looked so good.'

I'm pleased for her. I never should have put her through all of that.

'How's Shinji? The baby?' I ask.

'Eiko's in West Hospital and should be fine, and we're back above the wine bar; I'll let Shinji crash there for a while.'

The Roses gone and Shinji and Jiko taken care of. Look at us. Cut the story here and I'd call it a happy ending. For most of us, anyway.

'What's the plan, then?' I ask.

'Time to show the hyenas in office what idiots they are.'

It's sweet when kids take an interest in politics. 'How many are you expecting?'

'Couple of hundred,' she says. 'You in? We can find you a bike.'

I stroke my stubble and study her sidekicks. Blonde is still sporting bruises and Purple looks set to slit the throat of the nearest puppy.

'I've only just fallen off the wanted list.' I feel like an old man. 'The last thing I need is to join a bloody ride. You girls are cop bait.'

They smile like I've given them a compliment. Stupid kids.

'Your shiners are coming on nicely, Blonde,' I say.

I don't get the grin I expect, and they exchange glances before Blonde steps forward.

'My name's Su-young,' she says.

I'm about to laugh it off as I usually do, but their deadpan expressions shoot me down.

'The world isn't what it used to be, Dag. You grew up in a Sonaya where looks meant everything. Those days are numbered. My name's Su-young. This is Bo-min. Those are our names. Use them.'

Three to one, I'm outnumbered—and humbled. There's no witty comeback to restore a fossil's pride, and I'm stuck in aged amber, glued to the mistakes of my past.

I try to smile and regain my composure when Jiko steps up. She removes her vest and I'm struck by the rays of a Rising Sun.

'When I was fifteen I saw how fucked up Sonaya was. I wanted Japan to take us back, so I got this tattoo. To me it represented rebellion, Japanese pride. That was before I met Su-young and Bo-min, before I knew better. You know what this flag means to Koreans?'

Of course I do. It was a hundred years ago, but some things can't be forgotten.

'All this means to them is war and horror and disrespect. I found out who I was then: a stupid girl trying to look tough.

An ignorant kid who flaunted the symbol of oppression under the noses of her best friends.'

'So remove it,' I say.

Jiko pulls the shirt back over her head.

'We won't let her,' Su-young says.

'And they're right,' Jiko says. 'Whenever I see it I'm reminded of just how far I've come. This tattoo isn't me anymore, but it shows who I was, where I came from. We've all got mistakes etched in our skin; mine are just easier to see.'

'I don't like veiled advice,' I say.

'Fine, I'll pull back the curtain and make it simple. Move on, Dag. You can't rewrite history or delete what you've done, but you can learn from it.'

This evening just gets better and better. I started out as a lonely old drunk and end up being schooled into shame by the woke generation.

'After-party at ours,' Jiko says. 'But we won't be home before dawn.'

I manufacture a smile. 'That's my girl.'

Jiko winks and straddles her bike. They rev their engines and leave me cloaked in smoke. Alone again. I slip back into the shadows and stare up at the sky. The drones are out in force and the cops won't be far behind, like kids with electric kites. So it's just me with the backstreets of Sonaya and a shawl of sweet darkness. My two best friends.

I decide on a drink in Jiko's bar but when I get there the whole place is locked up. I'm about to head for Ganzo's when the dove darts up the alley.

'What is it now?' I ask. Pigeons rarely bring good news.

'The woman you asked me to watch,' she wheezes.

'Barnes,' I say. I'd almost forgotten I set the job. That was before I resolved to let things go. Maybe I shouldn't even ask. But to hell with it. 'What about her?'

'I saw her with the Roses, going into their pachinko place. But it's all closed up, lights out.'

I stare at the dove and consider. Maybe it's all just Dag-bait, another invitation to a game of cat and mouse that has no end. But maybe it's not. Usually my gut can be trusted when times are tough, and right now it's forecasting a fierce strike of lightning. One final fork of violet, and then I'm done.

'You missed the others,' I say, nodding over my shoulder. 'You better get your head down tonight; something tells me the time-bombs are ticking down.'

The dove examines me with a raised eyebrow. If she put a hand on her hip and tapped a foot she'd be a cartoon. I pull out some money, too much, and hand it to her. She counts every note and glares at me some more. Good Ol' Dag, saving the Sonayan street orphans one at a time. She flashes an impish smile and scrambles into the wine bar through a tiny basement window.

It's time for me to put this to bed.

#

What I really want is to disappear in a basement bar and surface at dawn. But I can't. Not tonight. Too many grenades have been thrown and it's finally time to count the bodies.

The eastern Rivers are still, but a few blocks away I can hear the protests along The Pulse. A couple of blasts go off, and they might sound like fireworks but the sky remains dark.

This is one of the biggest pachinko halls on the island. Two whole floors of flashing machines for zombies to feed with money and watch their lives waste away. The dove was right; all the lights are off and it looks like they're closed for the holiday, but I hang back in an alley to watch the entrance.

For a while nothing happens; no flickers of light or movement in the windows. But then I see them: ex-sergeant

Goichi Fujii, the man who stole the love of my life, side by side with Dustin Fairchild, my right-hand man. They saunter up to the front doors and disappear inside.

I wait a few minutes before bursting out of the alley towards the entrance; it's now or never, and I've never been one to sit on the sidelines and watch. I knock on the door and immediately recognise the Rose on guard.

'Your leg healing okay?'

He stares at me.

'Hurry up and let me in,' I demand.

His face screws up in confusion. 'I'll let them know you're here. Wait.'

I don't like waiting. As soon as his back's turned I liberate Old Trusty and hit him on the head with the handle. He falls to the floor and I step inside and close the door. The only source of light springs from the stairway at the far end of the room. It's like a graveyard in here, but instead of headstones covered in dust there's a legion of lifeless pachinko machines. I carefully pass through their unblinking faces and sharpen my sights for signs of movement, but there's no one down here. I reach the stairs and slowly start to climb.

The second floor is a ghost town, too. Nothing but endless rows of empty stools and silent machines. I glance around and continue on up. The door leading to the third floor is slightly ajar and a column of light spills onto the stairway. I press my back against the wall beside the door and strain to hear the voices inside. Another party I'm not invited to.

'Tell me. How did you get out of The Heights so early?' Silver Beard.

'I'm guessing the two of you cooked up some deal.'

'I did what I had to do,' Fairchild answers.

'So you helped set Kawasaki up at that party?' Silver Beard asks. 'I'm sure he'll be very upset to hear it. I thought you two were thick as thieves. Turns out he was just thick.'

'I didn't know anything about that,' Fairchild replies.

'No.' A third voice, one I haven't heard in a long time.

Goichi Fujii. 'Even I could tell that your time in The Heights made you untrustworthy. I knew you wouldn't have anything to do with pinning Ume's death on him.'

'But you knew about Earth Hour,' Silver Beard says. 'You accepted your role.'

'That was different,' Fairchild says. 'I was assured he wouldn't be hurt.'

'Well he got away, didn't he?' Another new voice. Sara. 'And now one of your Roses is headed for The Heights, strung up for the murder you tried to set him up for. Kawasaki can't be as thick as you think.'

'Shall we get on with it? Who knows how long we'll have.'

'Let's hear it then,' Sara says. 'The whole story.'

A brief silence. A chair is pulled out and someone sits down.

'You might know *how* Ume died,' Fujii says. 'But you don't know why. She discovered a secret, and it was my fault she found out.'

'What was it?' Sara asks.

'Twelve years ago a woman named Hana Nishi was murdered. Kawasaki was arrested and charged with homicide, but that fool doesn't remember what really happened. It was a set-up.'

Silence.

Silence as vast and empty as space.

My heart sinks like a stone in a well. Mouth dries out. Heart thunders against my hollow rack of ribs. Eleven years. Eleven years of doubt and despair in The Heights. Eleven fucking years of hating myself, and I didn't even do it.

'He was drunk. He was *always* drunk in those days, the bloody lush. It was easy enough to set him up. I sent him a message from Hana. Said she had something to tell him, and he came running like the ruin he is. She had no idea. When Dag woke up the next morning stuck in a cell and suddenly sober, he was convinced he'd killed her in a drunken rage.'

I retch and slide down the wall.

'So what really happened?' Sara asks. 'Who killed her?'

I reach for Trusty, grip the handle between my trembling fingers. If I'm going to pass out, I'm going to get my revenge first. All I need is to hear him say it.

'I suppose I did,' Fujii admits.

That'll do. I burst through the door and swallow the scene: a vast empty room with a solitary table in the centre, Fairchild leaning against a wall in one corner, Sara hunched over a pencil and pad, Silver Beard standing behind her with folded arms. Fujii is sat at the head of the table facing them, and now me. All four of them stare at me framed in the doorway, raging like a sky lit up at dawn. I know what I'm going to do, even if it means going back to The Heights. I fling my knife through the air towards Fujii's face, but he dives to the floor, leaving Trusty impaled in his chair. Within seconds Fujii's firing his gun in my direction while Sara, Fairchild and Silver Beard scream and take cover. I duck and roll and scramble to Silver Beard, take his feet from under him and wrestle the gun from his hand, elbow his lights out. Before I can take aim Fairchild jumps me, grabs my arm, but I can't stand the touch of a traitor and I've half a mind to blow his brains out. Fujii fires another shot across the room and it misses my head by one glorious inch.

'Weapons down!' Sara roars, but no one's listening. She aims her Baretta at Fujii, and then at Fairchild and me, but I strike Fairchild square in the face and he falls backwards with blood bursting from both nostrils. With my firing arm free I finally aim a bullet at the man who murdered the love of my life and stole eleven years of freedom from me. It whizzes past his ear; I'm too pumped up to aim straight. Sara fires two bullets into the ceiling but that only fires me up even more. I'm gonna end this right here, right now. I stand up and expose myself. Yeah, I'll take a few bullets in the chest if that's what it takes to deliver a bullet between that devil's eyes. I raise my arm and take aim, say a silent goodbye to my short-lived freedom.

Bang.

Someone else fires their weapon before I can pull the trigger, and it's a damn good shot for a journalist. Sara's bullet slams into my gun and knocks it out of my hands, leaving me unarmed, standing unarmed in the open like a duck with a target painted on its stomach. Fujii rolls out from behind his chair and shoots. Sara shoots back, but she's too late. Everything slows down and I watch the bullet fly through the air, the last seconds of my life slipping away in slow motion, and then I'm down on the floor, covered in blood.

Fairchild's body twitches on top of me, his eyes flickering a few inches above mine, spittle dribbling from his bottom lip. The traitor's saved my life.

'Don't move!' Sara bellows, but Fujii darts out the door and disappears downstairs. Sara rushes over and drops to her knees.

'God damn you, Kawasaki,' she says, cradling Fairchild's head in her hands. He's pale and getting paler. 'You fucked everything up.'

I drag myself up and stare at Fairchild, spluttering away with a bleeding hole in his chest. Yeah, big surprise. I fuck everything up, as is my wont. I grab Silver Beard's gun and pluck Old Trusty from the chair. I take one last look at the fading lights in Fairchild's eyes, and what I'd long suspected is suddenly clear: the heart inside my twisted rack of ribs isn't human. Yeah, it beats well enough most of the time, but that's not what a heart's really for.

I'm gonna kill that son of a bitch.

26

TWO WEEKS UNTIL RELEASE

There's a wiggle to his shoulders, like a playboy shaking the dust from his suit as he swaggers onto the dancefloor. I recognise the gleam in his eyes. From this day forward Dustin Fairchild is a free man, and his irises blaze again; bottle green and bright like neon, and he'll be seeing enough of bottles and neon soon enough.

He leans against the wall of my cell and smiles.

'I guess I'll see you on the outside, old man.'

I don't look at him. Just nod.

'You know…' he says, staring at my tiny window and lingering by the open door of my cell. Whatever he thinks I know, he can't seem to spit it out.

'Thanks for cutting my ear off,' I say. 'And for breaking my nose. I'm glad it was you.'

I look up at him and he's still fixated on the view from my window. He can't seem to drag his eyes away to meet mine.

We remain silent for several minutes, Fairchild standing by the open door, tapping the bars with his finger; me on the floor of my cell, watching him. Finally he looks at me. He wants to explain, to justify his actions, tell me everything, but he doesn't have to. I can read his eyes like a picture book. Whatever deal he struck before, the regret is pulsing in his pupils. Maybe when he's out of here he'll back out of the bargain, cut all ties with whoever he's working with. Maybe he'll welcome me to the Rivers like a long-lost brother, and we'll skip along, arm in arm like playground schoolgirls. Or maybe he's in too deep and there's nothing he can do. Maybe there's no happy ending for either of us. Maybe he'll sit back and watch my decapitation from the safety of the shadows. If he does, this is the look he'll have in his eyes.

I want him to know that I get it, that I understand why. There's no such thing as friends in this city; only people who get in the way of what you want, or people you can use to get a step closer. But sometimes it's nice to pretend. With these wrecked spheres in my sockets I send a message loud and clear: if you've let me down, I'll only do the same to you eventually.

He steps timidly towards me, the strut in his shoulders gone, and scratches his nose. He'll be scratching white powder off the same nose later tonight. He holds out a hand and I stare at it. I look at him. Fairchild. Friend or foe, life's too short to hold grudges. When I'm out of this place, we'll see how this one plays out. I shake his hand.

'Get the hell out of here,' I tell him.

The bottle-green glow returns to his eyes. He spins around and slips out of my cell. Fairchild's heading to the great ballroom early, but I'll be late to the party. I just hope he holds the doors for me.

27

I scan the streets for a sign of the scum who ruined my life, but he's nowhere to be seen. My mind's all a rage and I can't make sense of it. There's a thousand fires burning through my body, licking my skin and filling my eyes with flame. Sometimes I think we're more than just animals, but not tonight. Tonight I'm a bull with his tail up, seeing red at every turn.

I walk without thought, drawn to the lights and the noise.

I don't know how far I've come when Shinji scurries around the corner like a field mouse.

'The dove told me you were here,' he says, catching his breath. 'I saw him. Fujii.'

Congratulations, kid. The position of sidekick has just been filled. Grab a hold of my pocket, let's go for a ride into hell. 'Which way?'

'Follow me.'

Another goose chase, maybe, but it's all I've got. The kid scampers through the backstreets like a trained rat in a maze, and I stick to him as the brothel posters stick to the walls. We're only a couple of blocks from The Pulse and it sounds like the marches are getting wilder. Soon enough we hit the crowds, endless alleys full of angry faces, flags and placards and protests, police armed with batons and tasers. Happy Independence Day, Sonaya, and thanks for the cover. It's not a party in Sonaya until someone's dead, and sometimes one death just isn't enough.

We stand on the edge of The Pulse and scan the faces in the crowd, the water twinkling with light from lanterns lining the promenade. Fujii could be anywhere by now. We've lost him.

The red mist is fading and I don't like how it feels. I need to keep this hunger; I like the taste of it in my mouth, its sour ferocity. I need to be angry. I need to see Fujii's blood. I need to make him pay.

'Dag!'

I turn and see Su-young astride her green thoroughbred, her blonde hair wild and windswept.

'Jiko's got him. Jiko's got Fujii.'

I jump onto her bike. 'Take me there.'

#

The surrounding mayhem is all white noise. Su-young honks her horn and slices through the crowds, and pretty soon we're back at my attic. It's quiet. Jiko's crimson bike is parked on the curb and Bo-min is straddling her purple beast beside it. She watches Shinji and me dismount Su-young's bike, and flicks her eyes over her shoulder.

'Upstairs.'

I look up at my little attic window. Old Trusty is strapped to my ankle, Silver Beard's gun tucked in my belt. I tell the kid to wait outside. Don't want to lose two sidekicks in one night. Shinji furrows his brows and leans against Su-young's bike. I glance at the girls.

'Sorry to keep you from your party.' I look them in the eyes. 'Su-young. Bo-min.'

'Just finish it,' Su-young says. Bo-min doesn't blink.

I enter the building and take the stairs slowly. Clambering to my death, perhaps. The floorboards creak with every step and the smell of dust pervades the staircase. I run my hand along the wall. I've been climbing towards this climax for weeks. No, years. Twelve of them, in fact.

I linger outside the door. He's in there, I can feel it. I take a deep breath and push the door open.

A solitary candle flickers in the corner and I see a silhouette of someone standing at the window.

'Hope you don't mind,' Goichi Fujii says. 'Poured myself a drink.' His voice is hoarse; it's not his first drink tonight. My eyes adjust to the darkness and I spot Jiko nearby, pointing her gun at the back of his head. I follow suit and take aim.

'I thought maybe you'd killed him,' I say to Jiko.

'I already see too much blood when I close my eyes. I don't need more to my name. Kill him, put him in jail, I don't care which. All I want is justice for Ume.'

Jiko's never looked so young. She really is only eighteen. Maybe once Fujii's in the ground a line will be drawn under all this; maybe she can finally be free.

As for me, my hand isn't so steady and I'm not in a forgiving mood. Only a fool follows his own advice. I cock my gun and prepare to send Fujii flying through the window.

'Will you hear a man out before you send him to hell?' Fujii asks.

Twelve years. What's a few seconds more? 'I'll give you one minute.'

Fujii turns to face me. His movements are pained and slow, his eyes misty and bloodshot. 'A little privacy, perhaps?'

I glance at Jiko. 'Wait outside.' She nods and hands me a pistol from her belt. 'This is his.' She closes the door and leaves us to it, two sad sacks in a room full of dust and shadows, the ghosts of our sins closing in. The only thing we ever had in common was the love of an innocent woman, and her death is the reason one of us is about to die.

'I loved her, you know,' he says.

I'm too livid to laugh, and all I manage is an exhalation filled with spite. 'Don't you dare talk about her.'

Fujii peers into his glass like it's a window to the past. I recognise the look because I've done it myself often enough. 'I loved her more than anything in the world. You probably didn't know that they wanted her dead long before I ever met her. I was just a lowly uniform when they first approached me. They promised me promotions and a position of power, and at first I thought, why not? Why shouldn't I look out for myself? She was just some girl. But when I met her, everything changed. It wasn't long after she left you. We clicked straight away. It seemed like we were made for each other.'

My finger twitches over the trigger. There's no way I can hold out for another thirty seconds.

'I thought we'd be together forever. But when I found out about the baby, something snapped.'

I blink it away.

'You never did work out who they were looking for, did you? Who the Roses were hunting. She escaped from me several months ago. My fault, of course. I haven't exactly been the best father these past few years.'

I stare at him, and my heart pummels my chest like a pounding dancefloor.

'You knew Hana was pregnant, Dag. She was eight months in. That's why I thought you fled the scene so quickly. Couldn't bare the thought of having killed two people at once. But I was there. I got her help, got her to hospital. They couldn't save Hana, but they saved the baby.'

The minute has long gone, but I can't pull the trigger.

'No,' I say. 'They couldn't have…they…'

'They did, Dag. A little girl. A healthy, tiny little girl.' He's back at the window. I can barely hear him over the drumming against my chest. 'I was with her the whole time, right from the very first scan. I saw the baby's tiny fingers and toes, the beating heart. I helped Hana pick a cot for the bedroom, the clothes when we found out it was a girl.

'But Hana didn't tell me the whole truth until much later.

The night before it happened, in fact, and I often wish she hadn't. We might all have been happier if she'd kept quiet, buried her secret. If she'd never told me I wasn't the father.'

He turns to gauge my reaction.

'Yes. You had a night together, didn't you? I thought you were well out of the picture, but I suppose I was the biggest fool of all. I knew Hana would never forgive you for cheating on her, but one night she chose to forget, to exist in a world where you had never wronged her. One stolen night that changed everything.'

I can't think straight. I can't remember. All I want is to pull this trigger and wake up thirteen years ago.

'Ume's death was my fault,' Fujii says, turning away from me. I keep my quivering finger close to the trigger. 'But you know that already. It was a while ago now. I was drunk. This stuff,' he says, holding up his glass, 'always takes me back to that night. Always makes me weak. I lost control. And I told Ume too much.'

'What did you tell her?'

'I told her what really happened, that someone wanted Hana dead. I told her that it was all a set-up, that I planned to do it myself. Back then Ume was still a prostitute; up to her eyeballs in coke, boozed up all the time. I'm surprised she remembered anything. But she got out of the game, sobered up. I paid her off, of course, made it clear there'd be trouble if she told anyone. That's why her little biker friends never found out. She was protecting them. But she told you, didn't she, in The Heights? Or as good as, anyway. That was the only worthwhile thing Fairchild ever told me.'

Fujii smiles, not a drunken or a crazed smile, but a smile of curiosity, like he's been posed a riddle. 'You still don't remember how it really happened, do you? Well, I was a mess. I was drunk on hate. I hated Hana for carrying your child, and I hated you for coming between us. I thought I'd go through with it, too. I had it all planned out. I'd make it look like *you* killed her, frame you for murder and finally get you out of the picture for good, and then I'd take the promotion and forget all about it.

'But I couldn't. I couldn't do it. I couldn't hurt Hana, even after I discovered the truth. I loved her too much, Dag. But I wasn't the only one. You were there, too, kneeling in front of her, begging, like a wet dog in the rain. Pleading for one more chance. And for a split second there was a look in her eyes, a look that terrified me. She looked at you in a way she'd never looked at me. I was scared she'd say yes, take you back. That's when I stepped out of the shadows, tried to pull her away. I just wanted to take her home and forget I'd ever considered going through with it.

'But then you pulled out your gun. You pointed it at me. And fired. Everything happened so fast, I couldn't do anything. Hana stepped in front of me. She took the bullet and fell. There was so much blood. That's what I remember the most; the blood. It's a miracle the baby survived.'

I shake my head and try to focus, try to ignore the images he's put in my head, but I can't. They're brighter than ever, like old reels of film suddenly sharpened and sickeningly clear. He's telling the truth. I remember the bullet. I remember the blood. I remember the baby. Finally, I remember.

'Where's my girl?' I say. 'Where's my daughter?'

Fujii sips his drink and smiles. 'I thought you'd discovered the truth yourself,' he says. 'When you escaped Kosuke's party I thought you'd gone on the hunt for her, that you'd found her and gone into hiding together. I was *sure* you had her.' He chuckles wearily. 'But it seems I expected too much of you. I should have known better.'

'Where is she?'

Fujii picks up my bottle of whisky. 'I don't know, Dag.'

The door bursts open and I turn to see Sara in the doorway with her gun raised. She looks between me and Fujii and I'm far too slow to react. Fujii smashes the bottle and lunges towards me when the blast goes off. For the second time tonight I'm staring at my body, searching for blood and waiting for the pain to kick in.

But for the second time I'm spared. Fujii collapses to the floor, clutching his chest, the bottle smashing to pieces beside him. Sara rushes towards him, her eyes exploding in terror, as Jiko appears in the doorway, pale as the moon.

'No, no!' Sara screams, her fingers all over Fujii's fading face. 'Who was it? Tell me, you bastard! Don't you dare fucking die! Dag, bring me something for the bleeding!'

I stare at Sara cradling the man who ruined me. She did what I should have done. He splutters like a sick dog, can't even speak. That's it. It's over. I fall to my knees and watch him, Jiko's hand on my shoulder, the greatest]secret still unsaid.

Sara lowers his head to the floor and stands. 'Did he tell you?'

'About my daughter? Yeah he told me.'

'Did he tell you who wanted Hana dead?'

I look at her. Who cares who wanted her dead? She's dead, that's all that matters. Fujii was simply the stooge who tried to frame me for it. He didn't need to. *I* killed her. I'm the one who did it. Now he's dead too, and none of it means shit.

I close my eyes and deliver myself to darkness. I'm about ready to burst when I hear Shinji enter the room. I open my eyes to see him confronted with death yet again, panic and fear draining the colour from his face. He looks ready to throw up; the kid needs to get used to the sight of blood if he wants to carry on with me.

'I told you to stay outside,' I say.

'The cops are here,' Shinji says. 'If you've done something wrong, now might be the time to split.'

I look at Sara and then at the lifeless body on the floor.

'For once, I might be in the clear.'

28

'Who the hell are you anyway?' I ask.

Sara uncorks Ganzo's last bottle of red and fills our glasses; the panda's place is ours for the night, or what's left of it. The police were satisfied with our statements and let it go. As far as they were concerned, Fujii was complicit in Ume's death, and Sara killing him in self-defence made everything so much simpler. Outside, the coursing Rivers are calming; Independence Day is almost over.

'I was hired by someone in Tokyo,' Sara says, swirling the wine in her glass. 'When Ume found out that foul play was involved in Hana's death, she contacted my client, and I was hired to investigate. Of course, Sonaya's never been keen on letting private detectives from Japan roam around asking too many questions, but journalists from America? Not a problem.'

'I knew you were never just a regular hack.'

'Private detective, three years on the job,' Sara says. 'My client had long suspected that Hana's death was part of something bigger; that's why they sent Fairchild in a couple of years before me.'

'You were working together?'

'We did for a while, back in the States. He was a good actor, Dustin, but not everything was a performance. He didn't make enough progress with the case and, as you know, there were too many temptations for him here. By the time Ume's intelligence arrived he'd already been cut loose, but I tried to help him. You know, a favour for an old pal. I thought if he helped me with the case I could convince the agency to give him another go. But you know Fairchild. He didn't make it easy for me.'

I take a slug of wine and smack my lips. 'So you were both playing me.'

'You weren't the one being played, Dag,' Sara says. 'The plan was to get Fairchild locked up, make first contact with Fujii and slowly gain his trust. After what Ume told us, we knew he was our way in. Fairchild was supposed to get close to you, pass on information. Fujii didn't want you to get out of The Heights, at least not alive. Fairchild was meant to sell you out in exchange for early release. Of course, he didn't do anything to deserve it.

'We thought you must have had your own suspicions after Ume's death and your subsequent set up, but we were both disappointed to discover that you'd blocked everything out. You were next to useless.'

I take another hit of wine. I'm taking a lot of hits tonight.

'We had no idea it would be so hard to find answers in The Heights. Snitches and spies and bugs everywhere. Fairchild had to be careful who he spoke to and what he said, and so did Ume, apparently. We didn't get any answers we didn't know already, but eventually we made progress. Or you did, at least. Once you discovered that video of Ume's death and Fujii's involvement was exposed, we thought the whole thing would blow wide open. It wasn't long before Fujii lost faith in Fairchild, but by then we'd found a way in with the Roses. Thankfully, they always answer to the highest bidder, so after a bit of wrangling they set up our little meeting this evening. We were going to make a deal: Fujii would give us the names of the people who organised Hana's death, and he would receive a reduced sentence in exchange. He was about to tell us everything before you burst in and got Fairchild killed.'

Sara looks into my eyes and I look into my wine glass. It's not empty but I refill it anyway.

'I thought he was double-crossing me,' I say. It's too late now, but it's true.

'He may have been, in a way, but he was always on your side, Dag. We were only using Fujii and the Roses to get the answers we needed. Fairchild would never have done anything to hurt you. He said...' she hesitates, and I know the hammer's about to fall, '...he said you were the closest thing he'd ever had to a brother.'

I slug my wine and look to the ceiling and anywhere that isn't Sara's eyes. I think back over everything that's happened. It's like those last moments before death strikes; vivid images flashing before my eyes. Every word, every glance, every suspicion. I had it all wrong, and it hurts.

'It's only because of Kosuke that you're still alive,' Sara says. 'His money was the one thing stopping the Roses from blowing your head off when they had the chance. Even all of Fujii's influence couldn't compete with Kosuke's riches.'

I drink. Sara drinks. Every revelation makes me feel more and more the fool.

'So you never found out who was behind it all?' I ask. Sara shakes her head. 'Anyway, I don't suppose it matters now. Yeah, maybe someone wanted Hana dead, but *they* didn't kill her. Fujii didn't kill her either. *I* did. It was me all along.'

Sara leans forward. 'How can you say that? How can you say it doesn't matter? Can't you see there's something much bigger going on here? Everyone knows Hana was only months away from becoming prime minister. If you didn't do it, someone else would have. Someone high up wanted Hana dead, and whoever it was is probably still pulling the strings as we speak.'

I look sideways at her. 'Who hired you? This mystery person that cares so much about it all?'

Sara gives me that cool look that she could trademark. Detectives hate being on the wrong side of questions.

'Alright then,' I say. 'Forget it. But tell me this, and tell me the truth. Do you know anything about my daughter?'

Sara shakes her head. 'Fujii hired the Roses to find her, but they came up cold. They were convinced it was your doing, that you'd somehow managed to smuggle her away, but obviously not. It's like she disappeared.'

I lean back and try to imagine a miniature version of me running around the Rivers.

'But if she's alive,' Sara says, 'you're not her only family. There's one more, and it might just be time for a reunion.'

'I very much doubt *she'd* want to see me,' I say.

'Wrong again.' She stands, drains her glass. 'I'll leave you two to get reacquainted.' She places a hand on mine and looks me in the eyes. 'I sincerely hope you find your daughter, Dag.'

I watch her disappear up the stairs and sit alone, nursing my wine. Suddenly Ganzo's bar feels empty, the air heavy with the weight of Sara's words. I don't know how much time passes before the bell above the door rings. I see her black heels appear as she slowly descends the stairs. I know who it is long before I see the birthmark on her cheek.

#

Ryoko Nishi brushes dust off the chair. If she had a handkerchief, you can bet she'd sit on it. People can change a lot in twelve years.

'I like your suit,' I say.

She stares at me. Sleek black hair down to her shoulders, black suit to match. The birthmark beneath her left eyes looks bigger than I remember, like a smear of spilled tea on a silk carpet. She nods at the two bodyguards who followed her down the stairs and they leave the room.

'Charming boys,' I say.

She takes in Ganzo's empty basement, momentarily avoiding me and my words. It's strange to see her here, at the scene of our drunken dalliance, after all these years. I can still picture her waltzing down those stairs with her belly button on show and black feathers in her hair. How things change.

'You just couldn't keep your head down, could you?' she says, in her trademark husky voice. 'No matter how much I try to pretend you don't exist, you just won't go away. Like a fly, blundering around the walls of the dining room.'

'What can I say? We live in quite the playground. I just hope I haven't done anything to hurt your campaign.'

Nishi raises an eyebrow. 'I'm still confident in re-election, if that's what you mean.'

I pour her some wine and top up my glass. 'I wonder if your followers would be so loyal if they knew the truth. Me, you, Hana. The part you played.'

Ryoko Nishi watches me like a cat eyeballing its owner instead of the dangling toy.

'Yes, you're right, I did play a part. But there are different ways of dealing with grief, you know. There's your way: self-loathing, alcoholism, a life hiding in cells or shadows.'

Self-loathing? Has she met me before?

'Or there's my way: to respect the memory of that person, and use it as motivation to better yourself. I made one mistake, and it cost me the love of my sister, and my family. But I refused to punish myself forever.

'All those years you were sleeping in your cell, I was trying to build something. A better version of the life I had. My mother died shortly after Hana; she never recovered from the pain of losing her daughter. Then my father left to try and forget everything about our family. I was alone, abandoned with nothing but the memory of what we did—of what *I* did. So I ditched the bike and booze and bullshit black lipstick.' She smiles all the way to her dimples, and I'm suddenly aware of her obvious appeal to the great unwashed. 'I set off on the same road as Hana and made faster progress than I ever expected, though I had nothing like her talent, of course. It never came as naturally to me as it did to Hana, but I found my own way, slowly. It's been a long journey. I matured, I learned, I won. And now here I am.'

She holds out two hands to present herself. Maybe she's forgotten where we are: a dusty basement with cheap wine. I guess she's right, though; she's handled the grief far better than I have.

'I've done everything I possibly can to put my worst mistake behind me and get on with my life. What say we finally leave the past behind us, Daganae?'

'That all sounds nice,' I say. 'I for one am tired of looking over my shoulder. But don't you want to know? Aren't you curious who wanted Hana dead in the first place?'

Nishi shrugs, and it's the first time the coat hanger disappears from her shoulders. 'You know this city as well as I do, Dag. You think being prime minister permits me any real power? This government is a pyramid built on lies and secrets. Enemies will always exist, people will always plot. Thirteen years ago Hana was a shoe-in for this job. The possibilities of who wanted her dead are endless, but it doesn't matter now.'

I raise an eyebrow. I thought I was the only one who realised how little it matters.

'You want to know who killed her, Dag? *You* did. You killed her, and you suffered and served your time for it. So yes, it doesn't matter. My office is probably full of people plotting a similar end for me. That's just the way of this place. This is Sonaya, Dag.'

I consider this new Ryoko Nishi. If she truly knows how fucked up this government is, then she might just be the perfect person to lead our island after all. Weigh the anchor everyone, we're setting sail for the Pacific.

'You're a free man now, Dag,' Nishi says with an air of finality. 'A simple one, too, if you don't mind me saying.'

'I don't mind at all. If anything, I take it as a compliment.'

'What is it you want? Women? Alcohol? Sonaya is full of both. Stop chasing shadows and enjoy yourself. Go wild. Forget the past and start living in the present.'

I swallow the last of my wine. The bottle's empty.

'I didn't know what I wanted for a while,' I say. 'For eleven years all I wanted was freedom, but freedom's a hell of a hole, and the drink doesn't seem to fill the void.'

I finger my empty glass. I don't know why I'm suddenly spilling my guts. Maybe it's the wine. Maybe it's the memory of who we were; me and Ryoko together in Ganzo's basement, swallowing our troubles by the skinful, talking about love and life. Maybe I'm kidding myself that I can go back and do things differently—*be* different. Maybe I'm just a fool.

'The only thing I've known for sure since The Heights is that something's missing. I've been doing everything I can to avoid thinking about it, but now—finally—I *have* something. A flicker of light in a dark abyss.'

'And what is it you think you have?' Nishi asks.

'I have a daughter,' I say finally.

Nishi pauses to consider my words. 'Maaya's been missing for months. No one knows where she is. But I'm doing everything I can to find her.'

'She's your niece, Ryoko. Do more.'

'My people are looking for her. If she's still alive, we'll find her. And when we do, I think it's best you stay away.'

'She's my daughter.'

'She's *Hana's* daughter. You might be the father, but you're not father material, Dag. Tell me, what do you know about parenthood? What do you know about the daughter you so desire?'

I've got nothing.

'What can you possibly offer her? A mat on the floor of a filthy attic? Goichi Fujii was far from perfect, but at least he could offer Maaya some stability. I kept an eye on them from afar, just to make sure Maaya was okay, but I admit that in the last couple of years I haven't done as much as I should have. Unfortunately, those are the sacrifices I have to make for this job. If I'd had more maternal instincts, I might have smuggled her away myself, invited her to live with me, but I've never been good with kids.'

She inspects the nail of her index finger. Twelve years ago her cuticles were flooded with black varnish; now each nail is perfectly sculptured and painted blood-red.

'What happened to her?' I ask.

'I don't know. Goichi was a good man once, but heartbreak can do a lot to a person, as I'm sure you know. He drank too much, brought different women home each week. He lost his way. Maybe he beat her, too, but we won't know for sure until we find her. If he'd told me sooner, I'm sure I would have found her already. But it took him too long to come to me after she ran away. He wanted to sort it out on his own, the fool.'

'So she ran away? She wasn't taken?'

Nishi tilts her head to one side but keeps her eyes firmly fixed on mine. 'That's what Goichi said. No signs of a struggle. No note, either.'

'But you think she's still alive?'

'Yes, Dag, I think she's still alive, and like I said before, *when* I find her, I'll be moving her somewhere safe. And somewhere safe means beyond the clutches of drunks and criminals. She's had enough of those already.'

We sit in silence for a moment. Nishi takes a sip of wine and glances around the bar again.

'You must be busy,' I say. 'Don't let me keep you.'

She smiles. 'You've no idea. It's been nice catching up, Dag.' She stands and moves towards the stairs, leaving her wine glass half-full on the table. 'Remember what I said. You're free now. Move on. Let the ghosts go.'

I reach over and slide her wine towards me. 'I've never been good at letting things go.'

29

'She doesn't have any leads on your daughter, then?'

'That's what she says, and I think I believe her. But if she does find Maaya, she won't let me anywhere near her. I believe that, too.'

Kosuke puffs out his cheeks. We look out over the rooftops. He's putting me up in one of his guestrooms while they clean the blood off my attic floor.

It looks like the Independence Day celebrations are over. The strip's still lit up like a fairground on LSD but the Rivers are calm and quiet. Scooters continue to shoot through the streets but the heaving crowds have dispersed. It's gonna be one hell of a clean-up tomorrow.

Kosuke's elbows shuffle along the railing.

'I didn't know, Dag,' he says. I turn to face him. 'I didn't know about your daughter, I promise. Fujii knew I'd tell you. That's why he hired the Roses instead of coming to me. It was never my intention to work with him, Dag, you understand?'

'It's done. Forget about it.'

'He threatened me, Dag. At my party. I should never have gone along with it, I know, but—'

'It's not your fault, old man. Like I said, it's done. Fujii's dead. It's over.'

Kosuke places a hand on my shoulder as we stand in

silence and watch the lights flicker across the harbour. Without another word he turns to leave, and I watch him walk towards the stairs. The neon lights around the pool paint him a myriad of colours before he disappears below.

#

Sunrise.

The night is over, and that usually means the end of the fun. I've been nocturnal ever since I left The Heights. I love the night too much; the blazing neon and the smell of alcohol in the back alleys; the smoke that drifts from open windows, the aromas of char-grilled vegetables and noodles; the swinging signs and ringing bells of basement bars; the bright pink lights of bustling brothels, the eternal echo of raucous singing rooms, the endless yellow squares of crumbling apartment blocks; the idea that something is always happening. I can't help myself; I love Sonaya nights.

The city never looks as good in daylight. It's not as easy to hide the things you don't wanna see: the toxic yellow stains of piss on walls, mines of shit in filthy streets, grimy water spilling out from busted gutters, addicts skulking in receding shadows, the bloodshot eyes of businessmen, the permanent grey ceiling of pollution. Not a pretty spectacle.

But there's something beautiful this morning. The sunrise casts tangerines and fuchsias across the sky, creating silhouettes of the high-rises: banks, offices, apartment blocks, goshitels; cranes on crooked rooftops. The Pulse reflects the morning sun, flowing calmly through the heart of the sleeping city. There's still some life in Sonaya, and perhaps I'm not the only one perched on a rooftop, watching the city wake in a chrome haze.

I picture everyone out there, everyone I know. Sara Barnes stirring in her basement, alone. A private investigator and an ex-pat; there couldn't be a lonelier combination. No doubt the government will find a way to ship her out. PIs are too damn smart and nosy for such a corrupt and shady island. Shame. Just when we were starting to get along.

Shinji's down there, too, the little punk, worrying over his baby sister. That's a lot of responsibility on his skinny shoulders. The fool's taken a liking to me, and I could use a spunky sidekick, but I've got my daughter to think of now. Kids in Sonaya are forced to grow up fast, and maybe Nishi's right; I'm not exactly the best role model.

Jiko and her girls will be passing out soon, no doubt, returning home from triumphant rides in the golden light of morning. They won't rest up for long, I'm sure. Ume's death might be avenged, but their feuds with Fumiko and the Roses have only just begun, and if I know Jiko, then things will only get more interesting.

Then there's Maaya, the daughter I never knew I had. Maybe she's the only one who can save this callous creature I've become. If only I can find her.

So what's next, I wonder? What becomes of this broken little island? What becomes of this frayed old fool who's too scared to leave? What becomes of the nightmares? I've seen more blood this month than in all my adult life. Hana's death haunted me every night for eleven years while I shrank in a cell and scratched a tally into a stone wall. Now there are endless other screams and messed-up lives on this ragged, wastrel thing I call a conscience. Anchors hanging from hooks in my heart, making every day harder.

But I'll go on like before. Ganzo and Nakata are out there somewhere, pouring drinks for the drunks and the dregs. I like to think I'll be there with them, drinking basement bars dry and picking up whatever work I can find.

Maybe my life as Sonaya's most notorious criminal is over. Maybe I'll get my old job back, start climbing that old ladder once again, rung by rotten rung. Maybe I'll be the saviour of the city and stop the spiral of corruption. Or maybe I'll just be plain old Dag, skulking in shadows, tasting trouble at every turn. As long as I have Sonaya, there'll always be adventure: something to chase, somewhere to hide, someone to bail me out. I'm a father now and things are gonna change, but I've always been an optimist. It's time for a shake-up, and when it starts, I'll be bang in the middle of it.

The fuschia at the horizon slowly dissolves, and golden light consumes the sky. It looks damn good, I have to admit.

This is my home, and what a place it is.

TOMAS MARCANTONIO

Tomas Marcantonio is a novelist and short story writer from Brighton, England. He graduated from the University of Sussex with a degree in English Language and Film, and his fiction has appeared in numerous books and journals, both online and in print. Tomas is currently based in Busan, South Korea, where he teaches English and writes whenever he can escape the classroom. You can follow him on Twitter @TJMarcantonio.

Author photo by Seung-Jin Yeo

ACKNOWLEDGEMENTS

I owe a massive thank you to everyone at Storgy Books for believing in me, and for all the hard work that went into making this book a reality. Special thanks go to Anthony Self, who gave a home to Sonaya's first short story and saw the potential for more, and Ross Jeffery, for his ardent support and invaluable input from the start. I am especially grateful to my incredible editor, Tomek Dzido, whose dedication and skill made the lights of Sonaya shine all the brighter.

I am thankful to my friends in England, Korea, and elsewhere for their long-term support, especially Paul McConville, whose early feedback helped to keep this wayward train of a story on its tracks.

Thank you to my family, especially my wonderful parents, who I'm sure didn't realise how much of their retirement would be spent reading error-strewn printouts of their son's shoddy early drafts. Thank you also to my amazing sisters Lisa and Amy and their beautiful families, for their continued love and encouragement.

To my wife Jung-mi, thank you for your endless patience, and your questionable enthusiasm in closing me off in my "writing cage" every day.

Finally, I would like to thank one of my former students, a then 10 year-old Korean boy, who inspired Dag's first adventure. Our lively conversation about a man who bought an entire apartment block was the catalyst for Kosuke's rooftop party and the start of it all. So, thank you Henry.

ALSO AVAILABLE FROM STORGY BOOKS

SHALLOW CREEK

This is the tale of a town on the fringes of fear, of ordinary people and everyday objects transformed by terror and madness, a microcosm of the world where nothing is ever quite what it seems. This is a world where the unreal is real, where the familiar and friendly lure and deceive. On the outskirts of civilisation sits this solitary town. Home to the unhinged. Oblivion to outsiders.

Shallow Creek contains twenty-one original horror stories by a chilling cast of contemporary writers, including stories by Sarah Lotz, Richard Thomas, Adrian J Walker, and Aliya Whitely. Told through a series of interconnected narratives, Shallow Creek is an epic anthology that exposes the raw human emotion and heart-pounding thrills at the genre's core.

To discover more about SHALLOW CREEK visit STORGY.COM

STORGY®

MAGAZINE

ONLINE ARTS & ENTERTAINMENT MAGAZINE

BOOKS - FILMS - ART - MUSIC
INTERVIEWS - REVIEWS - SHORT STORIES

For more information about STORGY Magazine visit our
website.

STORGY

www.storgy.com

@fb.me/morest0rgy   @morestorgy   morestorgy